ACCIDENTS WILL HAPPEN

David stood beside Julie. He had never touched her before, but now he ran his hands in slow circles over her back and shoulders, above her cuffed wrists, and then started unbuckling the gag as he spoke softly into her ear. 'You know something, Julie? I think this has all been too easy for you.'

Behind him, Shalina was pulling the top of her dress down her arms.

'Up to now,' David continued, 'you haven't had to do anything. Everything that has happened has been done to you by somebody else.'

Shalina pushed the dress down to her waist and the top of her knickers appeared.

'Many people – and I think that means you – find it's quite easy to tolerate practically anything, provided they remain passive. That must change.'

Meanwhile, Shalina had unclipped her bra. When Julie looked over she was already turning back, her breasts now exposed. 'I think you're both going to enjoy this,' said David, as Shalina hooked her thumbs into the waistband of her knickers, dropped them to the floor and positioned herself in front of Julie . . .

By the same author:

DISPLAYS OF INNOCENTS
DISPLAYS OF EXPERIENCE
LESSONS IN OBEDIENCE

ACCIDENTS WILL HAPPEN

Lucy Golden

This book is a work of fiction.
In real life, make sure you practise safe sex.

First published in 2001 by
Nexus
Thames Wharf Studios
Rainville Road
London W6 9HA

Copyright © Lucy Golden 2001

The right of Lucy Golden to be identified as the Author of
this Work has been asserted by her in accordance with the
Copyright, Designs and Patents Act 1988.

www.nexus-books.co.uk

Typeset by TW Typesetting, Plymouth, Devon

Printed and bound by
Cox & Wyman Ltd, Reading, Berks

ISBN 0 352 33596 3

One

Eventually, rather more than half an hour late and with a final, 'See ya!' shouted from the porch steps, the front door was slammed shut. Immediately the voices and giggles were cut off but Julie continued to watch them through the window, their puppet mouths bobbing up and down as they skipped across the road, hand in hand like a television advertisement. The boy's car – new, white, gleaming – was carelessly parked opposite the house. It looked impressive, was doubtless expensive, better than Mike's car – better than any car any boyfriend of Julie's had ever owned. So what?

The boy unlocked the door on his own side and slid in before leaning across to let Gail in. Almost immediately the indicator lights flared out a vivid warning orange to the neighbourhood and the car started to move away. Neither of its occupants looked back at the house, but there was no call for them to do so. Their interest was entirely focused on each other, on how they would spend the next few hours with nothing spare for what they left behind, what was in the past, nor even what was yet out of sight over the horizon. They had already said they would not be home until very late, always assuming they came home at all. They might stay the night at his flat, wherever that was, if he even had one. Julie watched the car pull up in a blaze of red lights at the end of the road before it finally roared away and let the quiet of the street settle back into place.

Julie felt their going as a relief and released the long breath her lungs had been holding on to. She did not want to live Gail's life, knew she could not handle it, but was aware how much more of everything Gail managed to fit in, and she did wish that she could find as much joy as Gail did, that she could derive as much contentment and as much satisfaction in her work, her friends, her casual relationships. Gail was always looking for a long-term love and entered every new relationship with total confidence and enthusiasm, convinced that this would be The Big One, and she never lost that faith. Julie's experience was completely the opposite, for she had a long-term boyfriend, someone fundamentally good, reliable; someone whom her parents liked, to whom she had been engaged for nearly two years and with whom a future of security stretched before her. It should all have been so perfect.

She turned away from the window and dropped down into the big heavy armchair that was all she had brought from her London flat. She looked around the room, sighed and picked up the newspaper but after a superficial glance across the headings of the first half a dozen pages, she dropped it back on to the floor. She lay back, stared up at the ceiling and shut her eyes. Half a minute later, her mind made up, she quickly went to bolt the front door securely and switched the telephone on to the answering machine. She returned to the living room and the same chair, but this time she settled down deep into it, squirmed in, curled her legs up into the enclosing warmth and closed her eyes again.

It is a bright spring day at last, real warmth in the sunshine, real enthusiasm in the birdsong; the horse chestnut trees have turned overnight from bare skeletons to a green so vibrant that it practically glows. The

2

street is quiet but she always approaches the building from the opposite side, crossing over at the last moment. She tries to pretend this is just to stay in the sun for as long as possible, but there is more. It postpones for an extra few minutes the moment when she has to admit where she is heading.

The house is white stucco-faced, one of a terrace of identical buildings – none still lived in, all offices or medical practices. A brass plaque beside the door, on the right-hand side (it is important to keep all these details correct) announces it as the London Research Foundation for Female Sexuality. She runs up the few steps and into the cool shade of the porch. The outer doors are standing open and she ducks through, striding confidently across the deserted hallway. The brightly polished reception desk is deserted but a notice directs final-year candidates to the first-floor administration office. Julie can ignore that and rings the bell, even though she knows the routine perfectly from all those previous visits to this place. She knows where to go, how to behave and how to react.

After a short pause, a girl a couple of years younger than Julie – no, she is even younger than that, barely into her twenties – comes out of the dark inner office, her silhouette showing against the frosted glass briefly before she pushes open the connecting door and recognises Julie immediately. No, she is new.

'Good afternoon. May I help you?'

'I'm Julie Markham.'

'Yes, Miss Markham.' The girl is obviously confused. 'Do you have an appointment?'

'I've come for the exam finals.'

An utterly blank expression still sits serenely on the young girl's face.

'For the practical exam?' Julie puts all her most withering condescension into the question, and suddenly the realisation dawns.

'Oh, of course. I am terribly sorry. Please would you go up to room 23, which is on the second floor. The stairs are –'

'Yes, I know where the room is.'

'Yes, of course you do. I'll let Mrs Watson know you're here. Please go on up.'

She climbs up the familiar rich staircase to the first floor. On one of the doors at the top she can see a notice sellotaped on to the glass; that is the administration office and the notice is for the candidates so she does not bother to read it. Such things do not concern her.

Up another flight, and the nerves are now beginning to get worse. Displaying her experience to that silly young receptionist was so easy, but it will not always be like that. Mrs Watson has been here much longer, and Dr Reading too, of course. As she reaches the top of the second flight, the familiar mix of fear and enthusiasm settles lower in her stomach like a stone that will not be shifted. At the top, she falters briefly, but then she always falters briefly just here; if someone were there to see it, someone to be taken in by the show, it might have had a little more purpose. Mrs Watson appears from her little office at the back of the building and smiles artificially.

'Good afternoon, Miss Markham. How nice to see you again! It seems to have been ages since you were last here but I suppose it is only a few weeks. It really is so kind of you to keep coming back time after time. I really don't know how we would be able to keep going without you.'

Julie blushes obsequiously at her gratitude. 'That is very kind of you, Mrs Watson, but I am sure it is important for us to assist in these matters wherever possible. I can't pretend I enjoy it, of course, but then we must do what we can.'

'It's so kind of you to see it that way. There seem to be more and more candidates for our courses and they just get younger and younger. I must be getting old!' She laughs, and Julie wonders whether to join in the light chatter or to attempt some polite denial of her ageing. It does not matter. The woman carries on talking.

'What a lovely day, though! Really springlike at last and after such a miserable winter. I was really beginning to wonder if we'd ever see sun again. Now then, here we are. You can get undressed in here. Sarah seems to have forgotten to bring a gown; I'll ask her to bring one up.' She opens the door to the waiting room. 'We are running precisely to time, so you won't be kept waiting.'

She closes the door carefully behind her and Julie crosses to the window. The same road, the same square, same outlook, the same cars parked in the same places. Of course, how could it change? What is the point of being so melodramatic? It is the reassurance of the permanence that enables her to continue so easily with this process.

She puts down her handbag carefully on a table beside a big stuffed armchair and then hesitates, wondering whether to wait for Sarah to bring the gown before she undresses, but she decides against it. She pulls her sweater over her head and drops it on to the chair, then picks it up again and lays it neatly across the chair-back, smoothing the soft wool with her fingers. She kicks off her shoes and places them side by side, neatly. There is still no sign of a gown.

She unzips the side of her skirt, slips it down her legs and steps out of it, then lays it carefully across the chair. She fidgets, dawdles a few seconds over unbuttoning the blouse to allow time for the decision to be made for her, time for Sarah to arrive – but there is no sign of her and she dare not keep the examiners waiting. The pale blouse is arranged on top of the sweater, sleeves neatly laid out together. She pauses again, listens for any sound of someone on the stairs. There is no one. She rolls down her tights and, after straightening them out

5

again, adds them to her pile. This leaves only her bra and knickers. There is still silence outside. She sits down for a minute and waits. A door opens and feet – heavy, busy, masculine feet – hurry down the corridor, straight past and down the stairs. They do not pause, as if they were letting someone else pass, someone who might have been hurrying up the stairs. The silence settles back along the corridor and into her waiting room. She gets up from the chair, paces the room and then pauses to listen; a distant traffic hum, voices which could be a television. In the street outside, a car passes, its passage announced and followed by the low steady thump of its radio turned up too loud. She goes back to the chair, casually sweeping her palms up the length of her thighs as she sits. There are pictures on the walls; they are the same as last time she was here. The furniture is the same; everything is gloriously familiar.

Julie sits a few more minutes in her underwear, lightly teases her fingers over the swollen cups of her bra, but is becoming impatient. She can wait no longer. The hooks at the back of her bra unfasten easily. When she stands up and leans forwards, the whole bra slides smoothly across her skin and finally drops away. She glances down at herself, an automatic reaction to her nakedness. They are good, her breasts, full but firm and they retain their elegant shape without the bra. Her nipples too are attractive, long and thick, a rich red that has drawn the attention of many former boyfriends. She tucks the bra under the pile of clothes.

There is now only one thing left to do, so she slides her knickers off and quickly tucks them in under the sweater. Immediately she pulls them out again and checks; although they had been clean on that morning, she has been anticipating this appointment all day – at the office that morning, on the way home, during the hot walk up from the station – and she does not want to be betrayed. They are still reasonably clean and (a quick check to be sure) quite fragrant; she replaces them under the pile.

She stands looking about her and wonders whether to sit down; the chairs look too ready and businesslike to be sat on naked and she is not sure whether it would be entirely hygienic. Besides, supposing she made a mark? A mirror hangs on the far wall and she crosses over to check her hair, smoothing it down as well as she can. It is not a very long mirror, so it is only the upper half of her body that she can see reflected back at her. Her breasts hang attractively with just sufficient fold underneath to be full; at school she had been the first girl in her year to manage the pencil test. Her nipples are just a little bit swollen and respond easily to the pressure of a light pinch. Just right. She cannot see much lower than that in the mirror, but she fluffs out her little bush of ginger pubic hair where it has been squashed flat by her clothes. That too is neatly shaped: delicately trimmed and the sides and underneath cleaned away. She has used a cream, to avoid getting itchy stubble and to make sure there is no nasty red rash, no marks to show how much covering has been removed, how much extra soft tender skin is now being offered up. It feels smooth and clean and appealing and, although she is beginning to feel a little gooey inside, there is no dampness around the lips. The overall effect is satisfying, but she must think about something else, or the signs will become overdone.

She flicks through the magazines on the little table: mostly copies of *Cosmopolitan*, and a couple of bridal glossies, but she has looked through them all before, has already read what little there was of interest – and so she replaces them neatly and wanders away, her hands clasped in front of her where a single finger can slip out unnoticed and slide into the very top of her crease. Standing just inside the window, she leans forwards so that her breasts push against the net curtains. If

7

someone walking by outside happened to glance in, what could they see? She takes a step back again but continues to stare out at the real world beyond the glass, occasionally, lightly, imperceptibly stroking one little fingertip up and down the warm crease. A few more minutes pass and it is all starting to get unbearable so she returns to her chair to be ready.

Still she waits, dragging out the time for as long as she can bear, until at last it is time. She hears the door of the next room open and Dr Reading's clear deep masculine voice.

'Just wait one moment, please, gentlemen, while I fetch our subject.'

He paces heavily down the passage and at last arrives at the door to her waiting room.

'Ah, Miss Markham. So good of you to agree to assist us again.' He tries to ignore the fact that she is completely naked, but does not succeed entirely; his eyes are inevitably drawn down her exposed skin, only briefly, because he is thoroughly professional, but he is still a man, and she is a woman. All her skin feels caressed; tiny tingles have erupted everywhere his eyes have passed so that she knows absolutely that she has been seen. He looks up into her eyes again, his round weathered face peering out of his mass of curly hair, curly beard, curly moustache, and smiles at her. He is dressed in a formal dark suit, waistcoat buttoned across and a silk handkerchief poking elegantly out of his top pocket. He is about to invite her to join him when he appears suddenly to notice that she is not wearing anything.

'Oh, dear, have they given you nothing to put on? That is a very poor show, isn't it? They should have given you a gown or something.'

Just then, Julie sees the receptionist appear in the doorway behind him, her timid face peering round, as she clutches a white hospital-style gown to her chest. She is much more taken aback at Julie's nakedness than

8

he was and stares in at her, appalled at what she sees – although Julie wonders whether it is to a large degree fear of how much trouble she will be in for causing this outrage by failing to put out a gown. Dr Reading turns round.

'Ah, Sarah, about time too. Well, I am afraid you are really far too late with that. There is no point in her putting it on now. We are just going through. Be a little quicker next time. Our visitors should not be expected to sit around here naked. Please come through if you are ready, Miss Markham. No point in keeping you waiting.'

He leads the way out of the room and Julie follows him into the corridor. Sarah watches, jealous of her daring and confidence, envious of her figure, and perhaps a little scandalised that Julie so casually walks naked down the halls of this respectable Institution, her bare feet following quietly down the solemn corridors behind Dr Reading's heavy tread.

They arrive outside the little seminar room at the far end of the hall and Dr Reading pushes open the door and holds it politely for her to enter. Four or five students are gathered there who all look up expectantly as Julie enters. Are there any women among them? No, this time they are all men. Julie is introduced.

'This is Miss Markham, gentlemen, who has very kindly volunteered to be our subject today. You all know the routine so I'll ask you all to pay close attention and not to speak while the examination is in progress. Please wait outside and come in individually to conduct the examination when your name is called.'

They file out nervously, most of them unable to resist last quick glances across at her as they go. They are all impatient now, pleased, maybe even a little surprised, that their subject is someone young and so attractive. Dr Reading brings her up to the high examination couch at the front of the room and carefully shakes out a hygienic plastic sheet over the couch before he asks her to lie down. He even holds her hand while Julie swings her legs up on to the long couch and settles down on her back on the crisp clean sheet, but they both know this will not be enough and he hands her a small towel, which he watches her arrange carefully under her bottom. Finally he pats her thigh, smiles encouragingly and retreats into the corner of the room where he takes up his clipboard, assembles the relevant papers and calls out for the first candidate to enter.

A man appears round the door. He licks his lips as he glances at the doctor but he smiles at Julie when he steps up to the table. Young, perhaps about thirty, and tall, probably six feet: certainly he seems to tower over her where she lies waiting for him to begin. The man nods and smiles again, a friendly enough smile but perhaps more from habit than genuine concern. He knows he is in charge and evidently sees no need to hide the knowledge nor the power. He pulls up a chair beside her couch and sits down. But then he hesitates and turns to Dr Reading.

'Can I ask her questions?'

The doctor does not answer at first and does not glance up from his clipboard, then says simply, 'I am not here.'

The young man frowns briefly before he turns back to his subject and she settles down flatter on her back, her hands clasped across her stomach, as emotionless as she can appear. He stands up again and moves the chair away. 'I should like to examine you first, Miss Markham, to gauge your response to different stimulations and then take details of your history. I shall start with your breasts.'

He leans over and cups his hand around her breast. His thumb pokes up, just brushing the nipple but he ignores it and gently massages the main body of the breast itself, cradling its roundness, smoothing it back and forth in his palm, testing the texture, the resilience. He moves over to the other one and repeats the action:

10

squeezing, moulding, nursing her. He has still not touched either nipple directly but already they are responding to the promise of attention to come, stirring, awakening, stiffening. He takes hold of her wrist, raises her arm over her head and gently runs his fingertips down the sensitive skin of the inside of her wrist, forearm, elbow, upper arm. He even runs across her armpit, but for some reason this does not tickle. He brings up the other arm the same way, both now raised behind her head in a gesture of surrender, of submission, one hand grasping the other, total exposure to his eyes and hands. His fingertips trace down both arms, cross to her temples and cheeks, across her throat to her chest, down to her breasts again, circle round them and finally up over the nipple. He circles it half a dozen times; then at last the fingertips close tenderly over the raised point, pinching it into a full erection, responsive like a penis. He leans forwards and she thinks he is going to kiss her, but instead the soft hollows of his cheek sweep alternately across her skin in a wide all-embracing circle that takes in her shoulders, breasts and down to her stomach. His chin is noticeably coarser, a very slight trace of stubble that scrapes tenderly across her chest and only after the third or fourth circle do his lips home in on her nipple as he passes, nipping them painfully in a sudden pinch. The second time round he catches them again but this time the nip is followed by a flick of the tongue, so quick it is barely noticeable, a sudden dart like a serpent, gone before it is there, whose effect is unnoticeable until afterwards when the withdrawal of contact and sudden cold from the dampness is more obvious and more arousing than the actual touch had been.

He is good, this man, attentive and steady, careful not to hurry her; and yet she sees his eyes watching attentively for any signals on her face, on her skin, in her breathing. She suddenly becomes aware of his hands

11

again. They had been passing unnoticed until then but now she feels them moving so slowly and so lightly up and down the sides of her ribs, infinitesimally moving lower on every sweep, beyond her waist now and edging towards her hips. She lies as still as she is able, fearful that any sudden movement will drive him off, and keeps her legs straight and close together, even though she feels this man may be one of the rare exceptions who is able to produce a response on the first approach.

He is still gently nibbling on her breasts, but now concentrates exclusively on her nipples, drawing them into his mouth, licking around them, over the top and sucking them painfully deep into his mouth. Her breaths are getting deeper and she suddenly hears a gasp which she realises is her own. Behind her, the doctor's chair creaks as he adjusts his position. Dimly in the distance she hears a telephone ring twice before it is taken up by an answering machine; she shuts out the distraction.

The man's mouth starts to move slowly further down her body, still nibbling, sucking and licking at her skin, running his open mouth across her so lightly that it almost tickles; almost but not quite. He reaches her belly button, pauses and licks there, his tongue pushing in and circling into the dip, but then moves further down. She is aware of a fidgeting, a rustling from behind her – perhaps from the doctor, perhaps other spectators – but the man ignores them. Unintentionally, she realises that she has opened her legs a little: sufficient invitation for him, she hopes, for where she needs his attention and caresses. He ignores her and she feels his breath on the very sensitive skin at the join of her thighs and moving down her legs. At some point his hands must have passed her hips, for they are now much further down her legs, skimming to her knees and then gradually retracing the path, higher, higher. His hands twist round the tops of her thighs, slipping between them and, just when she hopes they will slide upwards, they

12

slide down. At her knees they twist round again, always caressing, always seeking new sensitive spots to stroke, to feel and experience, new sensations which shoot up to her brain and instil pictures there of these strange new hands running at will over her skin and all over her proffered naked body. There is a rushing swoop of his palms down her calves to her ankles and then at last the start of a slow, firm and unstoppable return up her legs. Her legs are now further apart than they had been but whether she moved them or he did, she is unsure. She should have noticed. At the thighs the hands slow a fraction but never stop altogether and now his mouth joins in too, little kisses nibbled up the delicate insides of her skin, following just behind his hands. At last they reach her opening crease. She sucks in a desperate breath, drawing deep as if she will draw him inside her as well.

The twisting fingers manipulate her and mould her, sliding her thighs further apart and hanging her legs over the sides of the couch so she is presented ever more accessibly to his reach. One thumb drops down the fold almost to her bottom and then, pushing in a fraction, just parting the swollen lips, slides up to scoop a sample of her juice. This gesture is so direct, so totally contrasting with the subtlety of his previous caresses and the devious way he had lured her body into responding to its own desires, that she gasps aloud, clutching the sheet in her fists. He circles his thumb around the top of her fold, running up over her swollen clitoris and back down to the bottom again. He pauses, hesitates, his fingertip touching so lightly that tiny point between entry and exit where he can choose his moves, dropping a fraction to tickle the delicacy that she herself has never dared to explore.

He waits. He makes her wait, makes her wonder whether he will continue or leave her panting. Her eyes reach up for him although his are concentrated between her legs. Her hands struggle to stay still, her lips start to

13

mouth words of begging and finally, after a lifetime, she sees him smile and feels his thumb worm its way in again, a fraction further this time, smearing her lips aside as it drives back up the crease to the top. This time he flicks his thumb right out of the fold, but the backs of his fingers, curled gently, float across her trimmed hair and trace their way up her body across her stomach, between her breasts, over her throat to her chin. The scent, her own scent, is carried like a trophy on the plump ball of his glistening thumb to hover beneath her nostrils.

For the first time their eyes meet; his are smiling, assured of his victory, but he does not speak as he drops his thumb on to her lips and then presses it into her mouth. The taste is strong, unmistakable, and sinfully familiar. He rubs his thumb across her tongue and then over her teeth, her gums, back to her tongue. Her taste is inflicted on her like a punishment that she longs to endure. She closes her eyes again to keep her secrets locked in safe from his sight, and in response she hears a chuckle from the man leaning over her and then the sound of movement from the doctor behind her again.

This time the doctor stands up and saunters round to watch from the end of the couch, beside Julie's hips. Still clutching the clipboard and making occasional notes, he studies the candidate's actions, then examines her, peering at her breasts, down at her sex. Suddenly he frowns, leans towards her and, with the sterile tip of his sharp pen, carefully separates her vaginal lips and slides it a short distance into the vagina itself. He peers inside for a moment before releasing her, removing his pen and making another careful note. He leans forwards again, scrapes the sharp point across that most delicate little slit of her urethra, but it half opens to him, like a little mouth offering kisses and he moves on. When he returns to his seat, he is sucking the end of his pen, not a habit she has noticed before.

14

The candidate is undisturbed by this and continues to run his thumb over her mouth before slithering a path back down her body, taking in a sweep over her breasts, a squeeze at her nipples: but the indirectness of the caresses is beginning to become unbearable. Her explosive gasp is more of frustration than anticipation and yet he is immediately responsive to the change of mood, glances at her face and then quickly returns to the task before him, one hand now homing in. He lifts one thigh and pulls it further towards him, opening her more to his inspection, to the view of the doctor and, by turning the entire couch on its little wheels, to the gaze of the row of waiting candidates who she finds have all returned to the room and are lined up at the back. He pulls up her feet and pushes her legs down flat so that she can see down the length of her body to the attentive watchers, sitting unblinking, craning forward towards her. She can visualise what they can see and tries to press her legs a little flatter.

His left hand floats down across her stomach and skims over her pubic hair to cover her open sex in its grasp. He rubs down the length once and back up again, and down a second time; then the fingers splay to spread her lips wide on the return journey. He stops then, still holding her wide open, but he does not look himself. This exhibition is for the line of men at her feet and for the doctor. He displays to them the results of his skill, the swollen pink wetness that he has induced, and she sees him looking over smugly first at his colleagues and then across at the doctor.

Keeping her angled the same way, with her feet towards the other men, he makes her turn over on to her stomach and to lift up her hips. She has never been asked to do this before but realises that, with her feet spread to the very edges of the examination couch, she is completely displayed, even more than she had been before, and that her careful depilation of the edges of

15

her sex will have further deprived her of any vestige of covering. She shivers and rests her head on the soft cushion under her cheek, feeling her blush burn in her face. He moves her knees even further up the couch and then, with both hands positioned very carefully, one on each side of her bottom, he pulls her buttocks apart. Automatically she clenches, but he waits patiently until her reaction has passed and then repeats the move. This time she can feel the tension in her bottom itself, feel even that tiny hole caused to open. One gentle fingertip tickles her there, right at the very centre where it is all so sensitive and forbidden.

He releases her but, still holding her open, his other hand slides down to circle the puffed rim of her outer lips and then, making a vee of his fingers, he traces up the very edge of her lips, back down both sides in the hot furrows. At the bottom the fingers close and the tips briefly pinch her clitoris before they run up together to spread her delicate inner lips flat and then to pull them open for the watchers to see deep inside her. On the return run, this time, he pauses at the middle and, with a sudden vicious twist, invades her body with both fingers at once. She is shocked at the suddenness of this assault – gasps, squeezes him, desperate to hold him in at last and, at the same time, she pushes her pelvis up against his thumb as it rotates over her clitoris, pressing from side to side. It is all too much for her – the public exposure in front of so many appreciative eyes, the lack of respect, his pride in her response and, after the hours of anticipation earlier in the day, the treatment she has received here in front of so many people is overwhelming. She feels the rapid swell of ecstasy not so much growing within her but materialising all over her body, in every limb, every inch of skin, every nerve, growing unstoppably and exploding out of her with something that is almost a scream as she loses all conscious control. She is panting for more and clamping her hands

16

across her sopping over-stimulated sex to hold in the wonder of the feelings that surge through her and pour over her and leave her shaking, quivering and so gloriously, pantingly alive.

Julie slowly unwound herself, turning back in the chair and sliding her feet back down to the floor, stretching her arms up over her head, flexing her muscles and smoothing the relaxation out along her limbs. Still flushed, hot and breathless, she lay back in the chair, squirming in the warmth and squeezing her thighs possessively round the little folded towel. She stretched her arms behind her head, legs pushed out straight in front, feet and toes pointed. A star. A star for her good behaviour.

It had been good, better than for many weeks, and yet also a little unnerving. This sequence – she never thought of it as a fantasy, because it was far too real for that – was very familiar. It had worked for her for many years, ever since she had been a teenager, and had maintained its irresistible power since then, with few changes. Sometimes the first candidate was enough; sometimes it needed more. On some occasions, the doctor himself had had to step in. There had even been periods – the last one had been a couple of years ago – when many of the candidates had been women. In the last few months, a woman had sometimes been there to watch, but never more than that. So far.

This time, and even though she had been careful not to picture him too clearly, the first candidate had looked much like Peter: too much like Peter. This time, all the others had suddenly appeared in the room to watch her; before, it had only been the doctor in the room with the candidate. This time she had been bent over and, although her bottom had only been shown and not used, not used in any way, she was unsure how that might develop. But it had been good.

17

She giggled to herself and combed the fingers of both hands back through her thick curly hair and then dropped her hands to the chair. Suddenly she realised what she had done and raised her fingers to her face. The scent lingered, pure and unmistakable. She smiled to herself. Supposing she were to wander around town with her hair smelling of pussy, even her own pussy? Would people notice? It would be very tempting to try.

She looked down along the length of her body, sprawled naked in the chair – her own chair, her special chair. Her breasts were still full and tender; her lips too, she found, and the carefully placed towel felt damp beneath her bottom. She tugged it out and held it up in the air where it displayed a clear oval badge of her excitement. That was what seemed so sad, so pathetically wasteful. There was so much she could do, wanted to do – and yet Mike asked for so little. He was so kind and generous and yet so bland. She really had loved him at first, and his concern and patience and attentiveness were such a contrast from the arrogant gropings of the boys she had grown up with. At first she had been carried away on a dream of romance and domestic harmony. But it had palled and, even though her mother had said all the right things about him, emphasised all that she saw as best, the picture that was painted for her – painted with the very best of motives – was not one in which Julie really felt she wanted to appear.

Suddenly she shivered, retrieved her blouse and started to put it on, but then lay it back over the chair. The room had already started to grow dark and, even as she looked out, the streetlamp at their gate suddenly sprang into startled orange life. Several of the houses opposite had the first of their lights on. It would soon be time for bed, and there was little point in getting dressed again for so short a time. Instead, she would scrape what pleasure she could from the loneliness and stay naked. She straightened the magazines on the small

18

table, tidied the cushions and the blanket on the settee and padded out to the kitchen with the mugs which Gail and her new trophy had left on the table. Standing in the gloom to rinse them at the steel sink, she gasped when the cold water splashed up on to her naked breasts and for a brief glorious second she turned the tap on even harder, watching the little drops sparkling on her skin. She set the mugs to drain. Beyond her, past the cold cracked glass, the little garden lay neglected and overgrown, and the houses behind were starting to glow with family lives and her bed was empty. For a moment she was tempted to walk out and savour her nakedness in the stickiness of the night as she brushed through the scratchy weeds and shrubs. But that was too much; she might be seen.

Julie returned to the living room and collected her clothes from their neat pile next to her chair, the shoes placed neatly under it, and made her way up to her room. As she passed the answering machine in the hall, she stopped to listen to the message that it had picked up. As expected, it was for Gail, so she left it, attaching the sticky yellow note they used for each other on to the front of the machine in case Gail did come back that evening.

She climbed slowly up to bed, deciding to read for a little before settling down to sleep, something to take her mind off the sadness she felt at the trap of her own making that was closing in on all sides. She also needed to decide about her escape plan, of flight to a new life in a new city in a new country – thoughts which had been growing ever stronger and more appealing since the seeds were planted three months ago. Besides, her sister would be arriving on Sunday; she could hardly admit total failure to her.

The days were passing quickly. Mr Collis would be back next week. If she was going to do anything, it had to be soon.

Two

Since the normal practice at Quinlon & Withers, Solicitors, was for the staff to knock as a courtesy but to enter without waiting for an answer, Peter Harrison did not respond when he heard a knock on his door in the middle of one Friday morning. He did turn his mind and his face back to a file staring up from the desk in front of him, but he didn't read it. The case had been occupying most of his time but none of his interest for a number of days and he was still struggling to scrape together enough enthusiasm to finish off the relatively simple report that was all it now lacked.

Peter was twenty-eight years old, close enough to six feet tall to be able to claim it, good-looking, unmarried and unsatisfied. He was even relatively rich, the result of a very lucky investment of a small amount of money he had inherited, while still at college, from an old friend of his father's. Now he was fully qualified, specialising in property law; and, although some aspects still interested him, most of the work had lost its novelty. However, unlike most of his contemporaries, he had outgrown the blind pursuit of money for its own sake. Having already accumulated a solid capital, achieved a secure and handsome salary and the prospect of an early invitation to the partnership, there seemed little to be gained in chasing mindlessly after more. As yet, no substitute interest had emerged and he was beginning to think that although, ten years ago, the view from the bottom of his professional ladder had been daunting, the view from here, not a great number of rungs from the top, was disappointing. He tossed the papers back on his desk and stared out of the window.

It was late summer, the last few weeks of what was becoming a regular series of record-breaking British summers: the driest June for so many years, the hottest July since whenever. The managing partner, Robert Collis, was away on his regular August holiday, leaving the rest of the staff to sweat out the long days from which he had escaped. The offices, three storeys plus an attic, had been converted from an Edwardian family house and, although pleasant enough, it was not very efficient and in recent weeks had been stifling. Besides, Peter resented being pushed up to the second floor with the two junior professionals while Collis ruled the first.

During Collis's absence, most of the work fell on Peter's shoulders, although nominally Douglas Withers was in charge. In practice, Douglas had taken little interest in the running of the office for several years and was perfectly happy to leave everything to Peter. He wined, dined and golfed the established clients and, Peter admitted in his more charitable moments, by doing so probably brought more money into the firm's coffers than Peter did himself. There was very little work in hand: it seemed that everyone was away on holiday for the summer, and Peter was looking forward to his own break, now less than five weeks away. The worst of the tourist traffic would have left Cadiz by then, and he would be able to walk and swim and ride along the beaches in relative peace. There would be other diversions too: good food, strong wine and a selection of impatient and lonely local companions for the evenings who would be lured by his almost perfect Spanish, delightedly shocked by his gutter vocabulary, flattered by his constancy and finally seduced by his sheer determination. He would bring home a selection of the food and wines, and, with convincing sorrow, leave behind the companions.

After that, he anticipated changes. Heavy hints had been dropped by both Collis and Withers that he would soon be moving on from his cramped office on the second floor. He had started to regard with proprietorial longing the huge, mostly empty, first-floor room that was still ostensibly Douglas Withers' office.

So the morning had dragged by while Peter, with steadily growing irritation, made a half-hearted attempt to correct the draft report that Janice had produced with such ill-deserved confidence. The number and extent of his corrections were rapidly rendering the draft unreadable until it would now be simpler to redictate the whole thing. At various stages during the interminable morning, he had picked it up, read it through and then given up and tossed it down again. He had not decided about the weekend; he had been invited to another gathering at the usual hotel in the Lake District and, although he could combine this with a duty visit to his parents – a visit which was long overdue – he could still not be wholeheartedly enthusiastic. He had been to three of these events at that hotel but always felt himself too much a spectator and not enough a contributor, so that the happiness and completeness of the others' lives only underlined the cold emptiness in his.

He returned to his desk and continued crossing through several of the more glaring errors – how could she have thought he would need 'site' of the plans?

He wished he could bring himself to get rid of Janice, but she had been part of his inheritance from Douglas. She had been there ten years, working her way up to secretary, and at this stage he could not sack her for incompetence without risking an Employment Tribunal complaint. By most standards she was competent enough for the tasks she was given, simple though they were, and Peter could guess how she had come to be recruited: Douglas Withers was as easily persuaded by a well-filled bra as anybody Peter had ever met. How the girl had ever managed to pass any exams was a different question.

Yet it was not her typing, or her spelling, or her excessive familiarity with clients that galled him; he was charitable enough to forgive her all of that. It was the one thing she could never correct. She was Janice: she wasn't Beth.

He still thought, dreamed, yearned and fantasised about Beth. From the moment she had arrived from the agency, walked into his office and sat down in that little chair, huddled into a ball of evasive fragility, Peter had been unsettled. Dark and barely reachable, her thick red hair billowed around a tiny sharp face set with eyes of jade, innocent and knowledgeable. They knew and understood everything they had ever witnessed, but were unsullied by their knowledge. She had worked there for only two weeks while Janice was on holiday, but what a two weeks. Not only was she good at her work, she had been so easy to get along with. She knew how far to go and where the limits lay.

By the end of the first week their silly flirtation had become serious and they went, once, for lunch together. During the following week it progressed steadily.

Tuesday had produced the first kiss.

Wednesday had been drinks after work. Beth had drunk two pints of strong beer and then sat squirming, too shy to ask for the toilets. He loved her sweet naïveté.

Thursday had been everything. They had gone for a drink before seeing a film, yet still she hadn't learned her lesson, and had wriggled through it in bloated discomfort before running to the toilets as soon as the film ended. Together they had eaten a late supper and then he had taken her back to his flat. She had been shamefully shy and shamelessly passionate. When he

23

leaned forwards to kiss her, her tongue reached out for his before their lips had touched. When he first peeled off her soft baggy sweater, her breasts, magically pale and freckled, so slight he could cover each one entirely in his cupped hand, had been so sensitive and responsive to his kisses that he was convinced she had actually reached an orgasm before she was even fully undressed. When he drew away her long skirt, long but insubstantial, slit almost to the waist, her skimpy knickers had virtually dissolved in her juice before he slid them down her legs. When he pressed apart her thighs and bent to kiss her there, to inhale the sweetest scent of pure desire, she opened herself, spread herself, offered herself so completely and so defencelessly that he licked and kissed and lapped and suckled until her tiny fingers gripped his hair, her slender thighs clamped his head and finally her savage cries screamed out into the night.

And then he had taken her into his bed and she had surrendered to him: slipped her hands up under the pillow and struggled just sufficiently when he held her wrists. Her pleas to be tied had been whispered in shame into his shoulder and, when a frantic search found nothing better than a tie, she had accepted the feeble substitute with only the mildest look of recrimination as she offered up her hands.

After that she was so passionate it was hard to believe this was the same girl who he knew in the daylight. Her body had responded to everything he offered her and when he could not offer enough she took it herself. She squirmed beneath him without once seeking a pause. Knowing it would be too much, he rested all his weight on her, pinning her beneath him, and she groaned for more. When he lifted away, she pushed up her torso, scratching her tiny breasts against his chest, reaching out to him with her mouth, her lips pressing to him, her tongue reaching for the sweat from his body, licking into his armpits and breathing him in. When he reached

24

down between her legs, her lips felt utterly full and soft but were so wet he could hardly hold her. When he smeared his palm across her, collecting a full handful of her honey which he spread over her mouth and cheeks, she savoured her own taste and aroma just as much as he did himself. Afterwards, when he was drained and he finally released her and she should have been sated, she sat astride him and, without shame or even selfconsciousness, crooked her long fingers between her thighs and masturbated herself to another screamed orgasm against her fingers, her palm, his chest and his chin, flooding him, bruising him, clawing him. Even then, after all that, she lay down in the crook of his arm, but lay on her stomach and pulled his hand over her buttock and wriggled, just once, so he wondered what more it was she wanted. The target was clear but the assault he would save for another day.

But there never was another day. He had been woken once in the night to find her buried under the bedclothes, where she had brought him to a full erection and within thirty seconds of a climax without even waking him. But she went on licking him beautifully and swallowed it all. He had woken a second time to find her in tears and had finally dragged out of her that she had only just broken up with a boyfriend of many years' standing. They held each other through the rest of the night and he had found himself reconsidering his determined opposition to marriage. At work the next day, the last day of her contracted fortnight, Beth had been back to her usual self. She refused to have lunch with him, although she swore that she had loved the night they had spent together. She refused to have a drink with him but said she would remember him to her dying day. It just would not be sensible to go on. It would never work. In desperation, he said he thought he loved her, but she had been adamant and, in the end, although he did not understand her decision, he had no option but to accept it because she had given him so much that he could now deny her nothing.

Yet he still thought about her, dreamed about her, worried about her. It had been more than a year ago, and he knew she was far too young for him, but every day he wondered what had become of her and who could now be enjoying that intensity of desire. He worried whether any spark that burned so bright could burn for long; whether, if he could find her – and surely the agency must have an address – if he did not ask her to work for him, he could ever persuade her to live with him.

Two months burned by and finally he did contact the agency, explaining how terribly important it was, that files she had been working on were lost and he needed to contact her: a matter of life and death. The agency was adamant in its self-protecting secrecy but finally agreed to forward a letter. A month later a reply arrived for him at home: no address, but postmarked Barcelona, it repeated the regretful but determined refusal.

And then that bizarre catalogue, which surely must have been her doing. It was at least six months after she had gone – yes, February, because when he first saw the big envelope he had wondered if it was an early birthday present – that a catalogue arrived for him. He had not ordered it but, when he checked with the company, someone had; someone had ordered it in his name, with his home address and paid for it. By cheque, no record kept of the account name. Nevertheless, the catalogue fuelled his imagination and fantasies anew, for suddenly it brought within his reach another world, a world of which he knew nothing but one that Beth had hinted at: belts, bonds, handcuffs, paddles, canes, clamps, clips, hoods. Convinced that Beth was intending to return, he started to explore this strange new world, determined that he should not be found wanting a second time. The catalogue produced the equipment. Discreet enquiries of colleagues and friends produced unlikely invitations and even less likely enthusiasts in a circle of parties and clubs and gatherings. Beth never appeared.

Yet those memories, the potential of that catalogue, the desire she had not dared confess, ate away like acid at his balance. They destroyed any pride in his work and achievements, illuminated the hollowness of all other pleasures, picked remorselessly at his composure and concentration while images of that tortured pale body danced through his mind. The elfin face, with mouth wide open and eyes tight shut, floated up out of the mist. The twisted limbs, wrists bound, tiny fists clenched, thighs spread wide and welcoming, hovered out of his reach. The pale breasts appeared, soft, eager and clamped in shining steel; the nipples . . .

And it was in the middle of this reverie that the knock sounded on his door, and when no face followed but instead the knock was repeated, he eventually called to the visitor to come in.

The face peering round at him was the last he would have expected: Julie Markham, Mr Collis's new secretary. She had joined the firm towards the end of last year to replace old Mrs Nelson, and made clear from the start that she considered herself to be due the same respect as was shown to Collis himself. She frequently recounted how she had previously worked at a much bigger company in London and implied that this work, this firm, these people, were beneath her. She was blissfully engaged to an absolutely wonderful man whom nobody else had met; they had known each other ever since university, were positively made for each other and would be getting married very soon.

And, worse, she was extremely attractive. At the overlubricated Christmas party a few weeks after her arrival, the consensus of the assembled males had been that she was the best-looking of all the women in the office.

27

She evidently shared this opinion and, in her dealings with both Collis and Withers, she played on it with huge success. She had once tried to play Peter the same way, had tried to create a bond by her own study of Spanish literature at university, but he had not been interested. Although not married, she was engaged and he had no wish to create complications in his life. Besides, his mind was still too full of little Beth's ecstatically complete surrender, that sweet defenceless obedience, to feel any desire for Julie's almost arrogant self-confidence. She never repeated the attempt.

Still, although he excluded her from his life and his bed, he frequently admitted her to a fantasy in which her prim superiority was turned to a sensual passion. When she was not looking, he watched her move, speculating about the body beneath her clothes; visualising the shape of her breasts, if he could ever free them of their bra; the texture of her nipples, the shape and extent of the areolae; wondering whether the thick auburn hair was as rich and as thick under her arms and between her legs as it was on her head. Bizarrely, shamefully, he pictured her body twisting in the leather bonds that he had intended for Beth, her arms and legs stretched wide to the corners of an iron bedframe; her breasts bound, her nipples clamped, her whole body offered to him, offered without restriction. He imagined the elegant tailored clothes ripped aside to allow better access to her skin; the delicate wrists rubbed red and raw from ropes cutting too tight at her flesh; her buttocks striped and purple, quivering and trembling as she knelt in expectation of more to come. He nursed fantasies of those neatly reddened lips crying out in an ecstasy of satisfaction induced from an excess of pain; the sneering voice screaming to be released and begging to be abused; the prim, cultivated self-control drowned by a wave of desire for which no mannered schooling, no London society, no stolid fiancé could possibly have prepared her.

28

It all stayed an idle fantasy and speculation. She was too tall, only an inch or two shorter than Peter himself – too sophisticated to release her inhibitions as Beth had done; too refined and glamorous to be the fragile submissive that Beth had appeared; even too pallid for, although Beth's fair complexion had seemed ethereal, a similar colour on Julie just looked pasty. Before Beth, she might have appealed. Since Beth, his tastes had moved on and the conventional stability represented by Julie's confidence and maturity now only taunted and did not tempt him.

So he was doubly shocked at the contrast when she sidled into his room, fighting back tears as she carefully closed the door behind her. However, it looked as if tears had been flowing only recently, for a crumpled handkerchief was still clutched in one hand, and a thin buff folder in the other. He invited her to sit down, less moved by her evident grief than by the sudden and utter change from her usual selfassurance. He could not help but feel some sympathy and surprised himself with his own tenderness as he set aside the caution that normally tempered his dealings and asked her to explain the problem.

As her tale tumbled out, he realised what the confession must have cost. Collis had gone away for three weeks' holiday and, she explained, just before leaving he had asked her to give Peter a letter regarding a development project that was needed urgently for one of the firm's major clients. She had completely forgotten about it until going through her desk in preparation for Collis's return next week. She could not hope to hide the omission once he got back, although Peter could well imagine she would have done almost anything to do so – so, if Peter did not cover for her, and in fact make a good stab at doing in a day and a half what should have taken three weeks, she was in real trouble, all her fine London experience notwithstanding. She frankly admitted it was her fault but asked if there was anything she could do to put it right. What she clearly meant was whether he would help her.

Her account dried up and she sat twisting the handkerchief in her lap, looking appealingly at him, her lips quivering but her eyes begging him to respond. He turned and gazed out across the carpark for a moment, an area of gravel where once had been a garden, giving himself time to consider the options.

He was tempted simply to refuse. He owed her nothing and he found himself rather looking forward to the prospect of her first having to repeat the confession to Collis and then being in a considerable amount of trouble. Collis was not a man who readily forgave what he would consider to have been a completely careless oversight. However, to be that cruel, particularly after the girl had made such a humble confession and so totally thrown herself on his mercy, would be not just unnecessary but dangerous. He understood enough of office politics to know that whoever antagonises the boss's secretary plays a very risky game. This was always assuming that she was not fired; he would not entirely put that past Collis, but it was unlikely. No, she would survive, but she would be looking for revenge, and rebuilding her own status could be achieved most easily by bringing others down.

Even so, he could see no good coming from allowing himself to be sucked deeply into the mess that she had made, and what she was asking was an impossible task. She was not just asking him to help; in reality she was squarely asking him to take the blame. Looked at from that viewpoint, he had no choice. He simply was not prepared to put himself so far out on a limb for her.

Peter turned back quickly but, in the split second before she turned her head down into her lap, he caught the ghost of a smile and that eliminated any lingering doubts. He could imagine her thoughts, her easy assurance that he could be lured by a tear and a plea and bent to her will. She would discover she was wrong; he was tougher than that.

'I'm sorry, Julie, but I can't help you. You're really asking too much of me to try to do this in so short a time. If you'd given me a little longer, even a few days, I could have made a fair stab at it. Now it's too late. If I were to try to do this now, it would simply put my head in the noose instead of yours – and, at this stage of my career, I simply cannot afford that kind of a blot on my record. Collis would be even harder on me than on you; you can plead inexperience, but he would not accept that from me.'

She started to cry and he stopped, hesitated and then took a breath and ploughed on, a ramble of words to cover the lack of feeling. He offered apologies but no help, explaining quite truthfully that he had tried to be helpful in this kind of mess before and it generally only culminated in the helper sinking while the real culprit swam away from the wreckage. He ended with an assurance that Collis would not mind too much but, in the silence that followed, he regretted the remark. They both knew it to be untrue and it cast a shadow of falsehood across everything else he had said.

She whispered, 'Please, Peter.'

He gently shook his head.

'Look, I know you quite fancy me – I mean, you do, don't you? I would be very grateful . . .' and she tailed off and looked down.

'What exactly do you mean?'

'If you help me, I would make it up to you.'

'Meaning . . .?'

'I would do anything you wanted.'

He looked at her sitting timidly in front of him; she recrossed her ankles. That chair was where Beth used to sit. Indeed this girl's posture was remarkably similar and the bowed head, nervous twisting fingers and soft voice rekindled dangerous images that beguiled him. The images of leather bands, of steel clips and whips pushed forwards out of the mist. If he could not have Beth, this could be the next best thing.

'What exactly does "anything" mean?'

But she said nothing, simply continued to stare down at her hands, clutching the folder tightly to her chest, tangling her handkerchief through her fingers.

He studied her through a few more breaths. Whatever silly mistake she may have made over this letter, she was by no means naïve, and must realise where so total a surrender was likely to lead and what the consequences would be. He probed a little further.

'Do you understand what you are asking me to do?'

'Yes.'

'And do you understand what I may ask in exchange?'

'Yes.'

'Are you quite sure?'

A nod.

'And are you prepared to deliver –' he paused '– anything?'

Another nod and a whispered, 'Yes.'

'For how long?'

She paused, obviously calculating. 'For this weekend? Until Monday morning?'

'Isn't Mr Perfect coming to visit?'

Her eyes darkened briefly at his description, but she did not rise to it. 'I'll tell him I'm busy.'

Her ready acquiescence took a few moments to sink in. 'I've been invited to spend the weekend with some friends.'

'Oh! I didn't know.'

'No. Why should you?'

'Couldn't you change that?'

'What makes you think I would want to?' But even as he said the words and she sat quiet and tearful in front

32

of him, he realised that a weekend with her could be just what he needed, and the change of plans would not be a problem at all. It would only take a phone call and a generous gesture such as this would raise his standing enormously. That prospect alone almost made the risk worthwhile. 'All right, this is what I will do. I make no promises, but give me time to look at the papers, and I'll see whether anything can be salvaged from the mess you have made. Meanwhile, you will go back to your office and you will draw up a contract, a clear statement, in detail, of your side of the agreement. Bring that back to me in ten minutes, signed. Understood?'

She nodded. 'Yes,' then corrected herself. 'Yes, sir.'

He grinned as the door closed behind her. 'Sir' was good; very good.

The folder she had left him with contained a five-page brief which presumably had come with some covering letter that was still downstairs but, when he started to read through the brief in detail, he found the situation was not nearly as hopeless as it had first appeared, nor as involved as Julie clearly believed. For one thing, the client was really asking more for an outline and a cost estimate than for a full advisory brief and, for another, the work was very similar to something Peter had done for a different client only four or five months previously. For the purposes of a brief, a very great deal of that could be reused almost unchanged. There seemed no real need to share that with Julie when she returned as instructed at the end of the ten minutes.

He held out his hand and she meekly passed a piece of paper across to him. He waved her back to the chair while he read her contract. It was very brief:

'I, Julie Markham, undertake that from the moment of signing this agreement until 9.00 a.m. on Monday, September fourth, I will serve without question and obey any instructions of whatever nature given to me by Peter Harrison.' Beneath that was the word 'signed' and a row of dots. There were no exclusions, no provisos or exemptions for her at all. The girl was clearly serious, putting herself completely in his hands, even though she must realise that he was going to exact a high price. He said nothing, but looked across at her, trying to pretend a reluctance that he no longer felt, and trying to maintain a clear mind as he reconsidered the options.

Rather than being a spectator with little to contribute, as had always been the case before, this time he could be just the opposite. For the next few days, this proud, arrogant body would be his entirely. The weekend was certainly starting to look a little brighter and he reached over for the phone.

Three

For Julie, the entire morning had been passed trying to find the courage to make this cold lonely climb to Peter's office. After abortive attempts over previous days, when she had fetched all the papers, checked her appearance, swallowed her fears and gathered up the emotion and finally started up the stairs, this one had to work. With every day that passed, the gnawing, nagging irritation at the back of her mind grew more insistent, goading her on with the knowledge that Collis would be back in the office in two weeks, then in ten days, then next week, finally on the following Monday – and so these were her last few days of freedom. She knew she had to make her approach to Peter now or lose the opportunity, probably for ever. Although she realised that her plan was far from ideal, and if she were to be rebuffed her position would be rendered even worse than if she did not try at all, she could see no other solution.

Now she was committed; she had made her appeal, laid bare her weakness and passed across the contract he had demanded. Sitting now in his office, grateful for both the scrap of security offered by the desk between them and the meagre comfort that her fingers squeezed from the sodden handkerchief, she watched him suspiciously unfold the paper and start to read the document which gave him everything.

Lying in bed the previous night, alone, hot and sweaty, she had tried to close her ears to the sounds coming up from downstairs, to the steady rhythmic creaking of some unidentified piece of furniture which ended with a crash of broken glass and an eruption of poorly suppressed laughter. A few minutes later the cries, grunts and giggles had moved up to the bedroom next door, where it was even harder to shut out the images that were summoned up, not to picture in vivid detail precisely what Gail must be looking like at this exact fevered ecstatic moment as she clawed naked at whichever eager and panting target she had shepherded up to her room. Instead Julie had reconsidered all the options for the hundredth time, systematically discarded all but this and promised herself again that today she would do it. She really would not let her courage fail her yet again.

With new determination, this morning she had reviewed again everything she had learned from her careful study of Peter Harrison; from listening to what he said, probing the books he read and the films he went to see. Viewed objectively, Julie was satisfied she had done her groundwork thoroughly and she was as certain as she ever could be that, if she laid the trail well, he would follow exactly where she needed.

She recognised that he thought her conceited, perhaps arrogant and, despite his voluble protestations, her experience in a large London firm clearly rankled. In consequence, he would no doubt exact a higher price, but both his dislike and his jealousy would inflate the temptation when presented with this opportunity.

And today, things felt right. If it would ever work, it would work today. So this morning she had finally managed to complete the trip and by the time she reached his office her face had been flushed scarlet, her eyes streaming red and, if there were no actual tears, she had been certain that she looked sufficiently helpless and penitent to secure his help. With this confidence, she had taken a deep breath, pulled the handkerchief from her pocket, knocked on his door and, for the first time ever, waited outside to be invited in.

Now he sat in front of her, still reading, still considering – but she could follow the train of thoughts as each trailed through his head: when his refusal weakened; when he hesitated; when he wavered – and then came the moment when he read through her declaration a second time and smoothed it out on the surface between them. She smiled to herself. Whatever words he might say from then on, whatever he believed himself, he had taken the hook. She had won. She had only to continue to play her part and he would do everything she needed.

Yet she did still have to play her part, to keep up her side. She managed a slight stutter. 'Will that be all right? Will you help me?' She presented her blotched eyes, tear-streaked face and quivering mouth.

'Yes, all right. Sign it.' And he handed it back to her.

Then it was her turn to hesitate. Just as he was now committed, so too would she be as soon as the paper was signed. This was her last chance to withdraw. No, she realised, that point had passed when she knocked on his door. If the path ahead was going to be hard – and doubtless it would be – the sooner she started on it, the sooner it would be ended.

She had brought no pen with her and reached across the desk to take up the fountain pen lying there. She had moved without thinking and held it in her hand before she realised fully what she had done. This man was about to become a partner in the firm, her boss, and she should have asked permission before helping herself; furthermore, she realised, it was his own fountain pen, real silver, and one he valued very highly. She must not be overconfident, must not overplay her hand. For this small point, it was too late, so she carried on, noticing that her fingers were trembling as she applied her name to the bottom of the sheet. She handed back the paper and carefully replaced the pen.

'Shut the door.' Still she could not trust her expression if she were to look him in the face, but she obeyed and returned to sit meekly like any good secretary would, waiting to see what he would need next.

'Take your clothes off.'

Julie felt her entire body seize up, her skin turning cold as she panicked. She had expected this request would come, but not yet; not within the first thirty seconds, and not here, in his office, in the middle of the day, with other people wandering about the building. If he demanded this now, what could he demand – what couldn't he demand – later? He sat there so calmly, practically sprawled in his chair, smug and superior while he waited for her to obey or, more likely, waited for her to admit she couldn't. It had all seemed so easy before; now she felt she was being carried away and she couldn't find any brakes.

She said, 'We can't, er, you know . . .'

He interrupted her, said, 'Goodbye,' and tossed the sheet of paper across the table. Then, picking up the pen that she had only just that minute laid down, he continued correcting the draft he had been working on when she came in. She watched the agreement slide off the edge of the desk and float down to settle on the grubby carpet where it stared mockingly up at her. She leaned down and picked it up carefully by the corner, wary in case even that could attack her.

Julie knew the contract by heart – every word in it had been considered and examined over several days – but she still read it through again. Somehow it had grown even stronger and more final now that it was typed and her name had been added at the bottom. Her hands were sweating, sticking to the paper, and already, from just the few seconds she had been clutching the white sheet, it was stained with the little round prints of her fingers. She quickly smoothed it out on the desk.

He was pointedly not watching her, concentrating stubbornly on some stupid file while she squirmed on his hook. Could she have misjudged him? Could he have adapted so quickly to his new role? If so, there might be no limit to his demands. With four little words he had thrown her resolution back in her face. Her fingers itched to reach out to the single sheet of paper lying on the desk between them. She had only to pick that up, walk out, and the matter would be closed.

But he would know. If she bolted, he would look up and make some snide comment, amused and contemptuous, as she walked out. He would know she had faltered at the first obstacle and, when he had called her bluff, she had failed. She had to prove that she was sincere or lose face entirely and for ever. Her heart was working faster and louder; she could sense the blood pumping all round her body and a tightening in her throat, in her stomach and in her breasts.

For a moment she was not sure if she could still move at all, but she could start with the easy parts. She leaned forwards and slipped off her shoes, placing them carefully beside her chair; his head was still bowed.

She stood up, watching him all the time, waiting for some reaction, but he simply turned over another page and ran his finger down a line of figures. She unzipped her dress, slowly, loudly, enticingly, slipped the loose sleeves over her arms and let it drop down to the floor. Nothing. She stepped out of it. He was writing something on the bottom of a sheet of paper.

She arranged the dress neatly over the chair and waited. It had all been so easy that morning. She had been so selfassured as she calmly selected the new tights (horribly expensive but very sheer) and the matching bra and knickers (delicate and flattering). Eager to impress him, she had studied in her mirror what he would see;

39

the outline of her nipples was visible, proudly erect and ready to be admired. Her pubic triangle showed through the tights and delicate lace knickers, little more than dark shadow, but enough to attract without being too obvious. But he was missing it all; he wouldn't even look up. If she had obeyed immediately, he would doubtless have watched her; but, since she had failed, this was her punishment: to be ignored.

Finally she rebelled against this display of arrogance and sat down again, saying nothing. After a minute or so during which he showed no reaction either to her having started to undress nor to her having stopped, she shuffled her feet, feeling quite as ridiculous sitting there in her underclothes as she would have done had she been totally naked. He still did not look up, but did at least acknowledge her presence by speaking.

'Why have you stopped?'

If that was all the recognition he was going to offer, it would have to be enough. She unhooked her bra and let her breasts fall out towards him, laid that over her dress and then slid down her tights and knickers in one movement to add them to the pile. She immediately sat down again, but without lifting his head he simply told her to stand up, and continued reading as she waited in front of him, clasping her hands together, not deliberately trying to cover herself but holding them clasped against the fragile warm comfort of her pubic hair. She had completed the first stage of the course and now stood patiently, waiting for his next instruction. She stared over his head out of the window at the heavy streams of traffic heading out to the bypass and the motorway, the houses and gardens, the pavements filled with normal people living normal lives – people who had not just signed themselves away entirely into another person's power. She glanced down several times, but he was totally engrossed in the task and not until he had finished with the file and tossed it into the tray did he lay down the pen and condescend, smugly, to look across at her.

Julie turned away, ashamed again of her initial failure to comply. Of course, they could not actually make love in his office in the middle of the day; he would have known that as well as she did. Already her automatic protest looked cowardly, and she wondered if his intention in making her undress had been to embarrass her, and perhaps to test her, to see if she really would obey. Now that he had done so, it was not surprising – in fact it would have been insulting – if he did not take full advantage, and he made no secret of letting her see his eyes run up and down her body.

She tried to meet his gaze but could not. He had won this round because, although she had been naked many times before, in the presence of several different men, that nakedness had been private, in a bedroom or a bathroom; somewhere expected and acceptable; somewhere comfortable, even mundane and commonplace. In an office the feeling was entirely different. Here the coarse carpet, the harsh lighting, the steel and leather furniture emphasised her defencelessness, mocked and threatened her fragile pale skin and together created a contrast from which a totally different picture was conjured. In spite of everything she was displaying, his eyes kept being drawn back to her face. Like a cat toying with a mouse, he savoured her nervousness, the incongruity of his being fully clothed behind his desk while she waited naked in front of him. It was an immediate illustration of his power over her that she could not imagine finding in any other way.

He seemed, as far as she could tell from his expression, to be pleased with what he was seeing and she hoped that she lived up to the expectation that his fantasies must have painted during the previous months. It was gratifying and flattering to be appreciated, and a contrast to the totally blasé reaction of her real boyfriend, who now seemed to take her entirely for granted.

41

Peter seemed impressed and appreciative and she hoped he would believe it was only cold and not excitement that caused her nipples to pucker under his careful scrutiny. Her arms and stomach and thighs were firm and fit, not muscular but not flabby, the product of regular swimming and irregular running. Her pubic bush was neatly tended, trimmed to an even triangle spread broad and low across her belly. She was proud of it and, without being asked, she moved her hands away to reclasp them behind her. He smiled at the gesture and she suddenly felt she had been transparent and needed to be careful if she were to continue to appear as victim and not bait.

Finally he sat back in his chair and spoke. 'You may place your tights, knickers and bra in the cupboard behind the door.'

She protested at this. 'But I'll . . .'

'No, you will not need them today; you can collect them this evening.'

So she went and put them away, deeply aware of the perfect opportunity this gave him to watch the movement of her hips and bottom as she walked away from him and the sway of her breasts and slide of her thighs as she returned. He allowed her to sit down and she listened patiently while he listed exactly what she had done wrong, and how much work was going to be involved in his trying to put it right. She did not interrupt.

'Good. Now show me your pussy.'

She lifted her hands from her lap and let her thighs fall apart a little, but it obviously was not enough because he was irritated, something she had never witnessed before.

'No, show me your pussy. I can't see a thing like that.'

So then she spread her legs the rest of the way and, when he told her to pull her lips apart, she barely hesitated before her hands reached down to obey that command too. They felt slippery already, in spite of herself.

'Now, remember, when I tell you to show me your pussy, that's what I require, understood?'

She nodded.

'Right. You'd better put your dress back on and go and get me the papers on this job.'

'Can I please have my tights back? People will notice.'

'No. If you like, you may go out at lunchtime and buy some stockings instead. I'll allow stockings, but no tights or knickers, understood?'

'Yes, Peter.'

At half-past twelve she returned to ask if she could go to get some lunch. He told her he would have to work through lunchtime so he gave her some money and told her to get him some sandwiches and something to drink. As she was going, he stopped her again.

'You'll be spending tonight at my flat, so make any arrangements you need to make. Don't worry about clothes – you won't need much – and we'll stop by at your house on the way.'

She tried to imagine what he had in store for her, but did not hesitate: just said softly, 'Yes, Peter,' and left the room, quietly closing the door behind her.

Back in her own office, she collected her handbag and strode out through the big front door, pausing on the top step. There she took a deep breath of fresh air and then could not help herself; she simply grinned, almost burst into peals of laughter. The relief that she felt, the load that had weighed down her soul over the recent days was magically lifted away and she was left floating. It had worked perfectly. Even when she had almost messed up everything, he was so securely hooked that she had been able to salvage the mess. On top of that, a bonus, she was wonderfully conscious of feeling physically freed by the absence of constricting elastic round her chest and waist and thighs. He would never

43

know, but this was by no means the first time in recent weeks that she had spent the day at the office without knickers. Much as she would have liked to, she could not go braless without it being obvious and encouraging attention and remarks that she hated, even while half of her thought that she ought to be flattered. From the men it was no more than lust, from the women no less than jealousy. So, although she seldom wore a bra at home if she could avoid it, she always did so at work.

On the other hand, nobody could tell what was under her skirt so she often left off any knickers and wore self-supporting stockings rather than tights during the hot weather. The sensation of being totally free and unrestricted appealed, but there was more than that. There was the secret knowledge of being naked beneath her skirt, of nobody else knowing what she knew. And then occasionally, very occasionally, they did know. Sometimes, if she was in the right mood, and the opportunity was right, and the man was right, she would let someone know. She was becoming very skilful at contriving the briefest of displays that left the recipient not entirely sure whether he had seen what he thought he had seen. More often than that, when getting into her car, she liked to pull the hem up to give her legs a bit more freedom. Sometimes, she would pull it up much further than was necessary, just to let people see, to make them look, and wonder, and dream, while she pretended that she did not realise.

Now her worries were all over, and she had been proved right in every way. She had laid the trail and he had followed, followed with enthusiasm because he thought that he was leading. How easy it had all been. How little she need have worried if she had only had more confidence in her assessment. She skipped on to the pavement and as she turned up the road, caught herself swinging her arms with such pure pleasure that other people were warily detouring to avoid her. Seeing that, she did laugh and set off merrily towards the shops before bringing herself up short. This was not the time to risk everything by losing the lead. She had reached this far by letting Peter think he was leading a most reluctant follower. She had taken care over the details, like wearing tights that day instead of stockings, and this all helped to build up the picture which he expected to see and so he believed it all the more readily when he uncovered details which confirmed his own view. If he were to suspect differently, if someone were to mention casually that she had looked particularly carefree, he would stop and re-examine the basis of his conclusions. The thought flashed to her that he could even now be looking out of his window, might be watching as she walked down the street and might have seen her earlier exuberance. She walked the rest of the way with her head bowed, but still could not keep from smiling.

The shopping expedition was not a complete success. With no time to go into town, she was limited to the little cluster of shops at the junction. There was a very small supermarket, which sold pre-packed, plastic-bread sandwiches, a chemist, a wool shop, a greengrocer, a launderette and a bicycle, sports and camping shop. She did try to get stockings but of course none of those shops kept such exotic items and she had to content herself with a pair of cheap and coarse tights from the supermarket. They only had to last a day, because she certainly intended never to wear them again.

Back at the office, Julie stopped off at her own floor to leave some fruit she had bought for her own lunch and to put on the tights. They proved as hot and uncomfortable as she had anticipated so that she almost took them off again, but decided that bare legs as well as no bra just looked too tarty and she would have to suffer. Besides, he would be sure to notice. She went up to deliver the rest of her purchases and found him working busily, poring over some graphs and sale charts. The sight made her feel so smug she only just stopped herself from joking about it. As she came round the desk to give him the packages, she felt his eyes roaming over her, pausing at her hardened nipples and dropping down to her legs.

'Lift your skirt.' She raised the hem to a little above her knees and then slowly further up; when he waved her on, she continued until the hem was at her waist. He said nothing but looked into her eyes, a question. He seemed unsure of himself, unsure if she was testing him, challenging him, telling him she would not comply with such extreme demands.

She let the hem drop and tried to explain, to help him understand. 'I'm sorry, Peter. I couldn't find any stockings. They're only small shops around here; none of them keep stockings.'

'I'm not interested in excuses, Julie, just obedience. I'll punish you tonight; for now, just take them off and put them in the cupboard.' He watched her as she meekly obeyed, silently adding these to the sorry little collection, and was about to leave when he stopped her.

'Wait a minute. Just to remind you before you go, come here. Bend over the end of the desk.'

She had discovered enough about him to expect even this, but again not so soon nor so casually. She had anticipated ritual and formality, not functional practicality; where was the glamour in this? She moved round to the end and bent forwards gingerly, inclined over the desk. It was not enough and his hand on the back of her neck pushed her further down until her head rested on her forearms and the edge of the desk dug into her. He stood up and she felt his hand at her knees, lifting her skirt again up over her waist. If anybody was looking in through the window, they would get a full view of her completely exposed bottom; she shuffled her feet apart a fraction. His palm was gliding across the surface, almost tickling, but with just sufficient pressure to be disquieting. Her bottom had been admired before – Peter was by no means the first to be drawn that way – but he was the first man who she had promised could do anything he wanted with her, and she shivered when she realised that could include what she had refused to allow Mike. A fingernail was now tracing straight lines across her skin.

'You must wear an extremely small bikini. It makes a lovely pale contrast to the gold of the rest of my target. Would you prefer me to use my hand or a ruler?'

Julie swallowed and tried to clench her buttocks together, knowing his remark about the bikini was only to humiliate her: knowing that clenching her bottom would only emphasise the attraction. She said nothing.

His fingers continued to doodle along the outline of the triangle made by her bikini but suddenly changed course and followed the cleft down to burrow between her cheeks. 'Well?' He may have been in no hurry for a reply but was obviously not going to let up until he got one. What could she answer?

'I don't know.' It came out as a whisper.

'Come along, you have to choose.'

'Your hand.'

'All right, and how many strokes do you think you deserve?'

She tried to think again, but her heart was beating too loudly, her lips were dry and she did not know what to say. She tried to remember all the speeches she had given herself over the last few days to build her courage, but here, faced with the reality instead of the fantasy, it was completely different. If she tried for too little it might backfire on her, but she had never been spanked before and she did not know how much it would hurt. Would it really be like she had read about? Better? Worse? How much could she stand? She was beginning to feel afraid.

Finally she whispered, 'Three,' and, as the words passed out of her mouth, her bottom started to clench

47

and send messages of imminent assault to her vulva. She responded to that but, even while she was concentrating on the physical reaction, she was still taking in his response.

'A very good answer. I'll give you three for now. The rest can wait until tonight.'

His hand stopped and rested gently on one cheek, only the fingertips stroked very softly; then, without warning, the hand whipped up and back down. The sound made her jump before the shock of the blow had registered. The sting followed quickly afterwards and so suddenly that she arched up without being able to help herself, but his other hand clamped straight down on her neck. He held her while the other two blows fell in quick succession on exactly the same place. By the time the immediate sting of the third one had started to disperse, she could feel the heat glowing beneath her skin and, when she put her hand back for protection, could feel the red tenderness with the backs of her fingers. She was determined not to cry in front of him but she could not speak when he let her stand up, could not face him, and could feel her chin was quivering.

He just said, 'Come back at the end of the day,' and turned back to his desk. She managed to get out of the room and close the door before the tears refused to be held back any longer.

It had been nothing like she had expected; nothing like her sister had promised her and nothing like she had read about in books. For one thing, it did hurt, it did sting – at least, it had at the time, although already that was passing. On the other hand, the other side of the pain was fabulously richer than she had expected. The complete capitulation to sensuality, the freedom from pretence because she had no freedom to resist, it all offered a complete liberation from all her old inhibitions so that she began to feel this would all be too easy, as if she had years of experience.

Down in her own office she shut the door, lifted up her skirt and tried to see what he had seen. It was not successful but, in the toilet next to her office, looking over her shoulder to the large mirror, she could see blazing clearly like a badge of experience, the livid red print of his palm and fingers. She moistened a tissue with cold water and dabbed it against the mark; it didn't help much.

Four

Most of the staff, the irritating Janice included, left on the dot of five; and, with a weekend coming and Mr Collis on holiday, many had already disappeared before that. Even so, Julie found excuses to go through the entire building and make certain that every office was deserted before she climbed back up to Peter's room. Given the complete lack of any boundary to Peter's rights, there must be no risk of anybody else seeing them, overhearing them or even knowing they were both still there. This time he might even want to make love to her in the office and, if he did, she did not want to risk it being known – or, worse, interrupted.

She knew from Janice's complaints during their tea-break that he had already completed a large section of a draft report which Janice was now having to type. Julie had smiled into her cup when she realised that this was causing Janice as much work as Peter, and Janice was getting none of the benefit.

Finally satisfied that everyone had gone, she returned to the second floor and knocked, but this time did not wait for his reply before pushing open the door.

'Can I have my underclothes back now, please?' Even as the words came out, she realised that the petulant tone was not very clever.

He did not even look up to acknowledge her entry. 'No. Sit down and wait.'

He worked on; checking the figures on file, glancing up at the computer screen and then tapping away at the keyboard, his agile fingers slithering over the keys so confidently she was envious of the proficiency at the same time as she found herself wondering what those fingertips would feel like skimming over her skin. Presumably it would not be long before she found out. He was paying her no attention, but his refusal to look up appeared unnaturally determined and it was not long before he tidied away the remaining papers, closed down the computer and finally stretched out his legs to turn and look at her. He replaced the cap on his pen and laid it straight across the desk.

'Where do you live?'

'In Meadowside Estate.'

'Ah. With your fiancé?'

'No, I share a house with a friend.'

'Why don't you live with your fiancé?'

'Well, he works near Bristol.'

'What does he do?'

'He's a teacher.'

'Do you sleep with him?'

She hesitated and looked down at her fingers, clenched in her lap. She could not answer that. The agreement was just between Peter and her; Mike should be left out. He did not prompt her straight away and they waited each other out through the silence. Finally he brushed his hair back with one hand, pushing his chair away from the desk, and sighed.

'Do you challenge my right to ask you any questions I like?'

'No.'

'Nor my right to punish you if your answers are unsatisfactory?'

'No.'

'To punish you in any manner I choose?'

'No.'

'Good. I'm glad we understand each other. Now, how often do you sleep with him?'

She swallowed. 'Not often.'

'Why not?'

'I don't know. He doesn't seem to want to sometimes.'

'So who do you live with then? Another boy?'

'No, a girl.'

'Do you have any other boyfriend?'

'No.'

'A girlfriend?'

'What do you mean?'

'Do you have an intimate girlfriend, a lover?'

'Not like that, no.'

'Have you ever?'

'No.' But he had not missed the tiny hesitation.

'Tell me about her.'

'I said I hadn't.'

'And I said tell me about her.'

She sighed. 'It was nothing really, just when I was still at school. We just kissed and that.'

'That?'

'Cuddled; sort of hugged each other.'

'Naked?'

'Not completely.'

'How much?'

'We always kept our knickers on.'

'So you kissed her breasts?'

'Yes.'

'And she kissed your breasts?'

'Yes.'

'And that was all?'

'Yes.'

He snorted, disappointed not just by the lack of any more interesting an answer but also, she felt, by her lack of adventure. 'And this girl you live with, what's her name?'

'Gail.'

'Right, Gail. What do you do with her?'

'Nothing. Nothing at all. It's not like that.'

'Describe her to me. Wait. Undo your dress and pull it down to your waist.'

Julie was not surprised at this – indeed, its predictability was a little disappointing – but she reached round behind her back to the zip. Aware of his gaze on her all the time, she pulled it part of the way down, but when she tried to slide the sleeves off she got caught. She had not unzipped it enough. He was amused at the awkwardness of her movements as she manoeuvred the zip down further and finally released the sleeves, pulling them down off her arms so that her breasts were now exposed. It felt so wrong sitting at his desk with her dress around her waist and, in spite of herself, her nipples already half erect. He made no secret of admiring them; raised his eyebrows then looked up and grinned at her, although so easy a victory did not merit such smug glee.

'That's better. Now, carry on. Tell me about Gail.'

Julie considered for a few seconds. 'Well, she's twenty-six, not very tall – I suppose about an inch or so shorter than me. She has quite dark hair, long, which she normally wears in a ponytail. Sometimes she wears glasses but mostly contact lenses.'

He seemed to digest this for a while, then said, 'Carry on.'

'That's all. What else can I tell you?'

'Do you see her naked around the house?'

'No, not normally.'

'But you must have done sometimes.'

'Well, occasionally, yes.'

'When?'

'Getting dressed or something. Sometimes. And we went on holiday together once and shared a room.'

'A bed?'

'No.' Again he made no attempt to hide his disappointment.

'Anyway, what does she look like naked? What's her figure like? Her breasts, her bottom, her pubic hair? Give me a full picture.'

Julie could not see the point of his questions. He could hardly be expecting or even hoping to embroil Gail into his arrangements, but if he merely did it for the pleasure of hearing Julie discuss subjects he must know she found uncomfortable, it was a very petty-minded game. She tried to decide what she could say that would satisfy his persistent probing without betraying her friend.

'Her breasts are quite small — well, very small, I suppose you would say. I mean, she hardly ever wears a bra; she doesn't really need to. She's quite slim, she just never seems to put on weight, no matter how little she exercises.' Julie stopped.

'And her pubic hair?'

She sighed. 'Well, it's dark, obviously.'

'Thick or sparse? A narrow strip or widespread? Come on, I want a full description!'

What had this to do with him, with her or with their contract? 'Well, I don't know,' she snapped back. 'I have never looked at her in that way.'

He didn't react to her little outburst at first, just watched her silently until her nerve failed and she looked down into her lap, to see the tangle of her dress and be reminded of what she had forgotten: her nakedness and his power. She swallowed. 'I'm sorry. I've just never noticed.'

'Maybe I should send you back to find out.' He let the words hang in her head for a minute. 'Kiss my penis.'

The calm tone and uncompromising words took her by surprise — yet it was that very calmness, that bluntness, which made the demand impossible to disobey. Besides, she did not want to anger him, genuinely did not want to be spanked again. She stood up, but the dress started to slide off and she looked up at him questioningly.

'Take it off.'

The dress was all she had. One single garment which all day had fluttered round her, brushing unexpectedly against her skin, rubbing across her breasts when she walked, catching between her thighs when she sat down. Thin and loose, it had allowed her easy access while she sat alone in her corner of the first floor but now, faced with this demand that she remove it, it became more substantial and more loyal a protection and its loss became more painful a defeat.

She unzipped the rest, pushed it down her legs and lay it over the arm of the chair, just where it had hung before, that first time in his office. She stood up, naked again, and moved round to his side of the desk and waited. He swivelled in his chair to present his legs and crotch to her but made no other move to help, just sat waiting for her to obey. She dropped to her knees in front of him and, seeing the soft swelling inside his trousers, carefully unzipped them and reached inside, up to the top of his underpants and inside the waistband. He was looking down at her, concentrating closely, and she glanced at him nervously a number of times, wanting to seem hesitant, to let him enjoy this superiority and so not push her for too much more.

Her fingers scrabbled through the tangle of hair, thick, damp and masculine, but then there was more than hair, there was skin, which felt hot and clammy before finally she touched him, touched his penis. He was not yet fully erect, still curled over but straightening eagerly as she pushed his underpants out of the way and pulled it out. He was thicker than Mike, and longer too, hardening as she held him, the pink round head emerging from under his foreskin as it woke and stretched and stiffened. She still just held him, squeezed gently but made no other move. Was this what he wanted? Would he believe this to be her first time? She bent her head to his lap to kiss him delicately. He asked for nothing else so she sat back on her heels, still holding and gently massaging his penis but no more. She did not want to take this too far, because the obvious demand, given their relative positions, would be for her to take him in her mouth – and, although she had done that once or twice, under protest, it always revolted her and she would certainly never want him to climax in her mouth. She relaxed her grip, hoping to allow him to relax and he took a deep breath again, almost a sigh, and ran his fingers through her hair and over her face.

'So between times, while waiting for your boyfriend to take you to bed, you masturbate.'

Julie looked down, swallowed and said nothing.

'Yes?'

'Sometimes; everybody does.'

'How often is sometimes?'

'Well, I don't know. I don't keep a log!' Again she immediately regretted her sudden flare of temper. Again he completely ignored it, just waited for a moment before pressing on.

'Every week?'

'Yes. Yes, I suppose so.'

'More than once a week?'

'Well, yes, probably.'

'Every day?'

'No! Certainly not!'

'So, two or three times a week. Good. Does Gail masturbate?'

'I don't know. I don't expect so.'

'Why don't you?'

'Well, she has a boyfriend staying most nights.'

'And he keeps her satisfied?'

'He seems to.'

'You listen to them?'

'No, I don't listen, but I hear them sometimes.'

He glanced down at her and she quickly carried on. 'You see, her bedroom is next to mine so I sometimes hear them through the wall.' Julie giggled. 'Gail is often quite noisy.'

He reached down to her, very delicately ran the tips of his fingers down the side of one breast and underneath, then pulled back his hand. 'And you masturbate while you listen to them.'

'I told you, I don't deliberately listen to them.'

'All right, you masturbate while you accidentally overhear them.'

'Yes. Sometimes.'

'Do you use a vibrator?' Even the traffic seemed to have fallen silent, waiting for her reply.

'No! I haven't got one.'

'You mean you only use your hands?'

'Yes!'

'No candles?'

'No.'

'Hairbrushes?'

'No.'

'Nothing?'

'No!' Destroyed by the relentless probing, she raised her voice in indignant protest that she could tell, even as she uttered the words, carried no conviction at all.

'Well, you will have to show me later on.' He paused, his dark eyes scanning across the desk, distracted but searching, until he reached forwards for his pen, the silver one, the one she had used to sign everything away. 'Here, put this inside you.'

She took it from him automatically, turning it over in her fingers as she tried to untangle his demand. The thing was cold, hard, angular and unforgiving, in every way the opposite of the place he wanted her to put it, so why did he ask that? At first Julie could not think how to continue, but finally she settled back, spread her knees apart a little and, by opening her lips with one hand, she was able to push it an inch or so inside, so that about half the cap was hidden. He watched her intently, but it was not enough.

'Right inside.'

Even though she was already very wet, it was extremely awkward kneeling down, and so she took the slim cold tube right out again, sat back on the floor and spread her knees wide apart. By a process of pushing and twisting she was then able to ease it inside, until she felt the hard narrow tip come knocking against her cervix. Half an inch of it was still protruding.

'Is that as far as it goes?'

'Yes.' There was no need for further elaboration. He could never know whether she might have pushed it in further if she had really tried.

'All right, well done. Now stand up.'

She struggled to her feet, trying to keep her legs together, knowing she looked awkward and clumsy, and knowing that was what he wanted. Having stripped away her clothes, it was now her dignity he wanted to take. She stood hunched, clenching as hard as she could the muscles in her belly and realising she could not do this without also clenching her teeth and fists.

'Put your hands on your head and stand with your legs apart.' He was clearly determined to make her drop it out. Why? So he could punish her again? Just for the indignity? She would not give in, would not fail. She stood up proud in front of him, just as he instructed and held his gaze. He actually seemed pleased.

'Very good. Now hold it in there while you go to collect your underclothes.'

At first she was not so confident walking, but after a few steps realised it was no different from a tampon. She even managed a little swing of her hips, just enough to show that his attempt had failed.

When she returned to his desk, he let her put her dress back on, but not her underclothes. Then he asked for his pen back and she suffered again as she first tried simply to release it, then had to reach inside and pull it out. Ashamed, she handed it back to him, both aware of the very visible white smear across the cap. She watched him, hypnotised as he held it, sliding his fingers up and down its glistening surface, and, when finally she was able to overcome her embarrassment and glance up, she found him equally entranced.

Suddenly he snapped together, seemed ashamed at his own display of weakness and quickly pulled a handkerchief from his pocket, wiped the pen and put it away but he still handled it delicately, almost reverently. He shuffled up the papers on his desk and put his calculator, rulers and notepads away in the drawer. His voice returned to normal.

'We'd better go and collect some things for you. Will your friend, Gail, be there now?'

'No, she doesn't get in until about seven.'

Julie directed them to her house, an unremarkable post-war semi which she and Gail rented. She did not like it much although she could not really explain why not. It was reasonably cheap and certainly not unattractive and yet both the house and its little garden shared the common distinctions of hotels, holiday homes and lettings: a practical prettiness that had been applied deliberately rather than having grown from within, from being the home of its occupants. Julie was nervous at letting him in. When she had left that morning, she had not anticipated that he would want to see her house, and so had made no attempt to tidy it up. The third bedroom was ready, of course, and she always kept her own room tidy, but she had no idea about the rest. In fact, she could have done little even if she had known, since neither Gail nor her conquest had emerged by the time Julie left.

She led him into the sitting room, glancing around as she did so, afraid of what might have been left out that morning. It was not as bad as usual: the odd coffee mug and some slippers on the table, a scattering of *Cosmopolitan*s and a fat paperback novel on the floor. She invited him to sit down but had to clear some bridal magazines from the settee first.

'Those are Gail's,' she apologised, and tried to make it a joke. 'She is ever-hopeful.'

'You're not?' he asked.

'For who? Me or her?'

'I meant you.'

'Sometime maybe, but not for a while. I'm not ready yet.'

'For her, then?'

'Oh, yes. She has got it all sorted out; once she catches sight of the right man, he won't stand a chance. Stuck in the web before he knows what's hit him. Would you like some coffee? Or there are some tins of beer in the fridge? We may have some vodka or something.'

'No, thank you.'

'Right.' The silence hung there, pressing on her, embarrassing her and she did not know how to break out. This was her home ground, where she was the hostess, yet their relationship was more complicated than that and her assurance was destroyed. She wanted to be finished and gone before Gail came home. Finally she found a subject and some words but had little confidence that she was heading towards safety. 'What clothes should I bring?'

'You'd better show me what you've got. Where's your room?' So she led the way upstairs.

'That's Gail's,' and she indicated a half-open door. 'It's probably a tip,' she added, trying to keep them moving past but to no effect and when he paused, pushing the door wider to look inside, she went back to join him. It was as bad as she had feared. The duvet was bunched up in the middle of a low and very well-used-looking double bed; a pile of delicately feminine clothes was tumbling off the single chair and had started to march across the floor but was halted, doubtless only temporarily, by finding a man's sock and underpants in its path.

Julie moved on, finding herself talking rapidly, frantically, any words to cover her embarrassment at the story of pleasures which Gail's room shamelessly revealed. 'This is my room and that's the bathroom. We did have someone else in the third but she left a few weeks ago and we haven't found anyone else yet.'

It worked. He followed, and they moved on into her own room where she felt more comfortable. This was much tidier, neatly laid out and the bed, a large single more than a small double, was made up. Even so she felt that she was on parade, awaiting his verdict, but in fact he barely glanced at her. He walked past to the little cluster of pictures on the chest of drawers and picked up a photograph of her parents with her dog.

He did not look at her, just said, 'Get undressed,' and picked up the next photograph. It was so quiet, so unemotional, that she was not sure if she had heard right; but when she didn't move he looked round at her, a slight raising of the eyebrows and that was enough. She obeyed but, instead of watching her, he continued wandering through the room, studying her ornaments and photographs, glancing back only once as she stepped out of the dress again. He picked up a photograph of her standing with her arms around the neck of a youngish man in a running vest and shorts. 'Is this your fiancé? What's his name?'

She was standing near the door, now naked, arranging her dress on a hanger. 'Yes; that was after the London Marathon. He's called Mike.'

Peter turned reflectively back to study the photograph, then replaced it on the dressing table and selected another: Julie, then nineteen, with her parents and, barely visible because she was sulking and didn't want to be seen, her little sister. It had been taken at the beach during their last summer together and, although it was fading and slightly out of focus, it was the only one she had of all four of them. He considered it carefully.

'Who's that?'

'My sister.'

He peered closer. 'I didn't know you had a sister. What's her name?'

'Liz. Are you sure you don't want a drink?'

He replaced the photograph and turned round. 'Yes, OK. Maybe I'll have a beer after all; don't bother about a glass.'

'OK,' and she reached behind the door for her dressing gown.

'Leave that; go down as you are.'

'But somebody might see me.'

'You'll need to be quick, then.' She glanced back once more at the dressing gown then quickly turned away and downstairs. What would he do in her room when she was not there to see? Nothing, she realised, nothing compared to what he might do when she was there to feel the invasion. Downstairs, she turned off the lights as she passed through the hall to make herself less visible through the frosted glass of the front door but still she hurried. When she got back upstairs, he was still standing by the window, seemed not to have moved. Nor did he move when she held out the damp can and she had to cross over to him. Presumably he realised that the bedroom curtains were open and caught her quick glance out of the window, but when she started to withdraw again he stopped her.

'No, stay there. You look good against the window.'

He turned over the pillow and pulled out her pale yellow nightdress; as he held it up to the light, she was ashamed by its transparency and dropped her eyes. He made no comment, pushed it back under the pillow and sat down on the bed.

'Well, now, I suppose you'll need some clothes for the weekend. What have you got?'

For nearly half an hour he kept her sorting through her wardrobe, often making her put things on and then take them off again, not only underclothes but dresses, blouses, shorts, T-shirts. He looked over almost everything she had, gradually assembling a small pile of items of which he approved. She would never have dreamed of wearing many of the combinations, the lace underclothes with sleeveless tops, the jeans with formal jackets but no shirt underneath.

However, she was getting increasingly worried at the prospect of Gail returning and tried to hurry the man along. Maybe he knew what she was doing, for her attempts did not work and it seemed that the more she tried to hurry, the slower he went. He sent her downstairs twice more although neither time really seemed necessary and could easily have been done in the hope that Gail would return while she was down there, and find her naked and embarrassed.

Finally, after hauling a very formal long dress out of the back of her wardrobe, he was satisfied and she packed the clothes into an overnight case. It was the case she normally only used when she was going down to stay with her mother for a weekend, and it was quite wrong, too strong a link to family life, to be standing completely naked while she filled it with this collection of her most revealing things. When at last that was done, he allowed her, almost as an afterthought, to put on a blouse and skirt, even some knickers, but he made her undo two more buttons of the blouse than she wanted.

As they turned to leave, she went back to her dressing table and, keeping her back to him, slipped off her engagement ring and slid it into the little top drawer. The next two days did not concern Mike and it was better that she have no part of him with her. When she turned back, Peter was standing in the doorway, watching, grim, perhaps angry. She realised her stupidity: with her back to him he had been able to see exactly what she was doing in the dressing table mirror.

'Why did you do that?'

She had no proper answer. 'I thought I should.'

'For my sake?' Silence. 'For my sake, or for yours?' Silence. He shrugged. 'Leave it here if you prefer.'

He carried her case down and put it in the back of his car, unlocked the passenger door and let her in. He turned the car round, backing it into the drive to do so, and as he leaned over his shoulder said casually, 'I don't think we'll go straight home. We might stop off on the way – a film perhaps, and then something to eat?'

'That would be lovely!' She smiled happily at the prospect, relieved to be gone before Gail returned. It would be another two days before she learned how attractively he could package hell.

Five

As they left the safety of her own house, the first few cars rumbling past had their lights on. On the opposite side of the street, the smell of barbecues rose from one or two of the houses where people were taking advantage of the dying stages of a hot spell that threatened to break any day. In others, the curtains were already closed in warm familiarity, safely enfolding those who knew what their evenings held. Peter drove back in to the centre of town, past the railway station but, without any explanation, he circled round and passed it again. Unsettled by his silence, she nearly asked where they were going but stopped herself. What would be the point? He probably wouldn't give her any answer and, if he did, it would not be one she could rely on.

After circling once more, they returned to the same dark street where, overshadowed by the high walls of the back of the derelict municipal baths, a parking bay seemed to satisfy him, although he glanced both ways before locking the car carefully and taking her arm. He led her up the street, past a couple of Victorian pubs whose frosted windows and cold green tiling held a menace even at that early hour of the evening. At the top he paused, but then turned away from the distant bright lights, the restaurants and late-opening supermarket and led her instead down an alley to emerge directly in front of a small tatty cinema. The display of posters, forthcoming titles and scenes from its current selection were unambiguous. Ranges of heaving breasts and ample thighs, plus gaudy banner titles littered with exclamation marks, all promised faithfully to deliver an impossible feast of sensual entertainment, and Julie was sickened to realise this was what he meant in suggesting they see a film. She had a vague memory of reading of the place having been raided some months before. Although sitting with him to watch a pornographic film was mild in comparison with some of her fears, he was still too calm, too controlled, to be comforting. Equally, if this entertained him, would it also inspire him? If so, what ideas would it induce for things he might demand later? While she hesitated, gazing longingly up towards the traffic and streetlights and bustle of familiar life, he thrust some money into her hand and told her to buy two tickets.

She took a deep breath and pushed through the doors, passing more displays of lurid posters, conscious of her heels clicking too loudly across the empty tiled foyer. The girl behind the ticket window – a girl probably a few years younger than Julie herself – was deeply engrossed in a magazine and had already pressed the button to produce one ticket without lifting her eyes from the page. There was sufficient novelty in the female whisper, 'Two, please', for her to look up and Julie felt the eyes examining her, felt the scrutiny as if this were the receptionist from the Research Foundation for Female Sexuality. Quickly she looked away; where was all that easy confidence now? For a moment she was afraid that the girl would take her for a prostitute bringing a customer into the darkness, that she would call the manager and have them thrown out, but she could not really believe she looked the part. Julie felt – and was sure she looked – too naïve. Giving over the change, the girl glanced across at Peter with more pity than interest. She saw only two rich kids who had come downmarket for a thrill and she clearly felt that in some way it would be a thrill at her expense, that she and her lifestyle were being made exhibits for their entertainment. She sniffed and returned to the magazine.

Peter seemed to know his way through to the auditorium, pushing with a disturbing confidence into the humid, smoky atmosphere that was all the management believed its clientele demanded. The house lights were still on, but so dim that Julie paused while her eyes adjusted to the darkness, smelling the age and dirt through the disinfectant wafting out from the toilets beside her. She let Peter lead down the tatty strip of carpet between the rows of seats. The sparse audience, barely a dozen men scattered across probably a hundred seats, sat with their heads bowed furtively, but they all looked up as she passed and she felt the pairs of eyes stripping her naked. There were no other women from whom to seek any support or to absorb any of the stares. Peter selected a place two seats in from the end of one of the rows where, even though they were a good five rows from the front, everyone else was behind them. Julie sat next to him, leaving one empty seat on her left next to the aisle. The music scratched on for another few minutes and then the lights started to dim even further, brightened momentarily and went out altogether. Just before they did so, Peter reached round and put his arm round her shoulders, a gesture she would have enjoyed very much more if she had not been so aware of the eyes still examining her, and known his action would have caught the attention of every one.

After an unsteady pause, a sequence of trailers for forthcoming films started, but she could see no difference between the various films being advertised. They all featured the same characters moving through identical cheap sets. All were designed to portray on screen the greatest expanse of flesh that the law would allow. None of them stood out as having anything special to offer and Julie really wondered what purpose the trailers served. The customers could assume that the theatre would go on showing films and could assume they would all be of one kind. The titles, the attempts at a plot and the scripts were meaningless.

However after three or four of these, the screen went dark for a minute and then the titles for the main feature came up. As if this were the signal for the start of a race, there was an eruption of noise behind them which made Julie look round. The auditorium had come to life like a disturbed ants' nest in a scurrying and scuffling, a creaking of seats as most of the men moved to new positions nearer the front, but not only that. They were also moving across the cinema into seats nearer to her and Peter.

She turned back and tried to concentrate on the film.

A young woman has come home to her flat: she immediately undresses and walks around the flat naked for a few minutes. The soundtrack is scratchy and distorted. The girl fetches herself a drink of milk, rubs the glass across her nipples for a second and then raises it to her lips but carelessly spills it out of her mouth. The camera follows the trickle down her breasts.

Behind her, the movement continued. Out of the darkness came the creak of a seat flipping up, a few shuffled footsteps and the creak of another seat being pushed down, but this one was nearer than the first. There was silence and then, from another part of the auditorium, another series of creaks, of shuffles. The whole audience, in a series of short jumps, was moving steadily nearer, closing in on them. She gripped Peter's arm and, in a whisper, asked him what was happening but he told her not to worry. He said that the cinema did not get many women and so the customers were bound to be interested when one did come in. She was little comforted, particularly when two of them took up positions no more than three rows behind her.

On screen, the girl has decided to have a shower; the camera pans over her feet in a pathetic attempt at artistry before closing in and climbing steadily up her legs as rivulets of water run down. As the shot approaches the top of her thighs, she turns demurely to the wall, presenting her flabby blotched buttocks to the camera. More footage of water running over skin.

From somewhere at the back of the auditorium came the steady shuffle of another customer working his way down. He sidled across the cinema and Julie realised he was heading almost straight for her. She waited, absolutely motionless, while he passed slowly down the row behind her, but she felt the slight tug at her hair as he passed. She heard him settle down.

The shower scene cuts suddenly, the music broken off and restarted in mid-bar, and now the girl is facing the camera again, spending long minutes ecstatically washing down her breasts with a ridiculously large sponge while she gazes dreamily at the ceiling. She shuts her eyes and sucks on her finger. It is pathetic.

Julie glanced across to assess Peter's response, but he wasn't looking at the screen. He was watching her and, as she turned, he leaned across and kissed her, a long slow kiss, that in any other location she would have wanted him to continue, but here she just wanted him to end before it was noticed by the eyes watching behind her. Peter either did not know or did not care, for he ignored the men circling closer, clambering over the rows, edging along, seat by groaning seat towards her. Like wolves, they had identified a visibly weak and defenceless prey and they circled and edged closer, ever closer. Nor could she find any comfort in Peter's lack of concern: he could as easily turn on her as protect her.

Finally she asked him again, 'What are they waiting for? I hate this, Peter. Can't we go?'

'Don't worry, they only want to make sure that they don't miss anything. They won't touch you unless I invite them to.'

She froze; his remarks could still knock her flat when his calm reassuring tone was applied to words whose meaning was the opposite; was too appalling to consider. 'Are you going to?'

He turned and smiled. 'I haven't decided yet, but I do think they deserve a little more than they have seen so far. Unbutton your blouse.'

'Peter!'

'Don't argue, please.' He was sickeningly calm.

She obeyed cautiously, trying to ensure that her actions were not too noticeable and carefully making sure that the sides stayed well together. He did not look at her for a few minutes.

'Open the front.'

She glanced back. 'Those men will be able to see me.'

'Open the front.'

She pulled it open a little way; she dared not look round to see if she was being watched, but could still feel the eyes. When he turned her head to kiss her again, she peered out to see that none of the audience was watching the film: all eyes were on her. Even so it was not enough for Peter and, in kissing her, he slipped the side of her blouse down off her shoulder so that her pale skin gleamed in the flickering projector light. The wolves behind would be able to see clearly the bare flesh, probably could also see that no bra strap was rising up her back and over her shoulder and therefore if they came round in front . . .

Someone else moved seats behind them, and then another came and took up the end seat of the row across the aisle. He barely glanced at the screen and Julie could take no more. She sank her face down into her hands, to let her arms conceal her breasts and her hands hide her existence.

Immediately Peter grabbed her wrists and pulled them down to her lap. For the first time he sounded genuinely angry, quite different from the tone at lunchtime when he had found her wearing tights. 'If you move your hands again, I will make you take your skirt off.'

She dared not move but meekly sat there, with her hands clasped between her thighs and her eyes fixed on the back of the seat in front. Even so the edge of her vision caught a surreptitious hand-movement in the lap across the aisle followed by a rhythmic flash of skin.

From the row immediately behind them came another creak of the seats as the man moved to take up the seat immediately behind her. She heard a rustle of clothing and a zip; a laboured breathing and the smell of an unwashed man hit her. She began to question how much longer she could stand it.

From deep at the back of the auditorium, other steps came pacing down, someone trying to pretend he was looking for a suitable seat, but as soon as he had passed where Julie sat, he turned and dropped the pretence, just stood in the aisle, staring, practically dribbling, his hands clasped in front of him but moving, twisting and writhing together like snakes.

It was hypnotic. Julie wanted to tear her eyes away but could not keep from watching. There was no pretence at concealment, no subtlety, just a blatant display of arousal that was being thrust at her. Sickened though she was, this was all because of her, because she was there, because her breasts were revealed. It was worse than her fantasy – a thousand times worse – and better, a thousand times better. She even let her arms drop away further, sat up a little straighter as she caught the man's eye and he leered, grinned and sniffed and the writhing became still more agitated. His hands were now sliding openly up and down, emphasising the contours of the bulge in the front of his filthy grey trousers, framing it for her, displaying and offering himself. His fingers started to toy impatiently with the zipper; his eyes watched and dreamed.

She knew that Peter was watching the exchange unfold and then she felt his hands on her, his fingers picking at her skirt and sliding it up, holding the hem and pulling it up across her knees, along her legs. Her thighs now stood out, pale and vulnerable in the darkness, and the expanse of bare skin was growing with every movement of Peter's hands. The hem was now more than halfway up the distance between her knees and her knickers. The eyes across the aisle were fixed on the slow movement and the hand was still pumping steadily at a penis that he was no longer attempting to cover. Peter's fingers were pulling at the sides of the skirt where it was caught under her bottom and, although he said nothing, she lifted herself up to let him slide the material up beneath her. The seat immediately behind her creaked and she felt the breath wheezing on the back of her neck as the man peered over at her. Something nudged her neck, something warm and clammy that might have been a hand but might not; she did not dare to look. Peter was now reaching under her skirt, his fingers probing between her legs, sliding inside the elastic leg of her knickers to press between her lips and discover the sticky wetness she could not control, could not deny and could not explain. Peter chuckled and pushed on up to the waistband of her knickers, pulled gently and, again unbidden, Julie lifted her bottom to allow these to be pulled down, to slide into the view of the crowding watchers. They were dragged across her legs, over her knees, down to her feet and then, one foot raised, the other foot raised and they were off. Peter bundled them into a little ball and handed them to her, watching her carefully, saying nothing.

It was now her move. This was her choice; she could even put them back on if she wanted to. No, she could never do that. She leaned across and held them out to the man wheezing in the aisle. For one second his hands released the slimy pallid erection and snatched the prize from her and, for one horrible instant, his fingers slid

72

over hers, and then were gone, the knickers clutched in his hand and he wrapped them carefully round his erection. Almost immediately she saw him erupt in a dribble of white froth into the scrap of delicate lace which had so recently nestled so closely and so intimately against her, which must still be warm from her own body.

Another man appeared on Peter's other side, leaning across to stare down at the narrow strip of rumpled skirt which still lay in her lap, hiding the last scrap of her modesty. She stared down at it in terror lest it be touched and then, as she was wondering how Peter would react if she slid the hem back down, inevitably, one of the wolves found the courage to take the empty seat right next to her. She did not dare look round as it creaked and a heavy body settled into it, sighed and immediately started to unbuckle his belt and unfasten the front of his trousers. The leg swung out casually, so very casually, to press against her own naked thigh.

Now Peter stretched across to take her hand and he unbuttoned the first cuff and then the second. He slipped the blouse down off the shoulder nearest to him, but it was another hand that reached up to tug on her other side, a hand which pulled the blouse down her shoulder, rasped down her arm, gripped her wrist and pulled her hand out of the sleeve before shoving the whole blouse down into a bundle behind her back. She was now naked from the waist up, her pale skin a beacon in the dingy theatre, a beacon that immediately drew another scurrying of feet, a renewed creaking of seats, wheezing grunts and another body dropped into place in the row behind her.

Suddenly an extra square of light appeared in front of them. Down beside the screen, a door had been pushed open and a man was held in silhouette. He stepped in, the rectangle behind him closed to blackness and he flicked on a torch. Julie watched it bouncing across the

73

floor as he crossed to the central aisle and then made his way up the slope through the auditorium. All the men had gone quiet. The one standing had scuttled away to a seat and everybody watched the yellow beam flashing across the seats, lighting on the faces as it approached nearer. It hit Julie's face square on so she was blinded and then it flicked across to Peter. Back to her it came, then shimmered down her body, rested on her exposed breasts, down further to her legs and lit them up, stark and bare in the harsh light. He slid the beam up her thighs as if the light alone could lift her skirt the last little bit to let him see beneath it, but then rose to her breasts again. Briefly it came back to settle on her face and she turned her head away, her eyes hurt by the brightness and her pride hurt by the discovery. Still silent, the man snapped the torch off and strode past her up out of the back of the cinema. The door banged behind him and the auditorium erupted again.

Glancing down, she was confronted by the lap of the man sitting on her left. His baggy trousers were entirely unfastened and a short stubby penis, no more than half erect, waved hungrily in full view. For a moment his fist wrapped round it, the foreskin slapping wetly as he slowly rubbed the length of his shaft half a dozen times; then he released it and the hand lifted away. She watched it, unable to tear her eyes away from the hand as it floated closer towards her, weaving through the air and finally it touched her. Polluted from contact with the man's own penis, it settled first on her shoulder before sliding slowly down, greasy, heavy and repulsive across her skin, to her chest, down further and then it was actually touching her breast, was slithering over the soft private skin as it headed inevitably towards her nipple. She felt the nipple hardening, erecting shamelessly in anticipation of his obscene touch as the hand crept closer and the foul contact became more imminent. She shivered, half pulled away, but knew it was ineffective

74

and insufficient. The hand crawled on until finally the fingertips were pushing at the nipple, the broken nails pressing at the delicate tender point and the hand was swarming across her, reaching round underneath her breast and holding her, gripping, squeezing and clamping her as tight as he could. Victorious at last, he turned to laugh in her face, spittle spraying from his lips and spattering her face and breasts.

Another hand reached over her shoulder on Peter's side, clammy fingers crawling down until this breast too was enfolded and squeezed, squeezed tight. A head appeared beside her, an unshaven chin rasping at her cheek as he scraped by, wheezing and chortling at the soft prize he grasped in his calloused hand. He turned towards her, broken teeth, stained and stinking, grinning out from a sallow skull.

'Come on, then, darlin'. What about a kiss, eh?'

She immediately turned away to be confronted by the leering face on her other side, which also broke into an evil grin as the man released her breast and the hand began to slide down. Her skin still tingled at every point where the hand had touched even as it continued its path down her stomach, edging inexorably inwards in a slow dive whose target was all too horribly obvious. Her preoccupation was broken as another figure appeared in front of her, another fat grinning face peering expectantly over from the row in front. Another hand reached out towards the nipple which had just been released, which was now available, which bobbed alluringly in the pale light from the screen, which pushed, shamefully erect, towards any hand that would touch it. The stubby fingers closed and squeezed and pinched and twisted, wringing a cry from her that the bloated face acknowledged with a slow licking of its lips.

On her left, the man's hand had reached her waist; it had tried to dig beneath the waistband, found it too difficult and was now starting to slide across the rolls of her bunched-up skirt. In front of her, the man had abandoned her breast and was now also making for her skirt. They reached the hem at the same time and, after landing on her thigh and waiting to see the reaction to that, the two hands began sliding up her legs simultaneously, steadily crawling higher towards the hem of her skirt and beyond: towards where her vagina was now entirely uncovered and unprotected but now seeped, opening in wet anticipation of their touch.

How could she cope with their discovering such a betrayal? And, if they did, what would they assume from it? That anything was permitted? This was too much to contemplate and Julie suddenly clamped her thighs tight together so that both hands were snatched away in guilt and fear. But Peter tutted disapprovingly and Julie did not even have to look up. She slid her thighs open again in a gesture that was absolutely clear. Anything they wanted, they could have.

The hands resumed their crawl. They reached her crotch together, the stubby fingers digging and pushing at her, fighting to burrow inside her, and then the contest was over and she felt an alien finger working its way deep into her while the loser pressed blindly on, prodding aimlessly like a sightless animal at every scrap of soft flesh, burrowing down lower towards her anus which, mercifully, was inaccessible as she sat.

Defeated, the finger crawled back up her crease. For a few seconds it tried vainly to shove its way in next to the other finger, the one that had already invaded her, but soon it gave that up and continued towards her clitoris, pressing brutally against that, scraping, scratching, gripping and twisting her. She cried out and tried to pull his wrist away, but it was no good: he was too strong and besides he already knew he was hurting her. That was the idea. The man digging inside her was no different. He must have known his crude and selfish probings were agonising on such a tender area, but he didn't care either.

Julie turned to Peter in agonised despair at the invasion, and suddenly his hands came down and pushed the two men away. He smoothed the hem of her skirt down and pulled up her blouse, arranging it across her shoulders as they stood up and pushed out through the waving hands which reached out, groping desperately for one final touch of real skin.

Peter shepherded her up the steps, past the white staring faces, every one of which, Julie now saw, was gathered around the seats they had just left. Yet even then escape was not entirely free, for as she hurried up the ramp, clasping her blouse closed across her breasts, determinedly keeping her eyes from straying to any of the foul sights on either side, a figure loomed up in front of her, blocking her path. She could have pushed by – he was not a large man – but she was held back by the horror of what he presented. The front of his trousers was gaping open, the sides pulled well apart and hanging from a thin belt, so that his penis and testicles were pulled out into plain view. His penis, long and crooked, reared up in front of her as his fist pounded up and down its length with a desperate determination to make her witness the climax which suddenly came. He opened his eyes and took another step forwards, gurgling in delight as the obscene fountain spurted up at her, flying hypnotically across the short distance between them to spatter on to her skirt, her blouse and then drip, cold and slimy, on to her hand.

Peter reached round from behind and pushed the man out of the way, then steered her on towards the exit at the top of the seats. As the swing doors closed behind them, he put his arm round her and hugged her as he whispered, 'Well done, you did very well,' and she collapsed in tears into his shoulder.

He kissed her then as he rebuttoned the blouse, and somewhere in his kiss she found genuine affection, which surprised her and warmed her and she found

77

herself feeling grateful to him for releasing her when she should have been feeling anger that he had brought it on her at all. They paused before stepping out of the darkness to tuck the blouse back into her skirt and Julie wiped her eyes. Their feet sounded back along the tiles of the empty foyer and the girl at the desk looked across, not hiding a little sneer. She had never believed that they would stay for long.

Outside the cinema Julie quickly recovered, and a few breaths of fresh air cleared her head. Peter still supported her, his arm round her shoulders, and she moved into his side comfortably and entirely at ease. He kissed the top of her head again. 'Now we'll go for a meal.'

While they had a drink in the little restaurant, he again praised her performance in the cinema. She was still grateful and enjoying the compliments and felt sufficiently confident to ask if they would do that again.

He smiled, not unkindly. 'I doubt it. That is the bottom to which we can sink, but there are heights to which we can rise if we want to. It depends to a large degree on you. You've promised to obey me fully, so I suppose it depends how you respond to different situations.'

'You mean if I misbehave you'll take me there again?'

'No, I don't mean that – at least, not exactly that. In the cinema no positive input was required from you; in fact your refusal to participate in the scene was in itself a contribution. That scenario therefore works whether or not you want it to, whether or not you make any contribution. Other scenarios would be different because they might call for you to take a more active and positive and willing role. If you fail in them, I am forced back on to those situations that do not make such demands on you.'

'So it was sort of a warning?'

He said nothing at first, then nodded a little. 'Yes, I suppose it was a warning, and also a test – a test to see how serious you are.'

'I am.'

'Evidently.'

'And what else have you in mind for me?'

'You'll have to wait and see.'

They ordered food and wine and Peter was so attentive that it was difficult to reconcile this man with the one who had put her through the ordeal in the cinema. After the waiter had taken the order, Peter refilled her wine glass. Then he looked over at her and his eyes had turned back to ice. 'Tell me about your fantasies.'

'What fantasies?'

'When Gail and her boyfriend are not there, what do you think about then when you masturbate?'

'It varies. You know. It depends.'

'What kind of things?'

'Well, lots of things.'

'When did you masturbate last?'

'About a week ago, I suppose. I don't know for sure.'

'So, tell me what you thought about then.'

Julie would have liked not to tell, but she could not think of a way. She would either have to make something up or reveal her private world. In the end revelation seemed easier than pretence. Besides, for three days, she had given herself to the man entirely in reality. What damage could there be in giving also the make-believe? So, urged on by his detailed and relentless questioning, she slowly unravelled the whole story of the London Research Foundation for Female Sexuality. She did not tell him the name, or even reveal that it had one, but gradually he wheedled almost everything else out of her until she was reliving it there, with him, in the public restaurant. In one way it was wonderful, exciting her as much by the public revelation of her desires as did the fantasy about the public revelation of her body. Yet it also frightened her because, after so detailed an exposure and examination, she wondered whether it would ever work for her again.

79

Just as she was finishing her tale, the waiter returned, bringing their food, and the mood changed again. Peter was open and appreciative; he enjoyed the food and the wine and he seemed to enjoy her company. The food was not just to fill his stomach, nor the wine to make him drunk; she recognised those signs, had spent too many meaningless evenings with that type and now recognised it readily and despised it. She had also been out with too many men whose only interest in her was physical, who viewed her as no more than a bed companion. Peter was different in that too, yet he should not have been.

She had given herself as no more than a companion for his bed – indeed, she had been the one who manoeuvred them both into a position where she was offered purely in that role for three days – and yet he was treating her as more. She began to wonder whether she had completely misjudged him, taking his arrogance as hiding immaturity when perhaps it was simply confidence in his own tastes and way of life. If this new assessment were right, it could greatly change the course of the remaining days of their contract. If he started to like her, perhaps going further than liking, where then would it lead?

So although she started the meal waiting for him again to use the power that her surrender had given him, he barely did so at all. It was not until the end when, not knowing what was coming next, she decided to go to the Ladies before leaving the restaurant, that the reminder came. He considered her announcement for a moment and then told her not to bother, that they would be going straight home. His tone made it not just a suggestion but a clear instruction and, although there was nothing really to it, she took his words as being intended as a further mild demonstration of his power, just to make sure she did not forget.

Still, that was all he did, and their evening, their date, seemed to be progressing along a path that was surely as clear and familiar to him as it was to her. So, when finally he had paid the bill and they walked out into a strengthening breeze that promised a break in the days of interminable sunshine, and she shivered just a little, it seemed entirely natural that he help her back into her jacket, and she was disappointed that he did not go on to put his arm round her shoulder as they walked back down through the skirmishing scraps of paper and the first leaves of autumn towards his car.

Six

In an area of town that had once been among the best and was even now labelled by estate agents as 'sought after', a modern block of flats squatted arrogantly amidst the assortment of Edwardian family houses. As Peter drove them back, the urban sounds dropped away and the pace of the passing traffic and pedestrians slowed; even the houses themselves had shuffled further apart so that, by the time they finally reached his road, the world had changed from a jumble of traffic and bustling humanity to a gentle tranquillity, leafy and secure.

The building stood confidently in its own grounds, square and solid but entirely uncompromising, the concrete frame and flat roof making no concession to the elegance or detailing of its neighbours. A square carpark in front covered what was a garden everywhere else in the street, but at least this was surrounded by towering horse chestnut trees whose massive branches hung down over the array of cars, their trunks lit to a warm orange in the horizontal rays of the last of the evening sun. He parked the car at one side of the door and, while she waited, took out her suitcase then led her inside.

The hallway was functional and dull. A cheap utilitarian carpet covered the floor and a few pictures were inadequately lit from a skylight somewhere high above.

The staircase filled most of the space, leading up one side and then turning back on itself before setting off higher. On each side of the hall featureless doors were closed firmly, the little tables and mats outside showing them to be the boundaries of someone's private world. From one side music could be heard and the voice of someone singing along. On the other, a television was turned up too high.

'There's no lift but I am only on the second floor.' He glanced up the flight of stairs. There was nobody in sight. 'Take your clothes off here, please.'

'Peter!' she started to protest – but one look at his face and she knew there was no point in continuing. He had not even waited for her, but turned and started up the stairs with her suitcase. She began to panic at the prospect of being left there naked and alone, and started ripping her clothes off as fast as she could. Having lost her knickers at the cinema, she did not have much but was still hopping on one leg to step out of the skirt while she unbuttoned her blouse at the same time. She did not bother about her shoes, but ran on to catch him up.

He was waiting at the first turn in the stairs, a half landing, as she came running up behind him, her clothes bundled up together and clasped in front of her. He resumed the climb but paused again just before reaching the first floor, and here he turned back to her and, without a word, held out his hand. She hesitated only for a moment then reluctantly passed over the bundle of clothes. She had been glad of the tiny protection they might have given if someone had come out of any of the other doors she was passing. He held the bundle in one hand but was not satisfied and nodded down at her shoes.

She could not stand the prospect of further humiliation by his rejecting yet another appeal so she silently squatted down to unfasten them and added those to the top of the pile. He offered no thanks just said, 'Good. Now fetch them' and tossed the whole pile over the

83

banister down to the floor below. She watched in slow-motion horror as the blouse floated silently and gracefully, the shoes bounced on the steps and echoed round the stillness, and the jacket and skirt tumbled over and over like a pair of dying birds. She hated the man's coolness and superiority but he was already striding on ahead and she glared after him, suddenly afraid that if she was not quick he would lock her out of the flat.

So she turned back and, doubled over, scuttled down the outside edge of the steps to the floor below to gather up the clothes again. Still there was no sign of anyone emerging from either of the flats on the ground floor and common sense told her that, once in for the evening, they would probably stay there. Yet scrambling naked around the hall of a strange building did not lead her to trust to common sense; more deep-rooted, primary fears took over. One shoe had come to rest right outside the flat with the television.

She ran back up the stairs, trying to stay bent over beneath the heavy banister, and while her ears were tuned to the sound of any opening door, she heard Peter's keys in the lock of his flat, the lock turning, the door opening and she reached the last landing just in time to see the door close behind him again. She was on the point of weeping. She knocked, and when nothing happened she knocked again, and rang the bell and called, but not too loudly in case it attracted the attention of the occupier of the flat opposite.

Then she stopped. Peter knew she was out there. He would open the door when he was ready and she could do nothing to make him do that any quicker. A frayed coconut mat lay outside the door and she sat down but it was so coarse that it dug into her in very delicate places. She moved off that on to the thin carpet but that was little better. It barely gave any protection at all from the cold floor and, sitting with her back against the door, knees drawn up and her clothes clutched to her chest, she felt the warmth being pulled out of her. For a moment she even considered getting dressed again, but was afraid of his reaction. He might simply make her undress again and then wait even longer, but he might do worse. No sound came from inside the flat, no indication of anyone moving about, and she wondered if he were simply waiting at the door. The flat opposite had a peep-hole in the middle of the door and, looking up, she could see his did too. Was Peter watching her? Was the man opposite watching too?

How long would he make her wait? How long could she make herself wait? Suppose fifteen minutes went by? God, supposing a whole hour, or even two? He might simply go to bed and leave her there. Would she just curl up and go to sleep there, on the mat like a dog? Yet, like a dog, she needed a lavatory before she settled down for the night and, although her need was not yet desperate, she could not wait forever.

Her own comparison with a dog became horribly apt. Supposing she just stayed there and waited – supposing she wet the mat, what would happen to her then? She shuddered at the prospect but, as she remembered how he had refused her permission to go to the Ladies earlier, it slid from a possible to a probable outcome. And what would be the consequence, his reaction? He might be angry and beat her like a dog and, although she shivered at the picture it brought her – a picture of her kneeling, naked, cowering and trying to smile to ingratiate herself – she knew also that it would not change anything; she would still be his dog.

And quietly and chillingly she realised how much he had changed her in just twelve hours. No longer was it unthinkable for her to squat naked outside his front door and relieve herself on to the mat like an animal. No longer was it inconceivable that she would submit to the beating that would almost certainly follow.

The only alternative was to give up and go home and take whatever punishment he later imposed, but she knew she could not do that because she was frightened of him. Already he had led her further than she had dreamed possible, and yet he seemed so entirely confident not only of himself but of her as well. Had she got it all wrong? Was this territory familiar to him? Or had Liz been right when she said any man would react this way?

She settled back, began to think that if she spread her skirt over the mat to protect her skin and used the jacket as a covering she could probably make herself reasonably comfortable. Sitting there, she felt the door behind her move and then slowly open but could barely bring herself to look up.

'What are you doing out here?' he asked. 'Come on in. The door's not locked.' He turned back inside without waiting for her as she gathered up her clothes and followed.

As soon as they were inside the flat Peter reverted to being as well-mannered and attentive a host as any man bringing home a new date for the first time, excepting that he was fully dressed and she was naked. He showed her into the bedroom where he had put her case, invited her to unpack her clothes, provided some hangers, and then left her in private. As soon as he had gone, she closed the bedroom curtains which he, no doubt deliberately, had left open.

She took her time over the unpacking, feeling safer in the bedroom than in his presence, even though the room was new to her. It was clean and impersonal, hotel-like, a room for sleeping. And if he did not always sleep alone, it told her nothing about its occupants: him, or her or them. The bed, black wrought-iron, was neatly made, the clothes all put away, and the top of the chest of drawers tidy and dusted. That was a little disquieting; it seemed to be too carefully prepared. What was worse was that presumably he must always keep it so, for when he had left that morning he could have had no intimation that he would be bringing her back there in the evening.

She stood in front of the mirror brushing her hair, more to delay returning to Peter than from any real need and her eyes were pulled by her nakedness, by the familiarity of her own body reflected back out of a strange bedroom. This was her first time in a man's room, other than Mike's, for nearly three years, but she did not want to think about Mike. She deliberately allowed the inside of her forearm to brush her nipple as her arm moved down, and then she ran the comb through her pubic hair, and was pleased with the effect. She believed that she looked better without clothes than with them; dressed she just looked heavy, whereas naked she seemed womanly. Her breasts were full but held their shape well and were flatteringly emphasised by her narrow chest. Her waist was slim, her belly neatly rounded and her soft auburn fleece balanced the golden colour of her skin. She combed the little tuft a few more times and turned to inspect her profile and back in the mirror. It was only then, seeing her own bottom, that she remembered that when he had spanked her at lunchtime, he had said he would spank her again in the evening. 'The rest can wait until tonight,' he had said. She wondered what that meant, and if he would remember. She could find little confidence that he would forget. She paused and listened to the sounds coming from the living room, soft music and a drink being poured. She carefully lay the brush and comb side by side and went back to him.

He offered her a drink, and told her to help herself from the sideboard. It was well stocked and she wondered again who else he might have entertained in this flat. He had never mentioned any girlfriends, but he was too confident, too much at ease for her to believe that he had none. Glancing up, a bottle of cognac in her hand, she found another mirror, a circular and convex one so that the room was distorted. Yet she could see that he was watching her.

He smiled as she returned, and she could almost believe that this was like any other date, could forget that she was naked.

'You seemed deep in thought.'

'Yes.' She did not want to tell him.

'About?'

'Oh, nothing really.' She left it.

'About?' and it was as if the last two lines had not been said. It was almost as gentle and polite. Almost, but not quite. She was starting to recognise the slight edge to his tone that meant he was not going to be put off.

She looked straight at him. 'I was wondering if you had a steady girlfriend, or indeed how many.' If he wanted to pry into areas she did not want to discuss, she would turn it back on him.

'And what did you decide?' He was clearly practised at this game, could see the traps.

'I didn't know.' A safety shot, unchallengeable.

'But what did you picture?' He was better at this than she had expected, and could turn her plays to his own advantage.

'I really don't know.' She knew it was not fair to repeat the safety shot, but she needed to make clear that he would get no further than a wall of assumed ignorance.

He did not answer straight away, and she smiled to herself as she raised her glass; few people could match her verbal skills. His next answer, so gently delivered, aced her – took the game, the set and the match.

'Lie down on the floor here and masturbate.'

It came like a slap across her face and, as with several of his earlier demands, with no warning, no chance for her to prepare, and this crippled her. She shut her eyes, wanting to scream that it was not fair, he had changed the rules and quadrupled the stakes without warning and it simply was not fair. But then she had not been quite fair and she had picked the game so maybe it was his right to change the rules. The contract that she herself had drawn up and signed only a few hours ago agreed to that. She opened her eyes to sip her drink as the full realisation of what he had demanded sank into her, dropped deep down into her; she could feel it like a cold lead weight sinking past her heart, through her belly to rest in her pelvis, pressing on her bowels from the inside.

Slowly she put down the glass. 'I need the toilet first.' Neither an agreement nor a refusal.

For a moment he stared at her in silence, then disappeared into the kitchen, returning a moment later with a large round glass bowl and a tea towel.

'Here you are, then.' He put the bowl down on the floor and arranged the cloth inside it. When she went to pick it up, he stopped her.

'No, leave it. Do it here, and face me, please.'

'What? Why?' He shrugged, but made no attempt to produce an excuse. 'Are you just trying to embarrass me?'

Peter shrugged again but, in the long-stretched silence, Julie knew that Peter held all the cards. 'Why?' she repeated, but still he made no answer, and she wondered if he were embarrassed himself at his own request. If so, perhaps obedience would be the best solution, pushing his own embarrassment beyond the point he could tolerate. He was sipping at his whisky, studiously not watching her as he placed the glass down carefully on the table beside him. She did not like to look at him, but slowly put down her own glass then went and squatted down astride the bowl, trying to keep her legs as much together as she could. When she was there, she waited, tried to concentrate, but this was too bizarre.

'I can't do it, not with you watching. It just won't come. I'm sorry.' She stood up quickly and returned to her chair, uncertain of his reaction to her defiance, but he did not seem to worry.

'Never mind. Leave it for a while and finish your drink. Perhaps you'll want to later. In the meantime, carry on here. I want to see you masturbate.'

She could think of simply nothing to defend herself. How could she argue with a man who was capable of taking such harmless requests and perverting them? It was not reasonable, not fair, what he demanded. He said nothing else, just sat complacently watching and waiting. They both knew that she had to obey.

Slowly she slid down on to the carpet until only her head remained propped against her chair, but there she stopped. From outside the window came the low hum of distant traffic. Inside was the sound of harsh breathing; Julie found it was her own. She looked down between her breasts where they fell to each side, down the length of her body and focused on the pale clump of hair where her legs were tightly drawn together. Still she barely moved. Still he said nothing. In some respects, she was not totally unprepared for this for, in preparing her appeal to him, while typing out the agreement, she had considered what demands he would be likely to make and known that this might be among them. In some moods, she had thought it almost certain. It had not concerned her greatly – had seemed quite easy then – but, now the reality was in front of her, she was less confident that she could bring herself to deliver.

How long could she stay? How long would he wait? She wanted to test him, and yet the longer she sat there the more her confidence ebbed away. If she failed him, she feared that he would simply demand something else, probably something worse. She could imagine, could almost hear, the soft and even voice saying they would go back to the filthy cinema. No appeal she could make then would have any effect. Not daring to wait any longer, she slid her hands down between her thighs.

She was very dry and, if only she had been alone, would have licked her fingers, scooping up a liberal coating of warm saliva to smear that all over herself. No such luxury was possible beneath his steady gaze. She brought one hand back up to her breast and rubbed over her nipples a few times, twisted them, flicked at them with her fingertips, but her body refused to respond. She tried to turn her thoughts to the scenarios she used at other times, but an image of Mike kept popping up, and yet she knew that to some degree it was because of Mike that she was now stretched out on that carpet in another man's flat, a man whose presence she could not block out. She consciously called up images of other men she had known, but none of them were what she needed now; few had been what she wanted then.

She turned her mind to Sarah, back at school: their childish whispers and promises and admiration of their slowly – far too slowly – developing breasts. She and Sarah had both sprouted pubic hair much earlier than any other girl in their class, and this had brought them together, made them allies and confidantes, reassuring each other at every stage as they nervously led the whole of the rest of their year into puberty. While their bodies matured and blossomed and filled, they had shared their secret worries. Together they had privately discussed the swelling of their breasts and, when more intimate changes began, taken comfort in listening to each other's similar reports, progressed to secretly comparing the similar appearance of the other, and eventually the similar feeling. Racked with guilt, each had offered up her clitoris and swelling labia to the other to be inspected, to be examined and finally, on that unforgettable wet afternoon, to be tasted.

Yes, she had lied to Peter about that. They had not always kept their knickers on, not after the first couple

91

of times. Thoughts of Sarah led her into thoughts of
Gail, of the noises behind the thin walls and the men she
brought in at night and led back out in the morning. She
was jealous of Gail, of her confidence and freedom and
the choices these brought her. That man last weekend –
far too young for her, a policeman or a fireman or
whatever, and yet he certainly had something about him
that made him worth an evening. That had been one
more in the succession of nights when Julie had brought
herself to her own pleasure, listening to the sounds of
theirs, and theirs had seemed so long drawn-out. The
silent pauses leading on to even more activity and
renewed cries. Sneaking downstairs after the house had
at last gone quiet, she found the piles of discarded
clothing, not just Gail's but a man's clothes too. She had
picked them over, trying to absorb some of the intensity
of the passion that the two must have felt as they stripped
each other's coverings away. How easy Gail found it all.

She ran through the events in the cinema earlier that
evening but the experience had not yet had time to
mature. It was still too fresh to sort out what had
excited and what had repelled her. Certainly she had
been aroused, despite the coarseness and squalor. Whatever fine sophistication she might like to pretend, her
body had willingly ignored all that and responded to the
offers and suggestions, to the proximity of so much male
arousal, all thirsting for her. When they had threatened
to maul her breasts, her nipples had erected to welcome
them. When their foul hands had approached close to
her vagina, she had grown wet in anticipation of their
touch. Her mind had still to sort through the images of
so alien an experience to determine which would be
rejected and allowed to sink back into the mud, but
which others would be retained, nurtured and embel-
lished to create the foundation of a new dream, just as
that day at the school swimming pool had led to the
Research Foundation for Female Sexuality.

She realised that several minutes had passed during which she had not been conscious of Peter's presence and yet had been obeying his command. Her fingers were wet, and when she moved them a greedy impatient slurping was announcing her desire. It was not going to be difficult to finish.

She returned to Gail, remembered as she had padded around the flat last Sunday morning in her tatty towelling dressing gown. It had not been fastened properly and the scratches and love bites over her breasts had been quite visible. Gail had caught her looking, had glanced down herself at her own body, shrugged, laughed, 'Men!' and retied the belt. Julie had blushed then but now she wanted Gail to be there, in Peter's flat – perhaps not right with them, but in the next room, not to take part but just to know how far Julie could go without her friend's help and guidance. She wanted Gail to be the one having to satisfy herself with her own fingers and having to listen to the sounds of others. Like the night during the height of the summer when they had both left their bedroom doors open to try to allow some air to circulate through the suffocating house. They had both been alone but the night had been too hot and she had been too restless. Some while after they had turned out the lights, she had heard Gail next door, the unmistakable sounds of Gail's bed, the soft moans and the gasps. The sudden silence, guilty silence – if Gail knew guilt. Suddenly a furtive and unsteady whisper. 'Julie, are you awake?' She had not answered and after a few moments the sounds started again, first alone then becoming a duet and if Gail knew that Julie was awake and heard, and understood, did it matter? She must have heard; she was meant to hear. When morning came Julie had hardly been able to face her although Gail showed no reaction at all, but that night, in the closeness of the heat and the darkness she'd been meant to hear. More than hear: to share.

She opened her eyes and looked at the man watching her and held on to the girl who had been listening to her and it was enough. Not shattering, not world-shaking, but ripples of satisfaction that crossed over her, quivering at her limbs and gratified her, and pleased him, watching. He let her settle for a while, then leaned forward and gently stroked her knee.

'Good; well done. Fetch yourself another drink, and another whisky for me, please.' He held out his glass.

She fetched the drink, feeling somehow even more naked as she turned and presented her back to him than when she had presented her front, even her front with her legs splayed. Back in the chair, she started to cross her legs, then stopped herself. Had he forbidden that? She was not quite sure, so she continued. She tried to think of something appropriate to say, but what was there?

'Supposing someone had come along when I was outside, on the stairs, earlier?'

'Unlikely, actually.' He paused. 'Unfortunately.'

'But what would you have said?'

He laughed. 'Me? Nothing. I wasn't there. I was in here, remember?'

'But what if they had called the police?'

He shrugged. 'Not very probable. Anyway, this isn't a public place. You were breaking no laws.'

She would not give up. 'All right, what if they'd complained to the supervisor or the landlord or whoever. What then?'

He laughed again, shaking his head. 'Very unlikely, that. I am the landlord of all these flats, so the tenants are scarcely likely to complain about what I do.'

She fell back into silence, wondering if he was lying, but could not make any advantage by it even if he was. He was watching her, and finally he spoke.

'In the office today, we started the punishment for your disobedience but we didn't finish, did we?'

She waited.

'Did we?' He demanded her acquiescence.

'No.'

'Have the marks gone?'

'I don't know. I didn't look.' She would have liked to sound angry with him but did not quite dare.

'Turn around and let me see.'

Slowly, nervously, she put down the glass, uncrossed her legs, stood up and turned her back to him. No, it was not her back – she turned her bottom to him and she felt very vulnerable, knowing that he was looking at her, looking to see if there were marks where he had hit her before and where he was planning to hit her again. She tried to think what her bottom looked like to him and she shivered.

'Put your hands on your knees and part your legs.' However vulnerable she felt, he knew how to make it worse.

Now she was staring down at the carpet, at her breasts hanging beneath her and, between her legs, the lips still glistening. She had no control. He kept her there for a long minute.

'How many more do you think you deserve?'

'I don't know.'

'Would you like me to decide?'

'No,' she called out before she even had time to think.

He laughed. 'I'll tell you what. You think how many you deserve and I will as well. When we have both decided, if my number is less than yours we will do yours and if yours is less than mine, we will do them both, yours and mine. All right?'

She considered. 'But you could just say any number more than me. That isn't fair. Whatever I say you could still say twelve or something.'

He laughed again. 'Yes, I could; or twenty or a hundred or whatever I like. You will just have to trust me.' She could not see him but could hear his glass scrape on the table. She tried to work out what the best thing was to say.

'Well?'

She hesitated, then, 'Eight.'

Again the little laugh. 'Well, I am glad you take your disobedience so seriously. I was only thinking of another three – but, if you want eight, then eight it shall be.' She blushed at being made to look so silly, and blushed more when she realised how pointless that was. Positioned like that, bent over with her legs apart so that everything she had always kept so primly concealed was now proudly displayed, why on earth should she blush over something so trivial?

'Spread your legs a little further apart, please.' She shuffled a few inches.

He came to stand beside her and ran a hand slowly down the gentle groove of her spine until he could reach to curve his fingers around one cheek of her bottom. His other hand came up underneath her and held one breast, the thumb idly caressing the nipple for a few moments before crossing to the other breast, but this time the caress turned into a squeeze and the squeeze turned into a pinch until his grip on her nipple brought tears to her eyes.

'Count them for me.' And, before she had registered the words, the first stroke of fire had spread across her bottom.

She gasped, and shook and wanted to stand up but his hand on her neck held her down. Then nothing happened. There were seven more to go and she waited for the next one but there was nothing.

He said, 'If you don't count, it doesn't count,' and he giggled as immediately the second one landed on her.

She was more alert this time. Even through the shock and the stinging burn across her bottom, she was planning how to make it stop. She screeched through gritted teeth.

'Two!'

'Sorry,' he said, 'You missed the first one, so that was only number one,' and another stroke came down. It felt as if it was right on top of the others, as if her whole bottom was burning. It was not fair but she did not make the same mistake again.

'One!' she called.

'Well, actually, that was number two – but we will call it number one if you like.' And the next stroke came down on her. He was a shit, a bastard and was deliberately playing games but she was not going to let him get away with it. She would ignore him and keep her own count.

'Two!' and was only just in time before, 'Three!' but she was really suffering now. It hurt much more than she had expected it would, than she had thought it could, and there was worse. She realised how much this cramped-over position and the punishment she was receiving reawoke her need for the lavatory. She needed it badly now and was not certain that she could wait for another five strokes.

'Four.' Half her mind was still concentrating on what it needed to do to keep the pain from being extended, but she was also having to concentrate hard to hold back her bladder.

As his hand landed on her the next time, she felt the trickle run down her leg but she was able to clamp it tight and remember to call, 'Five' but she knew it had come out quietly, and he stopped.

'Sorry, I didn't quite hear that.'

'Five,' she repeated.

'Right, five,' and immediately the next one came, so deliberately so unchanging and she felt another spurt down her leg. She would not last but she reached down her hand, clutching to hold it in just as he hit her again.

He noticed. 'Got a problem, Julie?'

'No, carry on.' She was so angry. 'Six,' she remembered.

'I can pause for a while and let it pass.' He knew that would not help at all; he knew that.

'No, I am fine.' She tried not to let him win, but she could find no way to stop him stealing the victory.

'I'll wait,' he said and went back to pick up his drink, leaving her bent over in the middle of the room.

She looked at him, sitting there, comfortable, smug, patient but she did not move. 'I can wait. Please finish this.'

He smiled. 'Well, I am not convinced that you can, and I certainly do not want an accident on my new carpet.' Still he did not move, and she realised that he was not going to. He could wait her out even if it took all evening. She gave in and, without daring to stand straight up, her hand still clutching between her legs, she hobbled, humiliated, across to his little basin and squatted over it. The first torrent gushed the second she took away her hand. It seemed to make so much noise but, having started, she could not stop. He watched.

'Turn to face me, please, legs apart.' She shuffled round, saw him watching her and decided to refuse to acknowledge his control. She pulled her knees as far apart as possible, and pushed her pelvis forwards. She dared not speak out loud but sent her thoughts across the room to him. 'You want to see me piss, then watch me piss. I don't care.'

Having resolved her mind, she could indulge the relief, at least until she became embarrassed afresh at how long she was going on. She found herself seeing cows standing in fields, seeming to piss for hours. It was only as she finished that she realised she had no paper. Never mind. She would face him out.

'Could you get me some paper, please?' He did not move, so she threw his words back at him. 'Unless you want me to drip on your new carpet.' He laughed softly, but casually got up and went to fetch some paper from the bathroom. When he came back, he squatted down in front of her.

'I'll do it.' Very gently he dabbed at her, then pushed the paper between her thighs into the basin. Then he grabbed her knees, pushed them still further apart and, with a fierceness that she had not met before, he kissed her, his tongue intruding far into her mouth, almost sending her over backwards so that she had to support herself on her arms behind. His eyes were open, watching her as he kissed, looking for signs of rejection, but in fact she welcomed this – it was more familiar territory to her and she knew how to react.

He seemed to realise that he was not going to get the reaction that he expected, for he pulled away. 'I think we have two more to go.' It took her a second to remember what he was talking about because she really felt no pain from the earlier blows. When he reminded her, she suddenly became conscious of the sting. She slowly got to her feet and returned to bend over again but, instead of coming across to her he went back to his chair and sat down.

'I think I'll do the last two across my lap.'

So she went back to him, stood beside him, waited to be told how to arrange herself, but he said nothing, just waited for her. When she did not move either, he only said, 'Come on, we don't want to wait all night.'

He read her, knew her. She was little affected by being told what to do, having all her freedom of will taken away; what she hated was having to make the decisions herself, having to work out in her own mind how he would like her displayed best and then arranging her body entirely for his pleasure. She hated it and felt the depth and the glow of that revulsion deep down in her belly, acting on her, affecting her involuntarily. She lay down across his lap, aligning her hips on one thigh, her chest on the other so her breasts hung down by his leg. She rested her fingers on the carpet as her toes dragged on the other side. He shifted his legs apart a little so that his thigh dug painfully into her breasts. She knew it was not accidental but refused to respond. His hand played over her bottom, tracing up and down the groove and round the circle which she knew must now be a burning red. He dragged it all out so long – waiting for what? For her to relax, for her to grow more tense? No, most likely for her to forget to count. She was ready, and waiting, and determined not to let him catch her out. He continued playing round the circle, gently up and down the centre.

'You know what? I really think I should have used a cane. You mark beautifully.'

The slap came down while the shock of the words was still sinking in, but she was able to shout, 'Seven,' just before his hand came down again. Her final call, 'Eight,' was gleeful. She had outguessed him. He had hoped to catch her out and win an extra one but she had beaten him!

As she thought.

'And one for luck.' He laughed as the ninth came down, harder than any of the rest.

It was the last stroke that destroyed her – well, not so much the stroke as the callous glee, almost spite in his voice as he claimed the final little victory. No, claim was not right, because it was not something to which he was entitled. He had simply snatched it, stolen it. He had set rules for her to obey and, when it suited him to do so, he disregarded them completely. Finally she wept for the pain – but not only that, although she did feel it. She wept for the hopelessness of her position: her defeat, his determination to win at whatever the cost to her.

She could not stand up but just lay across his lap, careless of how it appeared to him. She had never imagined, during the hours she had spent thinking out this plan, how total his control would be. She was no longer even sure that she could complete her side of the agreement. It should have been more delicate than this, more passionate, more beautiful.

He may have been genuinely shocked at the reaction, for he did not move at first. Then slowly he did pull her up, sat her on his lap and cuddled her. She was aware, even through her pain and her tears and her shame, of feeling his erection beneath her. She squirmed down, hard, and took satisfaction in his immediate wince. Even so, he did not reject her, but kissed her cheeks, her tears and finally, at last, her lips. It was a firm kiss, deliberate and with real desire so that, in spite of her shame and her anger, she finally allowed him, through her cries, to force open her mouth just enough to admit his tongue. Still she stayed on his lap, wriggling naked and, she hoped, appealingly as his hands started to explore across her breasts, pulling at her, teasing, pinching, squeezing. All the while she could feel his erection growing steadily stronger underneath her, and she kept the tears flowing as she snuggled into his shoulder. This was much better – more what she had expected and prepared herself for in her planning.

So when, after her sobs had finished and her tears had been dried, Peter took her through to the bedroom, she was completely ready for him, ready in her head and ready between her legs. She could not pretend to resist or even dislike his attention, and he was so very attentive, slow and understanding and selfless. He softly stroked her bruised bottom and gently caressed her skin all over from the top of her head to her toes; every part of her was stroked and kissed and soothed. As his caresses steadily became more focused on her tender swollen lips and clitoris, he still lost none of the gentleness and she felt she had never received such absolute and unquestioning love-making. By the time he finally entered her, after his tongue and lips and fingers had brought her to the very brink of an orgasm time and again, she was not just ready but desperate for him and for the release he gave her. Much later, while his head was busy somewhere down the bed lapping away the aftershocks of her third orgasm that evening, she found herself thinking of Mike – that he so seldom would do this even when asked, that he never brought her to more than one orgasm in an evening. She felt guilty both that she was in bed with Peter at all and also that she was thinking about her fiancé while in bed with another lover.

But she was also smug at the pleasure she was receiving and slept happily, securely and comfortably, content that the worst of her ordeal was finally over.

Seven

Julie, awake first, slipped as quietly as she could from under the light duvet and crept into the bathroom. There was a real shower, huge with a fold-down seat and a spray like a waterfall. She wallowed beneath it, relishing the size, the freedom and the luxury. As she washed, dabbing between her legs more gently than was normally necessary, she at last understood what Gail meant when she talked in her usual blunt manner of feeling thoroughly well fucked. Julie grinned to herself as she savoured the wickedness – and the appropriateness – of the words.

A few minutes later, the cubicle door crashed open and Peter stepped in. He wrapped his arms round her and hugged her back against his chest as his erection started to climb up the crease between her buttocks. Yet it was while they were in the shower that Peter pulled away all her security again, at first just with a slight suggestion of danger but then confirming the risk, the promise. She was standing beneath the jet while he massaged her entire skin with a huge soft sponge. He ran it around her ankles, briefly let it tickle the soles of her feet, but stopping when she protested, then travelling up her calves and back down and up again and round her knees. From there he moved on up the outside of her legs and flanks and then circled round to the inside, the sponge running down one sensitive thigh, the back of his hand running down the other. After the pleasure she had received last night, three times, and again this morning, just once, she felt totally contented but it was not her brain that was controlling her responses – it was a far deeper emotion that set off that feeling of softness, of her sex turning to jelly. Peter had washed both thighs very thoroughly: front and back, outside and inside, and was now sitting on the little seat in front of her as he turned to her triangle of hair.

'Have you ever shaved all this off?' he asked.

'No.' She shielded it with her hands. 'Certainly not.'

'I think we'll shave you.'

'Why? Don't you like it?'

'Yes.' He sounded doubtful. 'It's a good deal redder than on your head.' His fingers continued ruffling through the curls, pulling them out straight and then releasing them again, watching them spring back. 'Reminds me of someone.'

'Who?' Julie's question came out automatically.

'Nobody you'd know. Anyway, it'd be nice to have you completely smooth. It'd make you more visible, more accessible.'

Then he fetched an old-fashioned shaving brush, a bowl of solid soap and a brand new bright red plastic razor, disposable. He lathered up the brush and started brushing all over her triangle of hair. This took him a long time. It was interrupted by many kisses and, if he was spinning it out for the sheer pleasure, she could hardly complain. It did feel good, and the brush tickled and caressed her overstimulated flesh where anything harder than those soft bristles would have been painful. Did he know that? Maybe – but, if he did, it would have been more like him to have used something harder.

Once she was thoroughly soaped, a mass of frothy suds completely hiding her crease, he started with the razor, and in fact she could hardly feel it at all. She saw her hairs dropping away, surprisingly ginger against the white porcelain of the shower tray, swirling through the suds and spinning down to the drain, but he was so gentle, and so careful that she trusted him implicitly, obeyed his commands to sit on the little seat, to spread her legs further and further apart. He was slow; he stopped and relathered the brush and resoaped between her legs, down the outsides of her lips, and she did not mind. He made her push forwards further still so he could reach right into the valley between her buttocks. It was such a curious mixture of textures, the shaving brush, sweeping widely and liberally everywhere, the razor whose steel blade slipped over her stretched skin and his fingertips gently running back and forth over the area that the blade had crossed, checking for any remaining wisps or stubble. Finally he brought the shower head down and played it gently – but not too gently; it began to have a slight effect – all over the newly shaved area. He sat back, pleased with his work.

'There. Not a bad job, if I say so myself. They'll like that.'

She was shocked. 'Who will like it?'

'The people at the club. In the sauna.'

'What club?' She hated him for the easy way he tossed out these little pebbles, knowing the agony they caused, and then watched her grovel and scrape for every scrap of information.

His tone was sickeningly offhand. 'I told you! I had arranged to stay with friends this weekend. You're coming too.'

'Where?'

'Cumbria.' She frowned. 'The Lake District. There's a sort of health club, fitness suite-type thing nearby with a sauna. We often use that.'

She took in all the possibilities offered by his deliberately scant explanation. 'Please don't.' But he only laughed.

'Please, Peter. I really don't want to do that.' She paused, and decided to play her trump card, managing a small sob. 'I thought you were beginning to like me a little. Don't you care at all what I want?'

He had no quick answer to that. It had been a very clever question; whether he answered yes or no, he had to accept her right to some degree of consultation. He put his arms round her and hugged her against himself, his wiry pubic hair bristling against her bare skin. The pause went on as he gently stroked her back under the soft spray.

'I don't remember anything in our agreement about caring.' This time her sob was real, and he went on more gently still, 'It'll be fine. You'll see.'

She was not convinced and held a stiff silence as she submitted herself to being dried, a silence which he either did not notice or chose to ignore. She broke it only once.

'Will there be many people there?'

'Where?' He was back to playing games.

'At the sauna.' She tried to sound resigned but was aware that it only emerged as petulance.

'It rather depends on what has been happening during the day. If there has been a squash match, some of the players may be hanging on. The hockey team haven't arrived by then. Normally.'

She resumed her silence as she considered the meaning of his answers. She was determined not to give him the satisfaction of probing any further. She even wondered whether he was making it up or not. The two sports he had mentioned could just as easily be men's teams or women's, and she didn't know which would be worse. The men would at least ogle; the women would merely sneer.

'Right, we'd better pack!' He interrupted her reverie. 'I think we'll stop and do some shopping on the way.'

He allowed her to dress, but when she asked what she should wear he simply said, 'Suit yourself. No bra.' However, her choice was totally dictated by his decisions the evening before on the items he had allowed her to bring from her own flat.

Having no idea what was in store, she chose a full pleated skirt and a floral print cotton blouse that was loose enough to envelop her and conceal the lack of a bra. He had said nothing about underwear so she assumed he had no preferences, and selected a fairly ordinary, if modest, pair of white knickers.

They started by mid-morning. The breeze which had started last night was now blowing stronger and, after so many days and weeks of brilliant sunshine, the sky hung a little less clear. Heading back through the town centre and then out along what, in pre-bypass days, had been the Great North Road, they passed through clusters of factory units interspersed with small parades of shops and some little Victorian terraces. Occasionally a newer estate of 1950s council housing would pop up. Peter pulled up at one little parade which looked so much like all the others that there seemed no reason to have selected this, except for the last shop in the line, all pink writing and black paint and obscured windows. The sign over the door said only CONFIDENTIAL and although the painted-over windows hid the details the very nature of the disguise displayed its intention more clearly than any proud hoarding could ever have achieved. In case any remnant of doubt remained, a sign in Day-Glo pink advertised to the world: 'Books! Mags! Vids! Hottest Imports!!! See before you buy!!!' Its garishness and uncompromising enthusiasm seemed more a barrier than an invitation and Julie realised that, just as yesterday Peter had perverted the suggestion of their going to see a film, so today his concept of shopping was one in which even those familiar comforts would be denied her.

She remembered having passed the shop before. It was on the way to the sports ground where she had sometimes gone to watch Mike playing rugby during those weekends that seemed now so long ago and so far away from the life she was following. Of course she had never been in but, as the car drew up outside, she did wonder, just for a moment, just a flash across the front of her mind, whether Mike had ever entered. Had he ever experimented with something like this, with someone else? It seemed most improbable – even impossible – and yet, she realised, Mike would never imagine that she would enter such a place either.

Inside a counter ran the length of one long wall while opposite that stood racks of magazines and video films. A multi-striped plastic curtain was swinging and twisting gently across a small doorway in the middle of the back wall. The man guarding the counter looked up suspiciously and Julie watched his eyes as he registered their entry. Between thirty and fifty – or he could have been up to ten years outside that range – he glanced at Julie, back to Peter and then back to Julie and slowly down and back up her body. She shivered.

Peter was unembarrassed. He left her standing in the centre of the shop and crossed over to stroll happily down the length of the racks, occasionally picking up a magazine to flick through its minimal text and array of gaudy pictures. With nothing to attract her, she followed him. The videos looked to be little different from those on the top shelf of any video store but the magazines were new to her and she caught herself staring, trying to peer over Peter's shoulder at the blatantly artificial and amateurishly posed scenes. After a few minutes the man at the counter spoke over the top of his newspaper.

'Looking for anything in particular, sir?' He excluded Julie completely from his enquiry, his glance, his interest.

Peter had now reached the video section. He did not turn round. 'Well, a video, for one thing; I will see what you have got here, but my girlfriend wants a vibrator. Could you show her the range, please?'

108

Julie managed to remain unsurprised. This was the first that she knew of wanting one, but the man put down his newspaper at last; he folded it carefully and tucked it into the pocket of a scruffy jacket hanging beside him. He cleared some packs of cards, jars of creams and candles and ashtrays from the counter in front of him.

'What kind did you want, Miss?' He started pulling out all kinds of boxes and lining them up along the grubby glass counter top. Julie was reminded of the jeweller when she and Mike had gone to buy her engagement ring.

'These Japanese eggs are very popular with the ladies at the moment. Then there is the traditional personal massager pack which comes with a selection of interchangeable heads. This one has the additional tickler for extra stimulation, front or back. What sort of size were you thinking of?' He looked straight at her, straight in the eye; he did not hesitate or blush.

She looked down at the horrifying array in front of her. This was not quite as new ground as she would have liked to pretend, because she had used one, only once, while at university, borrowed without the owner's knowledge from the girl she roomed with. That had been plain and round, part black and with a gold top, quite unlike anything here. She sensed Peter looming up by her shoulder. He picked up one or two of the boxes and examined them, slowly, carefully and obviously – an examination performed for her embarrassment, not his enlightenment. She glanced down through the glass counter to see a face staring up at her, a life-size rubber mask of a girl's expressionless face, her mouth caught in a perfect 'O', blushed even deeper and returned her attention to the marginally more acceptable boxes arrayed before her on the counter top.

The man was still pulling out more boxes, some smooth and straight and others curved and kinked with

109

the most obscene display of veins, knobs and fringes. They came in pink, cream, black and even a deep red, and they all had grotesque names like 'Superman', 'Weekender', 'The Master'. The man never paused.

'This one's very discreet, fits into the smallest handbag; or, at the other end, this 'Rocket-man' at twelve inches long is the biggest I have.'

Peter seemed impressed; he examined the huge pink tube carefully and in the middle of this another customer came in, the archetypal dirty old man in a cap and a fawn raincoat. He was clearly very surprised to see Julie in the shop and to see her examining the spread of implements arrayed before her, but he scurried across to thumb through the magazines.

The assistant ignored the newcomer and continued his patter until finally it was Peter who insisted on her compliance by returning to the monstrous torpedo that he had admired before.

'This one could be rather nice, don't you think?' She refused to answer, but they both knew her silence was not agreement. 'Well, if you have no other preferences, I think we might settle for this one.' His tone dragged her further along the path he had laid out for her and, as he always did, offered her choices – but choices between bad and worse, relishing the way she was forced to participate in selecting her next humiliation.

She looked over the scatter of multicoloured plastic, tried to decide which one she would choose if she were really choosing for herself, and wondered how much freedom she really had. He probably knew already which one he wanted her to use and had asked her to make a selection for the pleasure of turning her down. If that were the case, she had little to lose, but maybe she could help herself a little by showing some enthusiasm. She picked up one called a tickler, which branched like a finger and thumb. To her surprise, Peter accepted the choice, paid for it and immediately unwrapped it, put in the batteries and twisted the bottom to check that it worked properly; it started to hum and briefly he held it enfolded in his fist before turning it off and handing it to her.

'There's a little office out there,' and he pointed beyond the curtain at the back. 'Go and try it out, but don't let yourself come.'

The man at the counter seemed to be about to protest, but then changed his mind. 'That is all most of the customers do out there while they pretend to consider buying a film – have a wank – so I suppose there's no harm if you do.'

Julie took the vibrator from him and started to the back of the shop when Peter stopped her again, calling out across the shop.

'Are you wearing knickers?'

The other customer stopped even pretending to read and turned to stare. She tried to think of something clever to say, some way to avoid answering but, in the hanging silence, under the insistent gaze of the three men, nothing came to her.

'Yes.'

'Well, you won't be needing them in there. Take them off.'

Given everything else that had happened, it was surprising there were any veins left to fill, but she felt herself blush deeper, again. She obeyed him. Of course she obeyed him, because she had agreed to do so in whatever he asked and she had no right of refusal. Meekly she slipped her hands under her hem, gripped the edge of her knickers and pulled them down her thighs, stepped out of them and passed them into his outstretched hand.

'Good girl. Have fun but, remember, I want the vibrator to come back nice and juicy but you are not to let your little cunt climax.'

She knew he was selecting his words carefully for maximum embarrassment, chosen for the benefit of the

111

other two men and not for her; it was not language he would have used otherwise.

She slid through the curtain and found a doorway on the right leading to the most filthy kitchenette and toilet that she had ever seen in her life. On her left was what passed for the office. From a tiny rectangle of unwashed wired glass high up in the back wall, enough light filtered through to see a stained and cigarette-burned table, a couple of wooden chairs, a black PVC sofa and a small black television perched on top of a video recorder. Beside it, among a litter of coffee mugs and an overflowing ashtray, stood a pile of tapes, some in boxes, some loose, many littered across the floor. Cautiously, using only the very tips of her fingers, Julie examined the top one: 'Farm Girls in the Hay'.

The sound of shuffling and low voices drifted through from the shop and the bell jangled – someone else arriving? Someone leaving? Julie quickly closed the door, pushed one of the chairs in front of it and gingerly sat down on the grimy sofa, certain that whatever she did with her skirt it would never be clean enough to wear again. She looked round.

There was the little black television screen staring blankly back at her.

There was some graffiti, the most blunt and unambiguous she ever remembered seeing, scratched between the torn Page Three pictures on the wall.

There was a filthy orange-and-brown piece of vinyl spread over the floor and a pattern of chipped ridges across the ceiling. Thousands of years ago it had been white; how had anybody reached up that high to chip them?

There was nothing else. That was it, nothing else to see, nothing else to do except either slot 'Farm Girls in the Hay' into the video or start what she had been sent in for. She leaned back against the back of the sofa; it was cold and felt clammy, almost slimy, to her touch and she quickly pulled away again.

112

She looked at the stupid object still clutched in her hand. It lay there in her palm mocking her, jeering at what she had chosen for herself. She turned it on; it functioned. She turned it off; it stopped functioning. It was just a machine. It was just a machine designed to work on her, to produce reactions in her as automatic as those she could produce from it. She tried to visualise the people who spent their working hours assembling the things and wondered what they thought of their work. Did the makers ever try to picture the users in the way that the users tried to picture the makers?

Julie really could not summon up any sort of sexual interest in this sordid setting and yet neither could she wait in there for ever. She lifted the hem of her skirt and was surprised to see her hairlessness; she had temporarily forgotten about that. She spread her legs and gently probed through the softness with a fingertip. Her vagina was completely dry, replete from the attention it had already received that morning and the night before. She grinned to herself, and to her reflection in the little screen facing her. How many times with Mike had she wished for more? Now she had received too much, and was asked to produce more and could not do it. She counted. Last night there had been one that she had been made to bring on herself, and two from him; this morning another one from him – well, one and a half. More than she would have got from Mike in an entire week.

Thoughts of Mike would not help her now. She spread her legs further apart, pulled open her lips and tried pushing the machine inside. That did not work; she was just too unready. So, ashamed of herself, in spite of being entirely alone and unseen, she dribbled into her open palm and twisted the gadget in her spit. This proved enough and, with the very tip of her forefinger strumming over her clitoris in the way that was familiar and comfortable, she let the small round plastic end roll across her lips and slip an inch inside. Beyond that, she was still too tight, too dry, too unaccustomed to so determined an invasion. She pulled it out again and then, playing out an obscene parody of desire to the mocking reflection, she raised it to her mouth and licked all round the shiny surface. It tasted of her own secretion and she lapped it round and pushed it into her mouth so deep she was almost choking. Maybe she could manage to take a real penis in there without feeling too sick. Maybe, but that was for another day. For now, she moved the vibrator back down to her open thighs and slid it, slippery now, back between her lips until it was deep inside. Finally she turned it on and the sensation was immediate. A quivering that juddered right through her and, when she had positioned the little projecting thumb right over her clitoris, had an effect that was almost overwhelming. She could feel herself swelling to embrace it, feel her lips tightening to hold on to it and feel the first pulsing deep inside whose imminent message was unmistakable. Frightened, she pulled it out and turned the thing off. As she examined its smooth shining surface, certainly wet enough now, she knew it was too strong for her, too powerful and could be utterly addictive. Just once, without turning it back on, she pressed it back inside and out again before smoothing her dress back down and making her way back through to the shop.

Peter was at the counter, waiting. The sales assistant looked up from his newspaper expectantly, and three other customers had appeared, all seemingly expecting something, all standing and watching as she emerged through the filthy little curtain. Peter said nothing but held out his hand and she passively handed the vibrator over. He inspected it.

'It looks nice and shiny. Was it all right?'

'Yes.' What else could she say to show she was not intimidated. 'It works.'

114

'Good. And what about your little twat?' He spat the word out with relish. 'Is that all wet and shiny too?' As he spoke, he hooked his finger into the front of her blouse, dragged her up close to him and peered down inside to her breasts.

'I expect so.'

Peter grunted. 'Hmm. I expect so, too.'

The salesman piped up. 'Had we better check, sir? You know what liars these little tarts can be.'

Julie's eyes begged Peter to spare her that, not to have to expose herself there in that squalid place in front of this gathering of disgusting men. For a long time, as she stared in silent dread, Peter said nothing, but he glanced round from one face to another as he considered the idea and finally nodded slowly.

'I suppose we should.'

The salesman enthusiastically cleared a table of its neat piles of magazines and came over to help her up on to it. Even his hands felt slimy. Once she was sitting on the table, with the other customers and the salesman gathered round, Peter stepped back again. When they looked to him for a lead, he simply grinned, shrugged and leaned against the wall. That was all the invitation they needed.

Immediately one man, bald but for a few glistening hairs plastered across his round head, started pawing at her breasts. He made no attempt at a sensitive caress; this was groping for his grunted pleasure alone, while his other hand massaged the swelling in the front of his trousers. Between them the others brought her feet up on to the table, hauled her thighs apart and pushed her skirt out of the way to give them free access to her most intimate places. Their hands immediately homed in, smearing the juice across her as they gripped her lips and pulled them open and out. The hand on her breasts had now pushed its way inside her blouse and was pinching and twisting at her nipple. She looked over at

Peter as he watched her. For several minutes, while the men toyed with her, their fingers pushing inside and their blunt nails scraping at her, exchanging comments that totally ignored her, Julie's eyes remained locked on Peter's. There was no affection in his gaze, not even desire, but he seemed to be entirely unmoved, simply watching to assess her reaction to everything they were doing to her. She tried to be equally calm as she found her breaths getting shorter and realised her mouth was open, her lips were dry and that she was panting with an urgency that shamed her. Without taking his eyes off her, Peter took a step forwards.

'Here,' he said and proffered the shining vibrator. 'Try her with this.'

The thing was snatched out of his hand and almost immediately the humming started again and she felt it being roughly pushed against her lips, twisted and screwed into her. She was so ready and so wet that her attempted protest convinced nobody. It was being drilled in and out of her so vigorously that she cried out, and reached down to try to grab hold of the thing and slow their efforts.

'Look at that!' one of them jeered. 'It's not enough for her. She wants to wank herself off!'

And she did. However much she wallowed in the callousness of their crude attentions, a much richer humiliation lay in doing it herself, in shaming herself so openly and starkly. There could be no excuse, no apology in this, so that when they left her to it and stood back, she continued working the vibrator in and out, twisted the head to make it go faster and more powerfully and opened her legs wide to show them everything as her greed devoured it and squeezed on it and gripped and held and milked it of every stimulation she could get.

Her eyes were wide open, feeding on the lust boiling up in the faces of the men watching her, and she saw

116

Peter step up again. Suddenly, as she was nearly there, his hand clamped down on her wrist and pulled it away. She wailed at the loss, panting for the last tiny touch which was all she needed to consummate her humiliation, but he had timed it exactly right.

'That'll do. I don't want you enjoying yourself too much, too soon.'

'Good idea, mate!' The salesman turned with a broad grin. 'She's got us to deal with first!' Even as he spoke, he was unfastening the belt of his great baggy jeans and fiddling with the zip. 'I'll give her something to squeal about!'

But Peter must have seen the real horror on Julie's face at this, for he stepped forwards again, considered the offer for some moments, looking from one to the other of the eager volunteers, and finally decided against it. 'No. I will do that myself, later. I've got a couple more jobs for her first.' Even so, Julie thought the decision was based more on his wishing not to gratify the assistant than on any finer feelings for her.

'You can put these on again.' He handed her back her knickers, holding them out to dangle on the end of an extended finger, and she felt the pool of surrounding eyes feasting their last as she scrambled down off the table and struggled, on one leg and with only one free hand, to get back into them.

Peter turned back to the counter. 'Right, we'll take it. No need to wrap it up; she will be using it in the car.' He also paid for a video film he had selected and Julie followed him out into the sunshine.

As soon as they were on to the dual carriageway he turned his attention back to her again.

'Lift up your skirt, please.' She lifted the hem, confused as to what he had in mind.

'No, I can't really see properly like that. I think you had better take the skirt right off.'

'What, here in the car?'

117

'Well, I could stop so you can do it on the side of the road – but I thought you would prefer the privacy inside the car.'

She had no choice, so unzipped the skirt and slid it down her thighs to leave it in a heap on the floor at her feet.

'And the knickers.'

She obeyed again, glad that there was little traffic passing but always aware that at any time he could redouble her trouble.

'Don't let your skirt get all creased; lay it out on the back seat.' It was a struggle for her to retrieve it but she managed and, leaning over into the back, laid it out as he directed. She knew that he only made her do it because leaning over into the back meant raising her naked bottom above the windows so she was exposed to any passing cars.

'Now the knickers.' As soon as she had them in her hand, he changed his mind. 'Throw them out of the window.'

She could not believe it. Yet he said nothing, just allowed the command to sink in as they continued down the fast lane, and she now knew him well enough to know that it was the lack of any emotion that showed how serious his command was. She wound down the window and patiently complied, but watching in the wing mirror as they were sucked away in a flutter of white debris, she felt more naked and irretrievably defenceless than if she had not put any on to start with.

All the way up the motorway Peter insisted that she keep her legs apart; he stretched over periodically to caress her and ensure she was still moist. He seemed determined to keep her just a little aroused at all times and so from time to time made her use the vibrator on herself again for a few minutes, sometimes making her push it inside, but mostly having her run the rounded end over her clitoris until she was almost ready to come again, but then he always made her stop and put it away again, continuing a gentle persistent stimulation with her fingers, always under the strict order that she was not allowed to reach orgasm. Although she realised – after considering the occupiers of the cars rushing towards them and those which they overtook – that she could not be seen from other cars, this provided little comfort or reassurance when she felt so naked. Even this fragile confidence was destroyed when enthusiastic hooting from a passing lorry showed that she was plainly visible to anyone at a higher level.

As the afternoon went on and they headed further north, the clouds thickened, the sky darkened from grey to a deep bruised purple and, as they skirted Manchester, the first massive dollops of rain splattered against the windscreen. Within minutes, the motorway was running with surface water, the wipers were racing entirely ineffectively at double speed and the heavy clouds had dropped so low that Peter turned on the headlights.

Peter had, inevitably, revealed nothing about the people they were going to stay with beyond that they were friends from university days. Julie struggled between dignified indifference and nervous curiosity but, in the end, as they travelled ever further away from any area which she knew, curiosity won and she tried to wheedle something out of Peter. He was typically unforthcoming.

'Not much to tell, really. I have known David and Chrissie since university. Oh, yes, and Barry too; he'll probably be there.'

'But what do they do exactly?'

Peter turned to laugh at her. 'That's a very open question! Do you mean sexually? Professionally? Spiritually?'

She tried to put enough patient resignation in her reply to point up the childishness of his remark. 'I meant professionally.'

'Oh, well, David works in London doing something to do with money. He may well be a banker of some sort or a futures trader or whatever but I don't think it's exactly that. He's always rather vague, so I expect it's illegal. Chrissie is a kind of historian, researches things, you know, don't know what exactly. You'll have to ask her!'

He ended brightly, but his avowed and careless ignorance was unconvincing and Julie had learned enough to know there was little point in pushing if Peter did not want to unfold. She tried alternative tacks, as much to keep some sort of conversation flowing as in any hope of getting information, but all questions about Peter's family or background met an impenetrable stone wall. She tried an oblique approach towards what lay ahead.

'Do you come up here frequently?'

'Chrissie and David come here much more than I do, but they come for the walking as well.' Julie was about to ask what it was as well as, when Peter threw in an afterthought. 'Obviously there will be others around the hotel.'

At first she took the comment at face value, but then realised that nothing Peter said could be taken at face value.

'We're staying at a hotel? I thought we were staying with your friends.'

'It's both, really. The hotel's pretty small, no more than twenty or so rooms – so if there are going to be many of us we often arrange to take it over entirely. Graham's a good friend of the owner and makes sure he does not lose on the deal, so it is not a problem.'

'But who are all these other people?'

'Oh, friends of theirs or people who share our interests.' He noticeably made no attempt to define what those interests were, but at the time the explanation seemed so innocent.

Although the rain had eased a little by the time they left the motorway, following signs for the Lakes, the day was still dark and forbidding, and as the road became narrower and more congested Julie's fear of her nakedness increased. Even after reaching the outskirts of Kendal, Peter refused to allow her to put the skirt back on and, when she tried to pull her blouse further down to cover herself, he insisted she pull it back up again, even threatening to make her take it off entirely if she tried to disobey. Eventually, inevitably, she was noticed. At one roundabout a van drew up next to them, and the man in the passenger seat, after an almost comic double-take, leaned over to call out, nudging his colleague and offering a variety of suggestions which succeeded in humiliating her immediately. She clasped her hands in her lap but the man still knew, still called, still drew attention to her state so that the driver too leaned across to see. Then a man on the pavement on Julie's own side came up close to the car and craned in, leering and grinning across to the lorry opposite at the view. The minutes seemed to last hours before finally they could pull away.

Peter sat drumming on the steering wheel through the whole episode. He neither protected her nor demanded more exposure, content just to let the incident unfold however it would. Even once they were moving again and leaving the town behind, he still said nothing, as if nothing remarkable had happened. Then he glanced at his watch and a few minutes later pulled in at a little tea shop – but not until he had carefully pulled the car into a space in its cramped carpark did he allow her to replace her skirt. He carefully placed the vibrator in full view on top of the dashboard as he led the way inside.

Eight

Julie felt she was beginning to learn the rules of the game, but sometimes it seemed that all she was learning was how little she understood. After selecting a table in the window, Peter took his time looking all through the menu, considering, reading it again and finally ordering. When the tea arrived, he poured slowly and drank slowly, declined a second cup himself, but insisted that she had a second and then a third so that, when he called for the bill, she stood up and headed back towards the toilets. He stopped her at once.

'We'll be getting there soon. You might as well wait.'

Since these were almost exactly the same words as he had used at the restaurant last night, presumably he was going to want to watch her again. For now, he just smiled condescendingly and told her to wait in the car. From there she watched through the windows as he waited until he thought she was out of sight, when she saw him take out his mobile phone and make a hurried call before returning. The act itself was not threatening; it was the secrecy in which it had been performed which frightened her, that and the growing fear that the whole purpose of their stopping had been to fill in time.

He came running out, too pleased with himself, and started the car with a cheery, 'Off we go, then,' that gave no reassurance whatever and started a deep fluttering in her belly that she could not, if she was totally honest, entirely term fear. There was a certain amount of anticipation as well.

The rain was letting up at last and enough breaks had appeared in the cloud for the evening to be developing into a lovely summer sunset. They had passed several small villages and any number of hotels and guesthouses before Peter finally turned up an overgrown drive towards the lights of a vast hotel blinking through the raindrops. The place was very much bigger, and with many more people bustling round its great porch, than Peter's description had led her to expect.

'We are staying here?'

'Oh, no. We just meet up here to use the sports facility.' As they circled the carpark, Peter nodded his head towards a separate entrance at the very end of the building whose illuminated sign indicated the sports club. 'After weeks away and the long drive up, a swim or a sauna or whatever is just the thing. We're staying at Scourfield Lodge, just beyond Ambleside, but it's much smaller than this, and has no facilities at all.'

In spite of all the empty spaces, Peter seemed to be searching out a particular space and finally pulled up next to a little white car, one with a long wing across the back. He switched off the engine and reached over to collect his bag off the back seat. Julie did not get out, but watched him, sitting with the bag on his lap, not moving. He seemed hesitant, reluctant. Then he resolved whatever was worrying him, took a deep breath, smiled at her and threw open the car door. He even crossed round to her side to help her out, putting his arm round her as he led the way up to the entrance.

The receptionist barely glanced up until she heard Peter's voice. After that, her attention was complete; she smiled up at him, a warm, genuine smile which, whether it was born of memories or wishes, carried an unmiss-able message of invitation. A single dismissive glance underlined her assessment of Julie's prospects. Peter

123

chatted to the girl happily enough as he signed them both in, collected towels and locker keys and then led her through to a long corridor, lined by several doors on the left and the glass backs of two or three squash courts on the right. The door next to them was marked as the men's locker room and Peter pointed out the door to the women's changing room next to that, with the sauna suite at the end of the corridor. At least there were separate locker rooms for men and women so she would not have to undress in front of a mixed audience.

He told her to wrap herself in her towel and meet him in the sauna and, right on cue, a young couple emerged from the suite. Both slim and blond, little more than teenagers, glowing and gleaming like characters from a Scandinavian holiday advertisement, each was wrapped in one of the club's huge towels. They were both laughing and the boy leaned down to kiss his companion, tried to grab her and hug her but she giggled, twisting away slowly enough to allow his fingers to trail across her breasts. When he caught hold of her towel, she giggled again and darted away to leave him holding the towel and allow the briefest glimpse as she escaped naked into the women's locker room. The boy grinned at Julie and greeted Peter as he came on down the passage towards them, but the radiance and broad smiles on both young faces made Julie wonder how fully they had been enjoying each other's company in the privacy of the sauna.

But as Peter pushed open the door of their changing room, a sound burst out that froze Julie's heart. Men – there must have been at least half a dozen – broke into a roar of laughter. Her hopes had been so insecure, so weakly founded but still the only security to which she had been able to cling. Now they too were shattered.

She despised herself for continuing to hope for anything better. Every time her expectations were raised, it was only as a prelude to their being dashed

124

back on the rocks of Peter's deviousness. Yet the disappointment was also partly her fault. He had warned her that there might be many people there, yet he had warned her in a way that had given ground, and was meant to give ground, for hoping it would be different. He did it all so well. He did not give her hope; he did not show her hope; he left her to find it all by herself so that, when she did, she could have total confidence that it was real, not one of his tricks. He knew – maybe he intended – that every time her hopes would be crumbled into despair.

Julie shuffled down the corridor and gently pushed open the door into the other changing room. It was not very big: a few lockers along one wall, wooden slatted seats down two others – one of these littered with squash kit and a racquet – and a large mirror on the fourth. The other girl had disappeared, but there was a doorway in the far corner, and from beyond that came sounds of running water. Julie hesitantly stepped through. The blonde girl was standing at one of a pair of basins in front of a large mirror, naked but for a very small pair of white knickers and some expensive trainers, unlaced. She looked up at Julie, smiled very cheerfully and said hello, not in the least embarrassed at her nakedness. Julie smiled back, but was uneasy in so small a room with a stranger wearing so little and would have left, except that as well as a pair of shower cubicles at the far end, this little bathroom contained something else which gave her despair a sudden lift: a toilet cubicle. She could use that now and so outwit Peter after all. Some things he could make her do whether she wanted to or not. Others were beyond even his control.

She muttered, 'Excuse me,' and pushed past into the cubicle, taking satisfaction in the feel of the bolt as she locked the world out. She pulled up her skirt and sat down but was still shy, seeing the wide gaps under and over the cubicle door and hearing so plainly the sounds of the other girl's washing. She did not let go until the girl had gone back out into the changing room, then she relaxed, sighed, listened to the sound of her trickle, knew that Peter would be displeased, and was gratified in that. If she was already empty, he could do nothing about it.

Even so, when she had finished and was wiping herself, the strange feel of hairlessness, of the emphasised nakedness, reminded her how easily Peter could find other ways to demonstrate his power.

Back in the changing room, the girl was now dressed and standing at the mirror, brushing her hair back into a ponytail. She would not take much longer so Julie sat on the bench and fiddled with her shoes, killing time until she could undress in private. With one quick movement, the girl suddenly bundled all the squash kit into her bright nylon sports bag, stuffed her hair brush into a side pocket and with a quick, 'See you later!' pulled open the door and swung herself through; the outer door swung shut with a slam. It was all so quick and fluid, emphasising the girl's vitality and happiness and health.

Julie glowered after her, only slowly realising that what she was feeling was jealousy. She was jealous of the girl's happiness, that she was so clearly in love with someone who so clearly loved her. What a warm and comfortable situation and yet, for Julie, how elusive. Also – and this was something she had never in all her life felt before – she was jealous of the girl's youth. The difference between them was probably no more than four or five years and yet what a significant few years they were. The other girl was, at no more than twenty-one or twenty-two, at her peak.

She slumped down, head in her hands. What a mess this whole weekend was turning into. Peter was simply using her for his own gratification. He had already said quite explicitly that he felt no obligation to care for her.

126

Worse, she could not object nor walk away; she still needed Peter's goodwill. She had offered the terms and could not be surprised that he took advantage of them. She cursed her stupidity in allowing herself to arrive at this awful position.

She was startled by the door swinging open again as another girl, shorter and darker but more athletic and stronger than the last one, strode in. On seeing Julie, she stopped short.

'Oh. Are you –' she faltered '– are you –' she glanced around again '– playing squash?' She finished brightly, but it was an artificial brightness and, whatever had been on her mind when she had started the question, it had not been squash.

'No, I am just going for a sauna.'

'Ah.' She was reassured. 'So am I.'

Julie said nothing but still made no move to change. The other girl also waited, then seemed to make a conscious decision to be casual and friendly. She smiled and pulled open one of the lockers to retrieve a small canvas bag, which she quickly unzipped and started to sort through. Her movements were fast, businesslike and determined. Her jeans were good quality, but not very stylish; her T-shirt plain, dark and functional; and her shoes old, well-worn sneakers clearly chosen for comfort not looks. She was at least an inch shorter than Julie, but so confident and relaxed that she seemed larger, more dominant. Her thick mane of hair, dark but not quite black, flew out untamed in all directions. When she was not giving out one of her grins, her mouth was firm, almost grim, and her eyes were harder than her smile would have liked. She seemed a couple of years older than Julie, and would have had even more cause for resenting the shiny young squash player. She had finished sorting her towel, some shampoo and a small make-up bag and started to undress;

but, instead of taking off her shoes and socks, she started immediately with her T-shirt. As she pulled it up over her head, her breasts came into view – small breasts, much smaller than Julie's, and with tight little nipples. Their eyes met and Julie realised she was staring, and had been caught at it. She was immediately embarrassed, fearful what the other girl would think of her, so she quickly pulled off her shoes and stuffed them in the locker, then carried on, all the while keeping her back to the room.

The other girl kept glancing over as if she were trying to find an opening into what she wanted to say.

'You didn't come up with Peter, did you?'

'Yes. Do you know him?'

'Oh, yes. I know him very well. My name's Chrissie, by the way.'

So this girl who Julie had been privately sneering at was her hostess for the weekend. To compensate, she made polite conversation.

'Is it usually crowded here at this time? The sauna, I mean?'

'No, hardly ever.' She faltered and looked round. 'You do know it is mixed, now?' Julie nodded. 'Right, good, I thought maybe you did not realise. Well, most women are put off by the prospect of there being men here. Equally, the men are shy or afraid people will think they have only come to watch the girls. There are one or two couples who come occasionally, but not many. I think they only keep it going because it looks right politically. Mostly it's just us.'

No definition of 'us' was offered and Julie didn't feel inclined to ask. She only had her skirt left now and, although she didn't think Chrissie was looking at her, she still hated undressing in front of anyone else, even another girl. Besides, she didn't want it known that she had nothing on under it. Behind her, the room had gone quiet, so she quickly slipped her skirt down, forgetting until after she had done so that she had left her towel over on the bench. She tried to fill time folding the skirt, arranging it neatly in the locker, but all movement behind her seemed to have stopped; Chrissie was clearly waiting for her. There was no alternative. Julie turned round and took the two paces to the bench as fast as she could, aware that her face was blazing red, taking in the sight of Chrissie sitting naked, relaxed and content on the bench, smiling, and yet also enjoying a good look up and down Julie's body, immediately drawn to the smooth availability of her clean shaved crease as Julie whipped up the towel and tried to wrap it round herself, away from the prying eyes.

When the towel was secure and there was nothing more to be seen, Chrissie casually stood up and leaned over to pick up her own towel, taking her time – perhaps deliberately letting Julie note the contrast of the thick bush spreading wide across her belly – but finally twisting the towel around under her armpits and leading the way down to the sauna suite.

Only one of the dozen or so seats was taken. Peter tossed down a magazine and stood up as they came in. 'Ah! You two have met, then, I take it?'

Chrissie answered before Julie had a chance. 'Yes, we introduced ourselves in the changing room. How are you, Peter?' In spite of their both being almost naked, she grabbed him enthusiastically, craning up to give him a big hug and a kiss that looked to be genuine. 'Nobody else here?'

'Only Barry and that girl he brought last time; I don't remember her name.'

'Linda? Barely twenty and short curly blonde hair?'

'Yes, that's her. They're in the sauna.'

Chrissie took hold of Julie's hand. 'Come on, let's have a shower first. I feel disgusting.'

They crossed through the first room and off the carpet, the floor turning to tiles, cold underfoot. Against

129

one wall was an open line of three shower heads above a single tiled channel and on the opposite side was the sauna itself. Chrissie hung up her towel, stepped into the shower and turned it on. After adjusting the temperature she turned to face them, her arms stretched above her head, and let the water cascade down through her hair, over her breasts and down her body. She grinned at them both, not in the least ashamed as the stream of water turned the hair on her head and her belly into straggled rat's tails. Julie watched her, noted the firm muscles in her arms and legs, and tried to ignore the casual ease and confidence with which she exposed herself to two other people.

Julie knew she would never find this so easy and, although she followed Chrissie's example, she stayed well up to the opposite end and kept her face to the wall as the water ran down her back.

Peter stepped into the centre shower and quickly soaped himself down then reached over and started to do the same to Julie. She wanted to stop him, but his hands continued to circle her shoulders, down her back and cupping under her buttocks, then back up to repeat the circuit. He did not make her turn round but pressed up close against her as his soapy hands circled around her throat, across the smooth top of her chest then progressed down to her breasts. Her nipples were still hard; they ached from being kept erect all day, but still he pinched them into yet harder points before slowly running one soapy hand down the front of her body to her smooth exposed crease. He slipped a finger down between her lips, and then a second one, and parted them to allow the water access to her swelling clitoris and moistening centre. One arm still hugged her close to him so that she could feel his erection growing against her bottom. He made no concession to the other woman standing behind them, watching them – surely watching them.

130

Julie was embarrassed at so public a display of intimacy, made worse when another thought hit her. Peter could not behave like this in the presence of the other woman unless he knew what her reaction would be – and the only circumstances in which a woman would not object to a man next to her so blatantly sporting an erection would be if she had seen it all before. The only possible conclusion was that he and Chrissie must be lovers, or must have been lovers in the past. Then something else. He had shown no surprise when she first walked in with Chrissie beside her. He had expected as much, had known she would be here. The deliberate delay at the tea shop; the furtive phone call; it all began to make sense. He had timed their arrival knowing when she would be here. The realisation that he had arranged this – and, if this, then what else? – caused Julie to shudder.

Peter misunderstood. He leaned forwards to whisper into her ear. 'I had better stop before something happens to you! In the sauna you are to keep your legs apart, understood? I want to see you properly.'

He slapped her on the bottom, turned off the water and stepped out, not caring that his penis, waving semi-erect as he crossed the room, was plainly visible to the two women and to anyone else who might come in. He collected his towel, wrapped it loosely around his waist and disappeared into the cabin. Julie was shocked to feel another hand on her bare shoulder and at the same time a nipple poked into her back. She immediately jumped away but the hand stayed on her shoulder and gave her a squeeze, it could almost have been a little hug.

'Don't worry, love. He's not nearly as bad as he pretends.' Then she picked up both their towels, but did not bother covering herself up, grasped Julie's hand again and pulled her into the sauna.

The heat hit her like a train. It had been many years since she had last taken a sauna and she was unprepared for the shock. As well as the heat, she became aware of other people besides Peter already there; she had forgotten there would be others. She needed to keep up with Chrissie, to get back her towel so she could cover herself up, to catch her breath and get used to the heat – but it was all happening so fast. She felt light-headed and stumbled on the slatted flooring, but a hand grabbed her arm and a man's voice, not Peter's, steadied her. She felt a bench beside her, sank down on to it and immediately stood up again; it was burning hot. There was a peal of laughter, and Peter called her over to sit on his towel but she still almost fell on top of him.

The other two people were facing each other from the opposite ends of a long bench running the width of the cabin. Their knees were pulled up and their feet met in the middle. The man smiled at her and Julie nervously smiled back before quickly looking away. He was about Peter's age – of course: he had told her they had been at university together – but his smile was dangerously self-assured.

'Julie, this is Linda and Barry. Julie's a friend of mine from work.'

They both said 'hello'. Linda, a quite delicate-looking girl, appeared embarrassed at being discovered but Barry was on the point of reaching across to shake hands when he thought better of it. At first Julie assumed that he did not think it to be really appropriate to shake hands on a first introduction when you were both completely naked, but then she noticed that he was keeping very hunched over and she realised the cause. Seated as those two were, it was very easy, if no one else was in the sauna, for either of them to stretch out a leg into the other's crotch. Clearly they had been enjoying their privacy and Barry presumably now had an erection which he was trying to conceal. She glanced at Peter next to her; the towel no longer covered his lap and his penis, although still slightly engorged – she surprised herself realising what an expert on its dimensions she had already become – had subsided.

He smiled at her and whispered in her ear. 'Sit like Chrissie.'

Chrissie had settled back along the bench beside the door, leaning into the corner, her feet up on the bench in front of her. It was clear what effect Peter wanted to achieve. He spoke out loud.

'Here, Julie, turn round and lean against me.'

He gave her no choice but pulled her shoulders round and she meekly followed Chrissie's example, lifting her feet up on to the bench. Peter kept his arm around her from behind, his hand resting on her shoulder where it could so easily slide down her arm and on to her breast. It probably looked like affection; she knew it was control. Her eyes met Linda's, now directly in front of her and very close. Julie had only to straighten her leg a fraction and she would be touching Linda's thigh. The thought repelled her, but she was afraid that might be what Peter had in mind. When he had been interrogating her in his office yesterday, he had probed for any involvement with other girls and had not disguised his interest in her childish fumblings with Sarah. That was all years ago, nothing she did now.

Peter's grip on her shoulder tightened and she looked round to see Chrissie slowly letting her knee drop down, opening her legs. Julie was mesmerised, appalled and fascinated, but Peter's grip tightened again and she knew she was expected to follow suit.

She dropped down her head and complied, despising the ease with which she obeyed his demands, but hypnotised by her own slow display. As her thighs parted, already sticky and glistening, she watched a slow trickle of sweat wind down her chest to be stopped on a crease running across her belly. Beyond that, her little swollen mound came into view, the top of her vulva was visible and the trickle broke free of her belly and carried on down into the vertical fold. By leaning forwards a

133

little, she could see the tip of the hood of her clitoris and the beginning of her inner lips. They felt puffed and open, ready to be pampered again. She was damp, and could not pretend the moisture was all from the sweat. A pulse was pounding down there, a throb of pressure building up steadily, but she watched it all from above, and felt it from above, as if she were witnessing the experiences of another person. Still a fluttering nervousness deep within kept reminding her that it was not someone else: it was her – entirely her.

She found she was breathing more deeply, and raised her head to meet Linda's gaze again. This time she could hold it. Linda stared; her mouth opened and a little pink tongue appeared momentarily, lapped round and slipped back. She dropped her glance down to Julie's open sex and then back to her face. Clearly Linda was even less experienced than she was herself and this transparent unease and naïveté gave Julie a confidence that she had not known since entering Peter's office the morning before. She shuffled her bottom forward along the bench, offering herself more blatantly to Linda's inspection. In the corner of her eye, Linda's leg was stretching out to her own lover, her foot dipping under his thigh and hidden, but the muscles gleamed and rippled beneath the length of pale skin as she subtly massaged the man. He too was watching her and, as his leg quivered, the tip of his penis flashed into her sight. She quickly looked away again, back to Linda, still gazing into her eyes; Julie became aware that the grip on her shoulder was relaxing as the hand slipped down her arm to encircle her breast. Again the fingers gripped the nipple and squeezed gently. The palm and fingers dropped below the swell of her breast and cradled it, lifted it, offered it forwards as the thumb gently rolled back and forth across her nipple.

Peter spoke so calmly. 'What do you think, Barry? Do you like Julie's shaved look? We just did it this

134

morning. Drop your leg down, Julie, so he can see properly.'

Julie dropped her foot down to the floor, allowing her legs to part further. In spite of the humiliation of having to display herself like this, she felt her body responding. She was the centre of their attention; neither Linda nor Barry could hide their interest and curiosity as they stared at the revelation.

Barry was less calm. Indeed, his voice sounded cracked and dry. 'It's very attractive. I like it.'

Linda's gaze dropped again, now to the breast, to witness the steady stroking of that one thumb and Julie realised that her breathing too was becoming laboured. More than that, she saw Linda's own hands come down off her knee to cradle her own breasts, her own thumbs take up their own caress on her own body. Peter's attention was growing harder. Where at first it had been a gentle caress, soon he squeezed more, tugged at the nipple, pulling her breast into contorted shapes, deliberately hurting her. Julie tried not to cry out but she could not help twisting in his grasp and pulling up her legs to rub her thighs together for comfort and relief.

But Julie was unsure whether this really was pain. The stimulation had been going on all day and at this stage too gentle a caress would have been no more than an irritation. Her whole body was ready, was crying out, to be treated more robustly, less forgivingly – and, although there was a pain there, it was causing more than that. She would not be able to stand much of this; there had been too much anticipation for patience now. Deep within her, she felt the build-up of more pleasure than she could tolerate and she shuddered again. Her open vagina pulsed and rippled and the movement immediately attracted Linda's eyes back, back to the squirming of Julie's buttocks on the hard timber slats, to the glistening lips and swollen clitoris. Linda's eyes were unstoppably drawn to the centre where, freed of its hair,

135

her sex radiated its beauty and revelled arrogantly in its true purpose, a talisman of desire. Peter's hand released her breast and dropped further down her body, so slowly, inch by inch, until he reached the crease. His fingers ran up and down the fold a few times then, with just the tips of his first and third fingers, he pulled her lips wide. Linda was utterly hypnotised and, even though her fingers were now fiercer in their caress of her own breasts, the action was entirely unconscious; her gaze and whole attention were focused on the movement of Peter's fingers. His hand stopped, waited, with the middle finger curled back like a snake waiting to strike. Slowly it straightened and hooked over the top of Julie's pulsing clitoris, pulled the hood back to show off even that to the wide-eyed stare of the girl in front of them. Then the finger curled back again and this time when it dropped forwards it pushed between her lips and twisted its way right inside her, as far as the first knuckle, the second and further until his whole hand was pressed against her opening. Inside her, the finger churned round and then, though Julie squeezed, it withdrew, again moving very slowly, ensuring Linda did not miss any part of the show. Peter ran his fingertips up her stomach, to her chest, between her breasts to her throat, her chin and her lips and only then he stopped, holding his hand up in front of her face, but the middle finger was unmistakably shiny. For a horrible moment, Julie was afraid he would push it into her mouth, here, in front of everyone. But he did not do that; he had something worse in mind.

'Lick,' he said quietly and Julie had to extend her own tongue and reach out for his finger, which he turned steadily in front of her mouth so she could lick every side of it clean of her own juices. When he was satisfied, he dropped his hand back to her breast again and resumed the gentle caress.

Timidly, Linda's hand reached out to touch Julie's knee and settled there, unable to continue. Her eyes still held Julie's as they begged not to be rejected and then the hand lifted off again and dipped down to hover, hesitant, quivering like a butterfly over the open flower that everyone had been admiring. Finally, it alighted on the smooth moist skin and that one light touch passed a spark between them which detonated the pressure of the day's long stimulation. Every molecule of breath left Julie's lungs in one grunt; all the muscles of her belly received the shock at the same instant and hurled waves of power and electricity and pleasure, rippling up her body and out along her limbs. As they passed, she lost all control of her body and slumped down between her thighs.

Linda too felt the shock. She gasped and snatched her hand away as if she had touched an electric cable, but Julie no longer cared. Now ignoring all the other people around her, she sank into her own needs, digging her fingertips between her own lips, plucking at her clitoris, squeezing the waves of pleasure from her sodden vulva. For a second Linda stared and then she fled, grabbing her towel, stumbling, crashing through the doorway and out of the sauna. Barry glanced apologetically at the others and then he too caught up his towel and made half an effort to cover himself before following her, hunched over, his erection waving from side to side as he ran.

Peter pulled Julie's head back against his chest and stroked her hair, kissed her again, cradled her breast again in his damp hand and hugged her close. She was certain that this time it really was affection. But they were not alone; someone else was there.

Chrissie moved across to the long bench recently vacated by the other couple. She arched her back and almost purred as she stretched out along the warm slats, settling on to her side. With one knee raised up, she ran her hands down the whole length of her body, but the gesture was for comfort more than stimulation, a reassurance of pleasure yet to come, patient like a connoisseur savouring the scent of his wine before starting to consume it. She peered, casually but quite unashamedly, between Julie's thighs; then as casually reached in a hand and gently ran the backs of her fingers up and down the smooth fold.

Julie flinched. She was still oversensitised and as her climax passed away was becoming more aware of what had happened, of what she had done, and with awareness came shame. Yet there was more than that. Chrissie obviously accepted a level of intimacy with other women that Julie could never tolerate, while her casualness in front of Peter showed not only that she had no reservations about it, but that she knew he felt the same way and even expected as much. Presumably he was in the habit of sharing girls with other people – even, it seemed, with other women. Perhaps this had been his intention when he had telephoned to arrange for Chrissie to be there.

Chrissie sighed and settled back into the heat, still watching Julie. 'Can I have her, Peter, if you aren't going to?'

'You'll have to wait; I may have her in a minute.'

'Go on, then.'

So Peter brought her round off the bench and in front of him and, resting his hand on the top of her head, gently pressed her down so his body passed in front of her sight. When she was kneeling and her face was directly level with his groin, he opened his legs wide.

The intention was unmistakable, but Julie dared not admit how much she loathed this act, for she knew that this time no excuses would be accepted and any reluctance she revealed would only cause them to demand more. He was already half erect, swollen and bobbing horizontal as his fingers curled around the back of her head and drew her in closer.

Peter pushed forwards until he was only just sitting on the edge of the bench, his thick thighs spread wide to embrace her, his testicles hanging beneath him like a bull's, stretching his scrotum so tight it looked painful, as if they were too heavy for their taut skin pouch. So too his pubic hair: dark and animal and glistening in the heat. She reached out to grasp his erection but Chrissie stopped her.

'No hands. Just use your mouth.'

Above her, Peter chuckled, and when she looked up he was grinning. 'Do as she says.'

So she opened her mouth wide and succeeded in catching the shiny tip and drawing that in over her teeth. She did not think she could manage much more than that, but she licked around the ridge as smoothly as she could and hoped he would be satisfied.

He was not.

He was steadily growing harder and more erect, and the hand on the back of her head was applying firmer pressure to press more of the thing into her mouth when all she wanted was to spit it out. From the corner of her eye she saw Chrissie sitting up to get a better view.

Julie knew she ought to feel disgusted but could not help feeling lifted. Mike had always asked for this instead of sex, not as part of it – not when she was already so aroused, when she could take pride in being the cause of the sleek shining erection waving in front of her face. She had done this and she was being watched, her skill admired, as she knelt at his feet. Maybe it would be all right. As long as she was able to pull away in time, she believed that this time she would manage. If only Gail could have been there to witness it.

She pulled her head back until he was free of her lips and then pushed forwards, lapping her tongue far along the underside. The rasp of breath through his teeth betrayed his rapid arousal as she continued to lap steadily along the underseam, around the head and under the hard ridge. Then she pulled right back to hold only the rounded end in her mouth, released even that and nibbled her way down the full length to his groin. She glanced up and met his eyes watching her and held his gaze as she stuck her tongue far out and slowly, strongly, pressing it hard against him, ran it back up to the very tip, round the ridge then opened her mouth wide and used her tongue again to hook him back between her lips and deep into her mouth. He suddenly twitched as if he would withdraw but she followed him forwards and, reaching up, lifted his testicles in her hands, feeling them twitch and shiver, lifting in their cool stretched sack. Almost immediately his grip on her head tightened and his penis swelled and quivered as he pushed further forwards right to the back of her throat. Immediately she pulled back but his hands would not release her. Like a vice, they kept her in place as he trembled again and his penis, huge now, was filling her mouth and suddenly her throat was filled with his foam. She choked and tried to spit but his hands were iron and there was more in her mouth so that eventually there was no choice left. She swallowed. And, as more came, she swallowed more. She swallowed it all.

Only as she pulled back from him did she see that Chrissie was not merely watching, she was caressing herself as she watched, and her gaze was fixed on Julie – on her face where the semen was running down her chin, on her breasts which Julie, unconsciously, was cradling in her palms, on her swelling vulva which of its own accord was already opening for something more. But when Chrissie looked up, Julie saw no sign of affection in those eyes, but a chill resentment, perhaps even jealousy. Chrissie sat up.

'My turn. Can I have her now, Peter – please, can I?'

His fingers continued to play and twist gently in Julie's hair as he considered the request. Evidently this was no mere formality. He enjoyed – he savoured – total freedom to grant or withhold consent. This demonstration of his absolute power, and of Chrissie's acceptance, was more frightening than his exercise of it. Finally he smiled across.

'Yes, all right, I suppose you've waited long enough. What do you want her to do?'

She grinned. 'Everything! But first, I want a wet! I have been waiting, too!'

He laughed. 'I think Julie does, too. Ready for that, Julie?'

Chrissie jumped up and grabbed Julie by the hand, dragged her to her feet and pulled her out of the sweaty cabin and into the showers. She didn't turn on the water. 'You can go first,' and pushed Julie back up against the wall but Julie didn't understand.

Peter came to help her. 'Come on, Julie, you wanted a pee as well, didn't you?'

Then she realised. She looked from one expectant face to the other, swallowed, no longer so pleased at having snatched victory behind his back, unsure of his reaction. There was no choice but to confess. 'No. I went while I was getting changed.'

In the sudden stillness, Peter's voice was acid. 'Chrissie, is this right?'

'No, I'm sure she didn't. I was in there practically the whole time.'

'Practically, Chrissie? Is practically sufficient?'

'No, Peter, I know, but I was only away for a minute, just to go up to the office to book a court for next weekend. I got here ahead of you; you hadn't arrived . . .' Her explanation, desperate though it had become, had run out of life. She looked across, hopelessly. 'You didn't, Julie, did you?'

'It was before you came in.' For reasons which Julie did not entirely comprehend, Chrissie was clearly in trouble and Julie found she did not mind at all being the cause.

Another silence. Peter finally broke it, calmly, but so icily. 'I gave instructions.'

'Yes, I know. I'm sorry.' Chrissie's voice trembled.

'I will decide what to do with you but you certainly forego all rights, don't you?'

Chrissie mumbled something, nodded down at the floor.

Peter went on. 'I think you wanted a wet, didn't you? I will permit that. In fact, you can repeat the trick you devised for the twins last month.'

For a minute it looked as if she was going to object, but in the end she just murmured 'Yes, Peter,' and started back to the sauna, but glared at Julie with even more hostility than before. Julie was quite pleased with that. Chrissie returned with the wooden bucket and ladle that had been standing in the corner of the sauna.

Peter moved back to the bench and patted the space next to him. 'Come and sit by me, Julie.'

Chrissie watched them warily and finally stepped into the shower tray. Still she did not turn on the water, but carefully laid the ladle out on the tiled edge and emptied out the bucket. Then she placed it carefully in the middle of the shower tray, turned to face the other two and squatted down over the bucket. At last Julie understood her punishment.

For a moment Chrissie looked down between her legs, she shuffled her feet and then finally a few drops appeared through the thick hair, a little trickle and then a yellow stream. Chrissie continued to look down between her legs but, once the stream was flowing fully, she looked up at them both, defiance in her eyes and, for Julie alone, resentment. When she was done, she said nothing, simply stood up holding the bucket, raised it high and then tipped the contents over her head. She screwed up her eyes and mouth as her urine cascaded down through her hair, over her face and body, running in streams between and over her little breasts and down her body. When it stopped, she stood still for a few seconds before Peter said, 'All right,' and she was allowed to put the bucket down again and wipe her hands over her face. She immediately went to turn on the shower, but Peter stopped her again.

'Wait, Chrissie. You have been playing with yourself all afternoon. You might as well finish off before you have the shower.'

Even Chrissie seemed shocked. This was clearly far more than she expected, and her plea was utterly genuine. 'Please, Peter.'

'No, you must learn to do as I say. Use the ladle. In fact, bring it here.'

Hesitantly, she brought it over and Julie was surprised at how strong was the smell of urine on her. Peter took the ladle and turned it over in his hands. It was quite roughly carved from a single piece of wood with a completely straight square cut handle emerging from the rounded cup. He turned and handed the ladle to Julie.

'Give her three strokes with that.' He shuffled backwards to make room. 'Chrissie, lie across Julie's lap.'

The two women's eyes met. Hatred in one, fear in the other. Julie wanted to say she could not do it but was totally caught up in the scenario that Peter was directing for his – and only his – pleasure. If she refused, he would simply reverse the command, have Chrissie beat her instead. Surely he must understand the depth of the enmity that he was creating between the two? Or maybe this was all part of the game. Chrissie did not hesitate; already she was leaning forwards. Her thighs, wet and slightly sticky, were rubbing across Julie's own lap and her pubic hair, thick and bushy but very noticeably damp, scratching across Julie's dry skin. These differences suddenly seemed so superficial when they were both being put through hoops by the ringmaster sitting quietly next to them. Julie had an urge to embrace Chrissie, even to kiss her, to comfort her, to become her ally, but she knew Peter would never permit that; he was starting to fidget impatiently already.

Julie had never beaten anybody in her life and had no idea how to do it – which end of the ladle to hold, how hard it should be. She really did not want to hurt Chrissie, but knew that to disobey could not help and in all probability would be worse for both of them. She stretched her arm around Chrissie's waist to pull her tight into her lap and show her some of the compassion she felt. Then she lifted up the ladle and brought it down on to the middle of Chrissie's bottom; the noise of the slap and the jerk came simultaneously, the first so loud and the second so sudden that Julie flinched, almost making Chrissie roll off on to the floor.

Peter was unimpressed. 'That doesn't count; it was nowhere near hard enough. Do it properly or I'll give both of you six.'

Julie tucked Chrissie hard in against herself again. It would be best just to do it quickly, before Peter could complain again, before Chrissie had time to react, before she herself had time to appreciate fully what she was doing.

She felt Chrissie's body stiffen in anticipation as the ladle was raised off her bottom and immediately brought it down hard, much harder than the first time, then back up and down again, this time leading to a sob from Chrissie and immediately for the final time.

They both lay still for a moment before Peter's hand snaked out to trace the three dark weals growing up out of the smooth, stretched skin. His penis was already erect again in spite of his recent orgasm and Julie tried to be disgusted, but somehow realised it was only to be expected. Unashamed, unfeeling, he sat naked next to them, his quivering penis the clearest possible proof of his will. Chrissie carefully lifted herself up off Julie's knees, a broad band across the centre of her bottom now glowing a deeper pink, and Julie was ashamed of what she had done, horrified at the marks she had inflicted and yet, when she went to cross her legs, she

144

discovered a stickiness between her thighs that mocked all her higher feelings.

'Now then, Chrissie, settle down in front of us and continue. Use the ladle.'

Chrissie looked up at him, evidently shocked by this; she glared at Julie, then turned back to Peter. 'Here? On the floor?'

'If you like.' He sounded so casual but, as Chrissie looked around, it was clear that there was nowhere else. This was yet another of his non-choices. She glowered at Julie and snatched the ladle from her fingers, then clumsily sat down facing them and lay back on the tiles. Slowly she pulled her feet back up towards her bottom, raising her knees and then, with a sigh, parted them to reveal the thick tangle of hair and, as that was parted too, to show herself fully, openly and completely to the other two.

Yet again Julie was unready for the sight that confronted her. Revealed between her legs was a vulva entirely different from her own, different also from what she remembered of Sarah at school; whereas Julie and Sarah both had a single crease with the entrance to the vagina tucked inside, Chrissie's vulva pushed out, grand and proud and dark. Where Julie had little more than a ridge down either side of her entrance, Chrissie boasted full lips that were really worthy of the name and, somewhere at the top, her clitoris was buried beneath a hood so thick and loose that Julie could compare it with nothing except – well, except Mike's foreskin. Yet even as she watched, Chrissie ran her fingers up the sides, inside her inviting lips, and when they reached the top they carried on, peeled back the hood and displayed her pink clitoris, open to plain view. She seemed to push down and the pink knob, as fat around as Julie's little finger, quivered and pushed out all on its own.

As if that was not enough, the girl's entire vulva was sopping wet, entirely covered by a thick, glistening wetness so much greater than Julie ever experienced.

Suddenly brought to face this, she felt both less of a woman herself and also small and naïve to have lived so long and yet to have learned so little.

Chrissie held the ladle in her fist but it was her fingers that travelled the length of her crease and finally one dipped in, leaving her thumb outside the vagina but working feverishly and noisily inside the cover of her clitoris.

'Use the ladle, Chrissie, like I said. Inside.' There was sufficient edge to Peter's voice to show he meant to be obeyed. Chrissie pulled out her fingers and moved the ladle up to her chest; for a moment Julie had the horrifying picture that Chrissie was to be required to beat her own breasts with the thing. This seemed not to be the case and instead she rubbed the hard edge of the handle across her nipples, quickly bringing them up in spite of the pain that the sharp edge must be causing her.

Then she drew it back down her stomach and ran the tip up and down between the puffed shiny lips and finally tucked the edge under the hood of her clitoris and peeled it back to expose the proud nub, deep pink, wet and inviting. The four sharp corners of the wooden handle circled around the nub and then ran back down the deep valley between her lips, turned, and pushed up inside the girl. It slid in deep, half the handle's length before Chrissie stopped and pulled it back out again, twisting it round as she pulled, then back in. This time, Chrissie brought her other hand down to gather up the folds of her lips between her forefinger and her ring-finger while the middle one stroked up and down the exposed length of her clitoris, occasionally swirling round it but quickly returning to the steady movement up and down the gleaming shaft.

Peter took hold of Julie's wrist and brought her hand over to his erection, silently but unmistakably indicating what he required. After everything else, this was not difficult. Peter was watching Chrissie, not her, and

Chrissie's eyes were shut tight, concentrating on her own pleasure. Julie gently rubbed up and down the length of his penis, taking her timing from Chrissie's steady movements in front of them. It didn't take long before Chrissie's breaths grew more laboured and, while one of her hands worked faster between her thighs, the other continued churning and twisting the wooden handle deep in her womb. Suddenly her feet lifted up off the floor, and with a sob she rolled over half on to her side, first curled into a foetal ball and then shooting her legs out straight as a succession of sharp grunts broke from her heaving chest and her fingers and thumb gripped, squeezed and plucked at the swollen knob of her clitoris. No more than half aware of the increased speed of her own arm movements, Julie was brought up short by the sudden oozing of semen into her hand and the tight clamp of Peter's fingers around her wrist where he tried to prolong the pleasure without permitting the pain it caused in his overexercised penis. They were both responding entirely subconsciously, their whole attention focused on the girl spread out in front of them.

Finally her convulsions subsided, her legs relaxed their rigid stretch and, just as she seemed to find calm, she sat up, snatched the ladle out of her vagina and flung it hard across the room into the corner of the shower. It was hard to tell whether the deep colour in her cheeks was the aftermath of her orgasm or rage, but suddenly Peter dropped down to the floor beside her and pulled her up in his arms and kissed her, on the mouth, deeply, warmly and with such obvious deep love. He cradled her in his arms, rocking her back and forth through her sobs. Julie was deeply embarrassed in the presence of such a display of intimate affection, but more than that she was utterly jealous of the manifest depth of Peter's feeling and, without either of the others noticing, she slipped away back into the sauna cabin where she sat cradling her knees to her chest and fighting down her tears.

Nine

Julie stayed huddled in the sauna. For no reason that she could define, except that it was the nearest thing to a home she had just then, she had returned to the same seat she had occupied earlier, and there she sat, waiting patiently. She jumped at the irregular cracking of the rocks in the heater, contracting as they cooled, and through the thick pine walls she could hear muffled voices, an occasional sob outside, then shuffles and finally silence. She began to wonder whether they had both gone and left her there, wondered whether to go out but was genuinely frightened at the prospect of meeting the uncontrolled anger that had flung that ladle across the floor. She hugged her knees up to her chest and tried to keep from crying. So much had happened since she had woken up, warm and comfortable and contented in Peter's bed that morning, so much that she had not been ready to confront.

She could cope with Peter's stream of demands; she had expected that when she started on this course of action, but she had envisaged it being the two of them together. She had never considered the possibility of others, like those men at the shop, or the lorry drivers or in the cinema. Most of all, she had never considered – not once for the briefest second had she considered – that there might be other women involved. It was well over ten years, fifteen almost, since she had last touched another girl in that way, and that had been so long ago, so childish and, despite their selfassurance at the time, so innocent that it bore no resemblance to this. But today, now, here, she had already been touched by two girls, touched everywhere, had touched both of them and found the sensation hypnotically pleasurable. Furthermore, all the indications were that there would be more such encounters. She could no longer remember how to be repulsed.

Suddenly the door was pulled open and Peter walked in, still naked and with a smear of semen on his thigh, but apparently quite unselfconscious. He paused before shutting the door and coming to sit down beside her. He put his arm round her shoulders.

'You OK?' She nodded. 'Chrissie's gone to get dressed; she's had enough.' Julie said nothing while the inadequacy of his explanation sank into them both. 'I'm sorry about that; she is quite upset.'

Julie offered a cynical laugh. 'I noticed.'

'Yes, well, she gets like that sometimes, but that was my fault, I am sorry.'

'But why?'

'Well, it's not easy to explain. I think she was upset because I was cross with her for not keeping a better eye on you.' He paused, seemed to be giving her an opportunity for an explanation, but Julie was not prepared to apologise. Eventually he carried on. 'She generally prefers to be in charge these days and, if I don't let her, she sometimes feels hurt. She feels it's not fitting for me to treat her the way I might – or she might – treat someone else. It's difficult to explain, really.' Again there was a pause. 'Normally, if she wants to be giving the orders . . .'

Julie interrupted him. 'I think the term is dominant.'

He quickly looked down at her, clearly surprised at her contribution. She smiled to herself, pleased to have impressed him.

149

'Yes, that's right, dominant. If she wants to be dominant and I start putting her sub, she makes clear that she does not want to play that. This time she didn't because I was cross about her not being there when you arrived. She'll get better soon, but I am afraid she is still rather angry and may take it out on you.'

'Will you let her?' Maybe she had no right to ask, but she could always try.

'She has rights too, you know.'

'You knew she was going to be here. You arranged that.'

He didn't falter or try to prevaricate or excuse. 'Yes.'

'Why?'

'Because I wanted her to be and I thought she would enjoy it as well. If all had gone as intended, no doubt she would have done.' Again he paused, giving Julie an opportunity to jump in with an apology for her disobedience, but she pretended not to notice, no longer confident that her action had been as clever as it had seemed at the time. She decided to change tack.

'But she's so . . .' Her voice gave up the struggle to express the full depth of exasperation at what she felt. There was silence but for the cracking of the rocks, their steady breathing and all the while Peter's fingertips circling round her shoulder.

He gave her time to find her words but, when the silence stretched on, he prompted, 'What is she?'

'Well, you must know!'

He laughed at this. 'She is many things, but I really don't know which of them you find so appalling at the moment.' She glanced across, not sure if she was being teased, but the smile seemed friendly, if tired, and was certainly genuine.

'She's so . . . big!' The word burst out and she knew it was not right but could not think of anything better.

'Big? No, she isn't! She acts wildly sometimes but not big.'

150

'You know, her . . .' she stopped again, not sure what word to use. 'Her vagina, her –' she felt silly being so clinical '– her cunt, it's so . . .'

He laughed, hugged her, cradled her further into his shoulder. 'Yes, it's magnificent, isn't it?'

Again she looked for reassurance that he was not mocking her; there had been many images dancing in her mind on the edge of being expressed, but magnificence was not one of them. The silence settled again; even the rocks had stopped for the moment, and in that quiet she found the confidence to express the insecurity she really felt. 'She is not like me.'

Again he laughed, softly, gently, but this time she did not need to be reassured. 'To be perfectly honest with you, Julie, she is not like anyone else I have ever met. Of course, all women are made differently. Your face is nothing like hers; your breasts are nothing like hers; your vagina is nothing like hers. She is very – what shall I say? – generously endowed in that area. She is rather flat-chested, but there is major compensation between her legs. Yes, she is unusually . . . full-bodied –' the obscurity of his words showed even he was embarrassed, something she had never thought to see '– and to be honest I have never personally known another girl with quite so much to offer in that department, although I have known of girls who make her look quite stunted. I'm making her sound like some kind of freak, which she most certainly is not, but you must realise that girls come in all shapes and sizes. You are neat, compact and lovely; she is full, generous and exceptional. I love you both.'

She did not react, not immediately, to those last four words, but ran them around her head for a moment, chasing the good and the bad, trying to separate them into distinguishable statements – but in the battle between pride and jealousy, it was jealousy that won. 'So you do love her? I thought she was David's girlfriend or partner or whatever!'

'Yes, she is. Now. But before that she and I were together for a while. I suppose it's opposites that attract and we are too much alike for the long term. It didn't last, but we are still fond of each other.'

'Is that why she's so angry?'

'She could be jealous, Julie. You must make allowances.'

'I don't see why!' She knew she was starting to sound petulant and childish but all the excuses were being made for Chrissie – none for her.

'Don't be silly, Julie. I hope I don't have to remind you of our agreement.' To reinforce the point, he took his arm away from her shoulders and leaned back against the wall, no longer touching her at all, and closed his eyes.

'But my agreement is with you, not her.'

'Your agreement is certainly with me and it is absolute. If I choose to pass some, or all, of those rights on to someone else, that's entirely my affair. It makes no difference whether I tell you to do something or whether someone else does. You have to do it all the same.'

'It makes a great difference to me!'

He still did not open his eyes or move, just lay back against the wall of the cabin, speaking into the distance. 'You seem to be forgetting that your wishes count for nothing. If I let her play with you, that's my choice.'

'Would you do that?'

'I already have.'

'What? What have you said? Exactly?'

'Just that – that she can play with you tonight.'

'Meaning what, exactly?' Julie was starting to get seriously worried and wanted to know precisely where she stood.

'Meaning just that. Whatever she takes it to mean. Really, Julie, I think you're beginning to make too much of this.'

'You mean there are no limits – you have virtually said she can do what she wants to me? But she hates me!'

He was unconcerned. 'Yes, I am afraid she does rather. As I said, she can be a little bit jealous.'

Julie contemplated this for a minute. 'Will you let her hurt me?'

Peter just laughed and sat up. 'Julie I'm not going to get drawn into a debate on what I will or will not allow. She was very upset at being punished for what she felt was really your wrong-doing. In compensation, I have said that she can share you for the rest of this evening. We will simply see what happens. Don't forget that, just as I gave her permission to share you, I can also take that permission away whenever I want, if I think it's going too far. Now, let's go and get dressed; we are meeting her up in the bar.'

He briskly stood up to leave and held the door open for her to show as clearly as it was possible to do that their talk was over. Julie tried to find comfort in those last few words, but what she found was very mixed. She was beginning to hope that Peter did have some feelings for her, but it had to be faced that his idea of 'going too far' was entirely different from hers.

Outside by the showers, they gathered up their towels and he led the way back to the changing rooms in silence. There was no sign of Chrissie but Julie was glad of the chance to shower and dress in private and prepare herself for whatever lay in store during the rest of the evening. She took her time in the little shower at the end of the changing room, and dawdled over putting back on the skirt and then the blouse, buttoning it methodically to all but the top two and glad that its looseness hid her breasts, concealed the fact that, in spite of everything that had happened, her nipples were still erect. She brushed her hair carefully and wished she had some make-up to cover her pink scrubbed face. Finally she could stall no longer and went out to the hallway, which was deserted, and through to the main entrance lobby. The receptionist looked up, saw her indecision and, after a moment's internal debate, decided to be helpful.

'Peter and Chrissie have gone up to the bar.' She nodded towards the far door and Julie felt the critical stare burning into her back every step of the way.

There were only a dozen or so tables but most were already taken, over half by one large party, already in very good spirits. She threaded her way through to where Chrissie and Peter were sitting with another man. This was David, the same age as Peter, naturally enough, but taller, an angular character who doubtless looked and felt more at home in a traditional city suit than in the open shirt and suspiciously perfect jeans that he now wore. Julie was introduced only as 'Julie from the office who I told you about'. David looked her up and down carefully as if he knew more than he was yet prepared to reveal.

'Glad to see you. Can I get you a drink?' He took a step back to let her squeeze into the corner, but Julie was aware of eyes running over her all the time. But Peter fetched the drinks, leaving Julie under David's scrutiny.

'Well, Peter's a dark horse, but then he always was.' The innocence of the tone did not entirely hide a bitterness behind it. 'So.' Julie felt the intensity of Chrissie's gaze directed at her while the questions were fired from her other side. 'How long has all this been going on?'

'I've worked with Peter since just before Christmas.'

'That was not the question,' Chrissie broke in with a hardness that clearly surprised even David. 'The question was, how long have you and Peter been together?'

Whether her question was born of irony or ignorance, Julie could not decide but tried, with little real confidence, evasion. 'Not long, actually. Only a few days.'

She caught David's quick smirk and, with a cold hollow dread, realised that in getting her invited Peter had also disclosed to David, if not to Chrissie, something of the background.

David stretched out his long legs. 'I understand, Chrissie, that Julie is repaying a debt of some sort and is to some extent at Peter's beck and call. Here he is. Peter, perhaps you can explain.'

After distributing the drinks, Peter did explain. As Julie felt herself withering beneath the amused inspection of the other couple, her face blushing red, her hands running hot and clammy, Peter spelled out in clear details her failure to pass on the message from Robert Collis and the price she was now paying. When he stopped, the other two sat in silence, staring at her.

David sniffed at last. 'This is even better than you suggested on the phone.'

Chrissie was at last looking more cheerful, but her grin was directed to the two men, not to Julie. 'You bastard, David! You didn't tell me any of this!' She turned to Peter. 'You mean she's almost like your slave?'

'Oh, no,' Peter corrected her. 'She *is* my slave. She has to do anything I tell her.'

'Wow! I think we're going to have fun!'

Julie could not carry on listening to this. 'Well, it's not quite like that. I didn't agree to other people being involved.'

Chrissie's disappointment was unhidden, but Peter calmly took a piece of paper from his back pocket, carefully unfolded it and started to read: 'I, Julie Markham, undertake that from the moment of signing this agreement until 9.00 a.m. on Monday, September fourth, I will serve without question and obey any instructions of whatever nature given to me by Peter Harrison.' He folded it up again and put it back.

Chrissie stared at Julie thoughtfully as she continued her probing. 'What have you done so far?'

155

And again Peter told them. In crushing detail he described taking her to that horrible cinema, making her undress in his hallway, shaving her, the shopping trip earlier that day. Everything was laid out for them to pick over and mock. Chrissie was still silent but a smile was hovering round her mouth and, when she did at last look up from the table, her eyes shone with an evil glow. In spite of the two men sitting quietly watching and listening, Julie felt it would be sensible to try to make amends before things became any worse. 'Look, Chrissie, I'm sorry if I've offended you. I really didn't mean to, you know.' There was no reaction, just silence. 'I really am sorry.'

Chrissie picked up her glass, turning it thoughtfully in her fingers as she spoke, letting the words fall out calmly but with a steadiness and seriousness that showed she meant every bit of it. 'No, you're not sorry, Julie – not yet. You will be later, but you aren't yet.'

She paused a moment watching Julie's face as the words sank in and finally completed the action she had started before, raised the glass to her lips and replaced it carefully in the middle of the wet ring it had already made on the table. 'I gather Peter has told you that we are going to share you.'

Her stare was an undisguised challenge to Julie to object and Julie was frightened. She knew Peter; they worked together and had a continuing relationship outside this silly contract. Chrissie was quite different; there was no long-term relationship there, nothing to place any limits on Chrissie's demands.

Chrissie reached for her bag, started hunting through it, then jumped up and half ran back through the swing door to the stairs. A couple of minutes later, she returned, worked her way over to the table, took Julie's wrist and, with a hurried, 'Come on!', pulled her out of her chair and out of the bar.

She dragged Julie straight into the ladies' toilets and slapped her hand down on the little shelf in front of the mirror. There were two wooden clothes pegs.

'Open your blouse.'

'What?'

'You heard. Open your blouse.'

Julie had no idea what Chrissie had in mind, but her tone was not one that invited contradiction and, still wanting if she could to make up their disagreement, Julie obeyed. Timidly she unfastened the buttons that she had so recently fastened up. When she finished, she let her hands fall to her sides and waited.

Chrissie reached forward and angrily yanked the blouse out of the skirt, pulled open the sides and took hold of Julie's nipple between her finger and thumb, pinching it hard, pulling it out, deliberately trying to hurt. This was no game and Julie yelled in surprise and fear and pain, knocking Chrissie's hand away and shielding her nipple. She had never had someone treat her breasts like this, with the clear intention of causing her pain, and was totally bewildered. Chrissie was completely calm; she simply took hold of Julie's wrists and, with a frightening strength, twisted both arms down and round behind her back. The action pulled the two girls together, so that her bare breasts were now pressed against Chrissie's shirt.

'Keep your stupid hands down!' she hissed.

'But it hurts!'

'Of course it hurts. It's meant to hurt.'

Chrissie waited a moment to let her message sink in then released Julie's wrists and again took hold of her nipple, pinching it hard with her fingertips. Julie cried out again, tears in her eyes now, and begged Chrissie to stop; yet, in spite of the pain, all the twisting and pulling had caused the nipple to erect, and it glowed there bright red and obvious. Suddenly Chrissie did let go, picked up one of the clothes pegs and, before Julie knew what was happening, she had clamped it on to the very nipple. Julie squealed and tried to snatch it off but Chrissie stopped her, again grabbing her wrists.

'Shut up and keep your hands down or I'll put a peg on your cunt and then you really will know what pain is.' Then she started on the other breast, again pulling, twisting and pinching for sufficiently long to make the nipple erect in spite of itself, in spite of the agony it was about to endure, and then clamped that with the other peg. She finally leaned back, satisfied.

'Right. Now you can do up the blouse.'

Julie was crying. The shock, the viciousness both of the act itself and the manner in which it had been carried out were too much for her, were much worse than the actual pain. Indeed, Julie was surprised to find that it actually did not hurt all that much and the initial stab very quickly dulled down to a quite bearable low, numbing ache like a toothache, but the horror of what had happened to her in the space of a mere two minutes was still excruciating. Gingerly she refastened the buttons up the front of the blouse. The pegs both hung down and so were not too noticeable, until she started to move; then every step pulled at them. Chrissie just stood and watched, smug and smiling. Finally she led the way back to their table.

Peter looked up. 'Where have you been?'

'I took her into the ladies.'

Peter said nothing but he raised his eyebrows. Chrissie finally broke into a grin. 'Pegged her!' and immediately raised her glass and drained the last of it.

'I'm going to have another one. Who else?' She could afford to sound bright and breezy now. Peter and David both declined but Julie said nothing and Chrissie did not even wait for her, simply wandered off cheerily to the bar while Julie sat still, hardly daring to move her arms for the stabs of pain she was afraid this would cause.

When Chrissie returned, she dumped her drink down on the table in front of her, the picture of carefree glee, but Julie's quiet misery was obviously too tempting. 'Come on, girl, things could be worse. In fact, they will be later on!' and she reached over and flicked at one of the pegs on Julie's breast. Julie yelped, and quickly blushed down into her glass as several other tables turned to stare.

Chrissie giggled. 'What a baby! Drink up!'

Ten

Having only just fought his way up through the weekend traffic jams, David insisted on a game of squash to unwind.

'All right,' Peter agreed, 'but then I must really be off.'

'Off?' asked Julie. 'Off where?'

'To visit my parents, but Chrissie can take you on to the hotel. Didn't I tell you?'

'No, you didn't!' It was typical of him to leave her in the dark and then announce a plan which appealed much more to Chrissie than to Julie – for, although nothing was said, both girls knew this meant Julie could not remove the pegs from her breasts.

'When will you be back?'

'About eight, maybe nine.' His carefree jolly tone invited further objection but Julie refused to give him the satisfaction.

A slow drizzle was still falling as Julie darted across to collect her things from Peter's car, and she had barely dropped them into Chrissie's car and climbed in herself before Chrissie sped off in a shower of gravel, scarcely slowing at the entrance and pulling out confidently into a gap that Julie would have said was far too small to take them. However, the car was clearly more powerful than it appeared and they were into the gap, through it and out into the fast lane before the cars behind came anywhere near them. That did not prevent one driver flashing his headlights and hooting in outrage, an anger doubtless increased by his inability to catch them up close enough for the gestures to acquire any significant value.

As soon as they were into the traffic stream, Chrissie turned to Julie and grinned. 'Peter tells me you have made a real mess of things at work. What will you do, assuming you don't manage to make it through the weekend?'

'I think I can manage.'

'I doubt it. How are the tits now?'

In truth, although every jolt of the car shook the vicious wooden jaws and pulled at the delicate skin, her nipples were almost numb and it was really quite bearable compared with the agony during the first few minutes. However Julie had a terrible fear that the sudden return of feeling when, in due course, the pegs were removed would be worse than the present steady low ache. Nevertheless, letting Chrissie believe she was suffering would be better than risk having the punishment increased. It seemed even worth risking a briar-patch gamble. 'They ache awfully, if you must know. Can I please take them off now?'

'Liar! I bet they're as numb as anything. Don't forget I've had it done to me often enough. You'll be able to take them off in a minute. I just need to stop for some petrol; we still have half a tank but there's no point in taking unnecessary risks, is there?' She laughed across the car.

Julie said nothing. The irony of the remark was perfectly clear and there was no point in further discussion on it. She saw Chrissie glance over, smiling to herself as she slowed the car and waited to pull across the oncoming traffic into a petrol station. Drumming her thumbs on the steering wheel in time with the click of the indicator, Chrissie spoke again, softly, matter of fact, as if it were the most natural thing in the world.

'Undo your blouse.'

'What? I can't, here.'

'Please do as you are told.' She must have learned the effectiveness of such total calm from Peter.

'But, come on, Chrissie, there are people all round. I can't undo it here.' Julie put a definite finality into her tone, a logical certainty that matched Chrissie's own and which she hoped would carry sufficient weight.

And in fact Chrissie only glanced across and did not answer, but concentrated on working the car quickly through a sudden gap in the oncoming traffic and into the petrol station. She swept in under the canopy and pulled up fiercely in front of the pumps, turned off the engine and yanked the key out of the ignition.

'You really must learn to do what you are told, Julie.' And then she slapped Julie once across each breast. In normal circumstances, that would have been agonising; with the little pegs biting viciously into her skin, it was excruciating and Julie immediately collapsed, tears springing to her eyes as she fought to keep from screaming out loud.

'Are you going to unfasten your blouse now, or shall I do that again?' In no doubt that Chrissie would carry out her threat, Julie quickly did as she had been instructed. Chrissie watched every movement and, as soon as the buttons were unfastened, she flicked the sides open to reveal Julie's breasts entirely before she casually stepped out of the car and started to fill up with petrol.

So Julie waited, her blouse hanging off her shoulders and her breasts visible to anybody who passed. Worse than that, it exposed her nipples, still held fast in the brutal wooden jaws which were now digging so deeply into her flesh.

In fact, Julie realised, Chrissie's anger helped here because she had pulled the car so far into the petrol station that they had come to a stop some distance in

162

front of the pump and there was nobody in front of them. Even so, it seemed to be taking Chrissie ages to fill the car, standing whistling happily and loudly as she did so, attracting what attention she could.

Eventually – this had to be too good to last – just as Chrissie finished filling the car and went over to pay, a van pulled up at the other side of the pump. The driver jumped down from his cab and glanced over as Julie quickly ducked forwards, snatched a road map out of the glove compartment and examined it intently. He turned to the pump and started the usual business of filling his own tank but, once the pump was running, he looked over again, saw that Julie was still ducked down and became curious. He looked round the petrol station to see who else might have noticed, whether this was some charade, a candid camera joke about to be played on him – but when he could see nothing he peered back, still unable to tell what he was missing, though his imagination filled in all the gaps. He kept trying to work his way further round the van to get a better view. Julie huddled down lower.

Suddenly the other door was thrown open and Chrissie jumped in. Immediately she took in the van driver, Julie's hunched posture and the unnecessary road map. Without saying anything, she busied herself with putting away her credit card and purse, leaning over to place her handbag on the back shelf, adjusting the mirror. The silence was ominous.

'Sit up straight.' Julie now knew better than to disobey, even though it meant she was visible to the van driver, who could see not only her breasts but also the pegs on them. Chrissie leaned over towards Julie, grinning. 'This bit is going to hurt.' And, without any further pause, she snatched away the pegs.

She was right, of course, and Julie collapsed down into her own lap as the blood surged back into her nipples and the nerve-endings reawoke with a scream of protest. Chrissie ignored her entirely as she steered the little car round the back of a queue of waiting traffic and roared on up the next hill. Hunched over, but determined not to weep in front of her persecutor, Julie nursed her bruised and throbbing nipples as they pressed on through the worsening rain and even managed to refasten her blouse without Chrissie stopping her.

Scourfield Lodge turned out to be typical of so many other small hotels that had come to litter the Fells since the burst of popular tourism during the nineteen twenties and thirties. A low, dark stone jumble of buildings, half hidden among the trees and rocks, it commanded an unrivalled view down to Windermere and it was this, coupled with the lavish comforts, which brought so many visitors to eat too much, drink too much and spend too much and then make peace with their consciences in an excess of sweat and exertion in one of the health and sports clubs or in puffing their way over the hills.

Yet Julie was new to all this. Never having been much of a walker, this was a foreign country and, as they pulled into the carpark, she ignored the lake glittering below, ignored the low cloud swirling round the peaks above, and merely peered out through misty windows to inspect the little gravelled square and count the cars which would have brought potential witnesses to her next humiliation. She was greatly relieved to see that the carpark was barely a quarter full, although a sign in the front bay window firmly repulsed any further potential customers with a defiant NO VACANCIES. She and Chrissie pulled their jackets round them, grabbed their cases and, bent almost double, dashed across to the shelter of the porch.

For a place with no vacancies, Scourfield Lodge appeared surprisingly empty but Chrissie skipped cheerily through the quiet to the only reception room the hotel seemed to have. This was both lounge and bar, a room twice as long as it was wide, that might once have been a ballroom. It had a fireplace and chimney at each end while all down the far side a succession of bays and French windows looked through to some sort of conservatory and, beyond that, to the garden and the lake. Before Julie had time to take all this in, they were hailed from the far end of the room where one of the fires was alight and a small group of people had gathered round, having tea.

There was just one man, introduced as Graham – at least fifty, and wearing a smart suit and tie that looked too formal for so small an establishment – and three women. One of these, Judith, was only a few years older than Julie herself and seemed to be the man's wife; second was young Linda from the sauna and the third was a quite severe woman named Margaret who might have been anything between thirty and forty and stared at Julie throughout with unsettling interest and self-assurance. They evidently knew each other well, and also knew Peter; so, after only the briefest of introductions, Chrissie launched into an explanation of Julie's presence which left out nothing except Chrissie's own part in any of the incidents.

However, Chrissie was perhaps less well-liked than she believed, because Graham and Judith made an excuse and left before Chrissie's tale was complete and Linda also hurried away when the story reached their arrival at the sauna. Margaret heard it out patiently enough from the comfort of her armchair, but was an unencouraging audience so, once the tale was done, Chrissie fell silent. Beyond the gothic windows, the day was darkening steadily into a miserable night; somewhere in the distance, muffled beyond several closed doors, a radio was playing for the hotel staff who had begun preparing the evening meal but, in their warm sitting room, the afternoon settled down to sleep. For several minutes no one disturbed the quiet.

'Put another log on, would you, Julie dear?' Margaret smiled like an aunt at Christmas, although her accent, a soft and very refined lowland Scots, came as a surprise. 'That's better; thank you.' She smiled as Julie returned to her chair. 'So young Peter shaved you, did he?'

'Yes.' No other answer was possible while Chrissie was looking over at her with that sour little smile.

'All of it?' Margaret pressed on.

'Yes, actually, all of it.'

The woman raised her eyebrows momentarily. It could have been surprise; could have been appreciation; could, in any other circumstances, with any other subject matter, have been no more than polite attention. 'How very interesting.'

Julie squirmed through the following silence. Margaret was obviously someone who had no notion of modesty or embarrassment and within a few minutes would presume an intimacy that would take Julie years.

'I think I'd like to see that.'

Julie started for a moment but then took the remark in the only way possible, given the quiet modest setting. She ignored it. The woman was not to be dismissed.

'Show me.'

'No!' The answer came automatically, but strangely not only did Margaret not argue, neither did Chrissie butt in. They both just let the silence hang so that the subject was unfinished and, as neither of them had anything to add, it fell to Julie. 'Look, there's a little bit more to this than meets the eye or than Chrissie explained, but it's between Peter and me and, if you don't mind, I'd like to keep it that way.' She glanced at Margaret and Chrissie and back again, unsure which posed the greater threat, so gave each of them her bridge-building, women-together smile. Neither smiled back.

Chrissie was entirely matter of fact. 'No, it isn't. I thought Peter had made that quite clear. You do anything he says, and that means anything I say. Show her.'

'But Chrissie, it's –'

'Show her.'

'No. I just feel that –'

'Show her.' She sat unmoving, unmovable, unpersuadable and for Julie, surrounded by people whose calm refusal to respect normal rules of behaviour showed her first that she was entirely on her own and second that this was nothing new for them, it was crushing. She knew herself beaten. All her objections would count for nothing in the face of such unchallengeable insistence. So if she was ordered to do this, to lift up the single layer of skirt which was all that had been permitted her as covering, she would do that. She could submit to the command and expose herself to the woman opposite and it would not be her fault or her choice; it would just happen. If the woman admired what she saw, or desired her or was shocked, there was nothing else Julie could do. But it was still so wrong. Julie knew she could, if she wanted, refuse. They could hardly force her physically to undress; even here there must be some limits, so she could simply get up and walk out. True, she did not have a car, but she could easily phone for a taxi or go down into the village. For a moment she considered that possibility; she could be out and away and on a train and home again; in her own bed for the night. But as she glanced at the narrow casement windows, the rain again pelting down against the glass as if it would smash its way in, she knew that was not an option. She would have to get through the night here the best she could.

And the rain outside in the darkening evening, and the log fire inside, hissing and popping in the glow of a safe comfort, turned her mind back to the little circle in front of her and she realised that she really did not want to leave, to abandon the warm security of this quiet world. Here she was cherished and looked after; she was fed and housed and ferried from place to place; told what to do and what to wear. This could, if it was played out right, be perfect – to be made to be naked in the lounge of this quiet country hotel, with the rain beating down outside but locked in among the scatterings of a conventional timelessness, surrounded by pretty landscapes and faded gentility. Here she could shine.

The impropriety would be emphasised by the quiet decency of the setting and the calm politeness of the two women. They were strangers, one she had known for a couple of hours and the other for a couple of minutes, yet they sat over their teacups, waiting for it to be time to dress for dinner and, in the meantime, for their entertainment, they had decided they would like her to expose herself. It was so entirely out of place that Julie found it was becoming extremely appealing. It would be as good as – no, better than – any of the times she had contrived to give strangers a quick glimpse of thigh, or of her underwear, or sometimes, when all the circumstances were just right, and the mood had been too strong, even of her lack of underwear.

Margaret prompted her again. 'If you please, Julie? No need to take the skirt right off; just lift it up for me.'

And that was what made it so exciting. That was what was hardening her nipples, was starting little spasms deep inside her which could, if they were allowed to continue, actually bring her to orgasm, without any further stimulation. There had been other people at the sauna, but then everybody had been naked. In Peter's office she had been the only one to undress – true the choice had not been hers, she had been required to do it – but then there had been only one person present. In the cinema, in that dreadful shop, there had been others but all men whose sheer indiscriminate obscenity disqualified them. This was better than any of those scenes.

This was richer, fuller. This was not her choice and this was in front of these strangers, these two women. This was wrong and it felt wonderful. The only way it could possibly be better would be if there were even more compulsion, even greater imbalance.

She looked back at Margaret, feeling that she understood the subtleties whereas Chrissie was simply blinded by her power. 'I really don't think that is necessary.'

But Margaret was determined; in fact, the lively gleam in her eye suggested she knew exactly what was required of her. 'Just do as you are asked, please, Julie.'

So she did. She slipped her hands off the arms of her chair down on to her lap and started to pull her skirt up, feeling the eyes on her legs, on her skin, watching and waiting as more appeared; knees, thighs and probably by now a deep shadow between her legs, a shadow where there should have been hair for extra covering and now there was nothing. She had reached the angle where her legs stopped, and then in a single rush she pulled it up the rest of the way to her waist. Sitting as she was, of course, little would yet be visible; they would have to demand more.

It was still Margaret who gave the orders. 'Stand up, please.'

In standing, Julie allowed the hem to fall a little, just to the tops of her thighs, just enough to cover her crease, just enough to mean she had to lift the hem all over again, to reveal herself all over again.

'Right up to your waist, please.'

Looking into the faces of each of her audience, at eyes which without exception were focused not on her face but on the steadily widening expanse of pale skin, drawing ever closer to the bunch of blue cotton at her waist, Julie pictured the scene they were seeing, pictured it as she had seen it in the mirror when she was dressing. She knew it looked so pale and fragile, so very naked in its hairlessness and so enticingly cleft, with a groove that

169

led through to promises for the future. Julie shivered as she waited.

This time it was Chrissie who spoke. 'Feet apart, please, Julie. No, further than that.'

Margaret interrupted. 'You know, I think it would be better if she sat down again, but sit right on the front of your chair, please.'

Julie complied; her legs were not pressed together but neither were they far enough apart. She would be ordered to show more. She glanced at Margaret and found her staring straight back. Julie realised that Margaret understood this game. It was not a matter of what was displayed but of how it was displayed. It was what went on in the mind that created the excitement; this was what made the difference and for Julie it was the orders given that made the game worth playing. Without taking her eyes off Julie's face, Margaret spoke again, calmly, slowly, evenly to let Julie savour every word.

'Spread your legs apart, please Julie.' She paused a moment to let the pleasure build. 'As wide as you can.'

That alone was almost enough to push Julie over the edge and she struggled to keep the strength of her arousal locked in, away from their inspection and perhaps their ridicule. She hinged her legs open and, when her thighs were stretched as far as they could, she carefully shuffled each foot out to give that extra inch. Only when she had done all she could did Margaret finally glance down to check, finding, as she had known she would, the consequence of her commands glistening between the taut thighs, glistening for anyone to see.

'Thank you, Julie. Quite delightful.' The woman's fingers slowly twined over and over each other as she sat there, enthralled at the sight which she had demanded to have revealed.

Eleven

Julie wasn't hiding – honestly, she wasn't, she was just keeping out of the way. She leaned on the little rail across the huge window at the top of the first flight of stairs and stared out over the sodden carpark. The rain had subsided to a sullen drizzle, dripping from the trees and shining through a scattering of puddles across the yards of broken patchy gravel. It was all so dull, so dismal, and so utterly different from the vision she had anticipated. She had pictured something glamorous, something bright and wild and glorious, brilliant sunshine as she and Peter strode out across the hills. Instead she was cooped up in a small hotel in a cheerless rain-filled valley; this was too much like so many miserable childhood holidays.

Then, as if things had not already sunk as low as they could, Chrissie, purely from spite, had refused to let her use the room that had been arranged for Peter and, presumably, for her.

'You don't need that yet. You can get changed with us; we'll look after you.' The promise rang as hollow as she intended.

Beneath her the carpark was filling up gradually and the new arrivals, some single, some couples, came scurrying across, dodging the puddles and banging the big front door right below her. David had arrived about ten minutes ago, bounding in across the unmade ground, and now Julie could hear the receptionist talking to Chrissie down in the hall.

'That's everyone Mr Worthing said he was expecting and the day staff have all gone. Shall I close up?'

She didn't catch Chrissie's reply, but now heard her coming up the stairs.

'Ah, Julie! I was beginning to wonder what had happened to you. Do come up. It'll be time for dinner soon.' Julie felt the firm pressure on her elbow and, rather than face further argument and humiliation, she silently allowed herself to be led upstairs to their room.

'Right!' Chrissie must have known how much her artificial jollity grated. 'Here we are!'

Julie's spirits sank even further when she found it only had one double bed. Unless Peter came back, she would either have to share their bed with them or sleep on the floor. That was certainly the more preferable.

The hotel had been built in the days when visitors were still willing to pay for quality, so it was a large room where Julie could tuck herself away in the bay window. At first, she was virtually ignored, left to read one of the collection of predictable bedside whodunnits that the hotel supplied while – for almost an hour – Chrissie took a long bubble-filled bath, put up her hair in an elegant braid and dressed up in silk stockings, embroidered suspender belt, bra and knickers and topped that with a sleek full-length evening dress, while David, fresh from his shower in the health spa, put on a tailor-made dinner jacket, bow tie and silk dress shirt. During her soak in the vast iron tub, Chrissie left the bathroom door open and she and David chatted happily about the other guests, names which meant nothing to Julie at all. The way Chrissie kept rekindling the conversation on subjects of which she knew Julie knew nothing, seemed intended to emphasise her exclusion.

Eventually not even that was enough, and Chrissie called out from the bathroom for Julie to come through, where she found the woman lying back in the suds. Julie could not keep from looking down at the little nipples which barely broke through the surface and the thick mat of dark pubic hair covering Chrissie's plump vulva. However, she was shocked to see Chrissie's own hand down there, idly but quite openly playing with herself.

Chrissie casually lifted one leg clear of the water. 'As you're not doing anything, you might as well wash my feet.'

An objection would have been ineffective; a rebuttal would have been demeaning, so Julie knelt down and did as she had been told. She kept being uncontrollably drawn to stare at the full vulva which this stretching of the legs had pulled so far open, but she resisted as much as she could, concentrating on soaping each of the short stubby feet and nasty crooked toes.

At the end there was no word of thanks. 'Now my back.'

Chrissie sat up, her skin pink and wrinkled from so long in such hot water and leaned right forwards to present her back. Julie took up the flannel again, soaped it up once more and rubbed it vigorously across the woman's shoulders and down over her ribs. The surface of the deep water made a clear boundary below which she need not go and Julie had reached that, was about to rinse off the soap when Chrissie heaved herself up out of the water. She turned to face the wall and presented her bottom at the level of Julie's eyes, standing with the water running off her, glistening like a beached seal. This was a much plumper bottom than Julie's own, she was sure of that, but what really gratified her was to see a broad red band across the middle which was definitely pinker than the rest and through the middle of that were three thinner bands blotched with a pale bruise.

'Carry on.'

Julie tried not to hesitate. She knew Chrissie's intention was only to humiliate her and that would only succeed if the humiliation was acknowledged. She carried on with the flannel from the point where she had stopped, down the small of her back to where Chrissie's buttocks jutted out. A neat line showed where her bikini had started and Julie took that as the mark, turning back up the rib cage.

'Carry on,' Chrissie repeated.

So Julie carried on, washing down across the plump round bottom until it was well covered in trails of white soap suds tracking across the whole surface.

'All right?' The question was probably unwise, inviting a further rebuke, but Julie was not used to this role.

Chrissie twisted round, craning over her shoulder to see. Then, without a word, she turned and picked up the bar of soap, plucked the flannel out of Julie's fingers and proffered the soap. 'You've missed a bit.' She turned away to face the wall again and then carefully, pointedly, moved her feet apart.

Julie looked down at the bar of soap and considered the task that had now been given her. If she did this, could there be much more? Nothing she could think of. She rubbed the soap in her hands until she had worked up a good lather and then placed her palms squarely in the centre of each cheek of Chrissie's bottom, rubbing in small circles over the fullest part, but rubbing over the top of where she had already used the flannel. Chrissie leaned forwards, resting her hands against the tiles, and pushed out her bottom. The crack opened a little, just enough to make a shadow down its length and to uncover, right at the bottom, the darker little smudge which Julie was now required to wash. She slid her fingertips into the crease, running them down the length and pushing in as she went. The softly rounded sides parted willingly to receive her and then she was there, feeling the harder little ring of muscle under her fingers and she was touching the little wrinkled opening. For a few seconds Julie swirled her fingers round, for a few

174

seconds more she toyed with the wickedness of pressing inside – and then she knew that was too much and pulled away again. Chrissie made no objection, no comment at all, when she stood up to rinse the soap off all the way down the woman's back, and Julie scuttled back to her books in the bedroom before Chrissie could come up with anything else.

David behaved as if Julie were not there, or were simply a dog whose presence in his bedroom was of no significance. He undressed out of the casual clothes he had arrived in, took off his underwear and for several minutes walked around the bedroom entirely naked, careful at least once to approach so close to where Julie was huddled that she could not, even if she had tried, avoid seeing him.

Chrissie was still splashing round in the bath and then it went quiet. 'Julie? Are you going to want a bath before you get changed?'

'Yes, please.'

'Right. I'll leave this water then. It takes ages to refill these baths; there's no water pressure right up here and I doubt if there's any hot water anyway, since everyone else will be having baths.'

It seemed an unnecessarily full explanation at the time, but Julie duly went through when summoned to where Chrissie was still reclining luxuriantly.

'Come on, then. Get undressed.'

That took very little time, given that she still had no more than the blouse and skirt, but even though Chrissie had seen her getting undressed earlier at the sauna she made no secret of watching again. Even after Julie was naked, standing with one arm over her breasts and the other over her pubis, Chrissie was in no hurry to get out and let Julie wait, casually rubbing the flannel up and over her breasts from time to time. Eventually she pulled herself upright and, without a trace of modesty, stood facing Julie. She shuffled her feet apart

175

and those thick ripe lips came into view again but Chrissie reached down and even pulled them open a little wider, displaying much more than Julie wanted to see of the rich pink inside. For a second she stood entirely still, showing herself off as if it were the most natural thing in the world, and then Julie saw a little trickle of pee appear. The trickle faltered and then started again and rapidly grew into a steady stream that splashed down into the bathwater while Julie could only stare in horrified fascination, disgusted at the obscenity of the action and the complete lack of selfconsciousness on Chrissie's face. As the stream squirted down into the bath water, it splashed up a turmoil of bubbles that rose and burst and were instantly replaced, but even over Chrissie's bath oil the sour smell was unmistakable. Conscious of Chrissie's cool scrutiny all the while, Julie could scarcely believe what she was seeing and would have turned away, had she not known full well that Chrissie had only called her in there so that she would have to witness the action. Eventually the stream died away to a last few drops and Chrissie stepped out, her shining wet shoulder brushing against Julie's arm as she reached for a towel.

'Right. In you get.'

For a few seconds Julie stared in disbelief but Chrissie was calmly wrapping the towel round herself as she spoke. 'Of course, I could ask David if he wants to go as well.' In no doubt that Chrissie would do just that, Julie cautiously stepped into the bath and, since Chrissie was obviously going to stay there until she was satisfied, eventually sat down, hoped that would be enough but found it was not and finally lay back.

'There now!' Chrissie's jolly tone was back with a vengeance. 'Not so bad, was it?' She reached down to dabble her fingers in the water and suddenly splashed a wave of it right up over Julie's face before walking out, laughing and urging her to be quick.

Being quick would not be difficult and, anxious to stay in the foul water for as short a time as possible, Julie immediately started washing and used the shower to rinse off both the soap and Chrissie's pee. Inevitably, as soon as she had pulled the curtain across and turned on the shower, Chrissie found a pretext to come in again and peer round as Julie shivered under the lukewarm trickle. Finally, after being as quick in the shower as she could be and wrapping securely round herself the one small towel that Chrissie had left behind, she returned to the bedroom just as Chrissie and David were finishing dressing. For a minute they stood admiring each other.

'Put those on –' Chrissie nodded towards a pile of clothes on the corner of the bed '– and don't be long. We'll see you in the lounge.' She twined an arm possessively round David's waist and left Julie standing alone. A second later, her head reappeared. 'By the way, you can use the loo if you want to. In fact, that would be a good idea; do as much as you can.' Then she was gone again and the footsteps headed off down the corridors. Julie shut the door.

Sorting through the pile of clothes, Julie found not only the long dress that she had brought from home but also – surprisingly – full underwear. She was glad Peter had included something formal – had she been allowed to do her own packing she would not have thought to do so – but it was still much less glamorous than the creation Chrissie had just walked out in. She started getting dressed, discovering that she was already getting used to being denied a bra or knickers and wearing them now felt uncomfortably constricting.

Although she was as quick as she could be, and took the advice to go to the toilet herself, Julie was only just coming down the stairs when she met a scowling Chrissie coming up.

'Where on earth have you been? We're all going in to dinner now.' They had reached the ground floor, now deserted save for the receptionist still guarding her desk, and Chrissie led her on through to the lounge. 'You'd better wait here while we get things organised. Have a drink and I'll come and fetch you in a minute.'

Chrissie disappeared back into the dining room and at first Julie just stood about, waiting for her to return. As five minutes passed, and ten and fifteen, it became clear that this was just another trick to wrongfoot her so, since no one was serving at the bar, Julie selected the chair that Margaret had used earlier and settled down to wait.

The room held little of interest; a disarray of unmatched stools, chairs and sofas were littered round a number of small tables. A small bar occupied one corner, its garishness only emphasising its emptiness. The walls, a sensible plain white, were liberally dotted with conventional Lakeland views except where, at both ends of the room, an area of authentic stone had been left exposed on the matching chimney breasts, each crowned with a matching mirror. At the far end, a forest of dried flowers filled the grate, but at this end the fire still crackled and glowed in warm comfort, a pile of thick logs waiting their turn in the hearth. The low ceiling was crossed by oak beams whose pale honey colour and neatly shaped edges showed their authenticity; they actually served a purpose beyond pretending that, in this part of Cumbria, Tudor architects really had lived on into the early twentieth century. Even so, the last beam in front of the fire carried a line of iron rings and cleats which, if not actually horse brasses, suggested a disappointing ambition towards kitsch decoration.

An occasional burst of laughter rang through from beyond the closed door, threatening her that at any moment Chrissie might come bursting out with further degrading instructions, but Julie soon began to wonder if she had in fact been forgotten entirely. She went over to peer out towards the garden. The French windows, now locked, led out to what had originally been a flagstone terrace, but at some time this had been closed in and now formed a narrow sun porch running the whole length of the building on that side. From there, two other sets of doors opened out on to the garden. The glass roof reverberated under a swirl of pounding rain, pouring from overflowing gutters down the half-glazed walls to create a second skin outside. Through that, filtered through the thick clouds rolling off the hills above Windermere, the last angry purple of an unsettled sunset washed across the stone floor. The elegant cane furniture and magnificent potted plants showed that, on a better evening, this would have been a magnificent setting in which to see the sun go down or, on a fine morning, to see it rise.

Yet now the daylight was fading fast and it was not long before the receptionist came round to close the curtains and turn on the table lamps and wall lights, sending an even mellow glow over the whole room. She lit half a dozen slender candles ranged along the mantelpiece and, as she worked, enclosing the room tighter and warmer against the foul night beyond, Julie searched for words to create a bond with someone other than the strange crowd who Peter had left her with. No words came and, when the girl left, closing the door behind her, Julie was more alone and further from hope of escape than she felt she could ever bear.

It was a full hour before Chrissie returned, invited – no, instructed – Julie to accompany her and, in silence because Julie was unwilling to admit even to being interested in let alone ignorant as to the plans, led the way back out to reception. There Julie was left again, perched on one of the little chairs ranged along the wall opposite the desk, while the receptionist, a fire of youthful enthusiasm, scurried backwards and forwards from the back office with no more than the occasional glance and polite smile towards Julie. Chrissie went back through to the dining room and, as she opened that door, the sound of voices and laughter poured out to emphasise Julie's exclusion. She sat there idly reading the publicity brochures, learning the delights of a weekend break in this intimate, family-run hotel, with its à la carte menu and excellent wine cellar. The cover showed 'The Lounge with its Well-Stocked Bar'; the grinning chef and sullen staff were photographed in front of the 'Breathtaking Backdrop of England's Finest Lake'. Ten minutes later, Chrissie was back.

'We're just about ready. Get undressed and I'll come to collect you in a few minutes.'

Julie stared. If the receptionist had not also fallen into horrified silence, she would have wondered whether she had heard right – but surely they could not both be mistaken, could they?

'I'm sorry. What?'

Chrissie's smile was as warm as an October frost. 'You heard me.'

Julie felt the receptionist's stare swivel round on to her, realised how stupid she must be looking and finally shut her mouth. Even so, at first she couldn't find words as the instruction sank in, yet Chrissie had not moved. She was standing with that calm smirk on her face, clearly without a scrap of doubt in her mind that Julie would obey. Well, Julie would not. She shook her head. 'Look, Chrissie, I'm sorry, but I don't know any of those people. I made a deal with Peter, and there was nothing about including anybody else. There was nothing about you, for that matter.'

Chrissie smiled, shaking her head. 'I was going to punish you anyway. The longer you dawdle, the worse it will be. If you have to be handcuffed and carried in screaming, I will handcuff you and carry you in screaming. You don't have a choice over whether you go in, only how you do it. Get undressed and be ready when I return in ten minutes. Perhaps five.' With that Chrissie ducked back through to the lounge and the dining room door opened and fell shut behind her again.

Julie sank back down into her seat. The receptionist jerked into life again and immediately busied herself with retidying the empty desk, no longer daring more than the briefest of surreptitious glances towards Julie. When the phone rang in the office behind, she dashed out in undisguised relief and, through the mist of bewilderment, Julie was vaguely conscious of hearing the conventional normality in there: the apology; the hotel was full this evening, some suggested alternatives.

While waiting before, Julie had already done the arithmetic. The hotel had – according to its brochure – eighteen double and six single rooms, so if, as the caller was being told, the hotel was full, the dining room now held forty-two people. All were strangers and, although she had seen several of them arriving, Julie had no idea who they were, where they had come from, or what connection there was between them, if any. Only that they were all sitting in there having dinner and waiting for her to take her clothes off and walk in, completely naked.

It was unthinkable.

It was unbearable.

It was like her fantasy.

She had been worried that describing it all to Peter yesterday would have destroyed it. What, then, would living it do? What was planned? What would happen? Could she actually go through with it? No, of course not. But could she live with herself, knowing for the rest of her life that she had run away from the one chance she would be likely to have? This was her choice; she had composed the agreement. In exchange for Peter's help, she had allowed him 'anything' and, although she had never admitted it even to herself, she had known that 'anything' would take her much further than she could imagine. It had done so already. A dozen men had seen her half-naked in the cinema. Four men had groped her and watched her masturbate in the sex shop. Peter had even watched her urinate. The choices were back with her.

Julie stood up, glancing nervously round. On one side of her, the front door was solid, shut tight and firmly bolted, but the broad windows either side looked out into the dark so if she did undress, anybody out there would see her. On her other side was the archway through to the lounge; any one of forty-two people could come through there at any moment. In front of her was the reception desk and beyond that the little office where the receptionist was still chattering, but she would soon return. It was just a typical hotel reception area and as unsuitable a place to get undressed as any she could imagine.

First the shoes; there could be no harm or shame in slipping her shoes off and placing them neatly by the chair but, having done that, there was nothing more she could do without being committed. For her visits to the Foundation she had often worn a sweater or a jacket that could be slipped off as a halfway stage. Now there was just the dress and her underclothes. What had been the point of giving her all this to put on? She might as well have stayed in the simple skirt and blouse that she had been wearing all the rest of the day. She might as well have come down from her bath stark naked. But Chrissie had prepared the deceptive pile, and must have known even then that it would all end like this. Of course she did; that was doubtless part of her scheme as well. The more Julie was given to put on, the more prolonged would be the process of undressing; that explained why she had unexpectedly been permitted underwear. The thought also made Julie realise something else; she could take off the underwear first, still covered by the dress as she had been for much of the day, and nobody need know how little she had on underneath it. Quickly she pulled up the skirt and tugged off her tights and knickers in one go. As she turned to disentangle the bundle, she heard the receptionist finish her telephone conversation. Presumably she would now come back out again, so how could Julie stand there and undress with that girl so close? Yet it was what she did every time the Research Foundation for Female Sexuality beckoned her. That was fantasy; this was real. For a few seconds, while she was still alone, Julie turned away and allowed her fingers to drift down, reach under the hem of her dress again and slide back up to the warm familiar welcome of her soft gooey crease, hairless, she was reminded. When the time came for her to go through and stand in front of all those strangers, there would not even be that to cover her. The receptionist still had not returned. Just two items left.

Julie pushed the straps off the top of her dress although, since the back was still zipped up, it hung in folds round her body, leaving her entirely covered from the waist down, but her top was bare except for the bra. For a few minutes Julie stayed like that, savouring the imminence of her complete exposure and the indecency of being dressed in no more than a bra in so public a place. She teased her fingers lightly over the swollen cups, and then she needed more, half wanting to wait for the girl to come back out and witness the event, half wanting to see the shock of her returning to find her naked. Julie could not wait and reached back to the hooks which her fumbling fingers managed to unfasten. She turned to drape it over the back of the chair, feeling her breasts sway and ripple with each movement, and for a moment she stayed half bent over the chair to watch the reflection as they swung beneath her. Full breasts; round breasts; proud breasts whose eager nipples were already erect and hardening further in her rolling fingertips. She glanced up to see the startled red face of the receptionist.

'I'm sorry,' the girl whispered, 'only I'm meant to stay at the desk.'

Julie smiled and released her breasts, noticing the girl's eyes automatically drawn to the displayed nipples. 'It's OK.' Then she continued, trying to reduce the girl's embarrassment but realising even as she spoke them that her words actually hinted at something far worse. 'I'd rather it was you here than all of that lot in there.'

The girl blushed again and said nothing, but turned away to try to concentrate on sorting the room keys in their pigeonholes – most of which, Julie noticed, still held their keys.

A sudden burst of distant applause brought her up short. Possibly five minutes, Chrissie had said, and Julie had no doubt that no opportunity for criticism would be missed if Julie were not ready.

Only the dress left now, and Julie, ignoring the girl with her, not because of her, slowly unzipped it at the back but continued to hold it in place to savour a little longer the moment when she would let it fall and be standing naked in a hotel bar hundreds of miles from home and preparing to walk out in front of a crowd of strangers. She took a breath and then slowly lowered the dress, watching as the neat curve of her stomach came into view, the pale skin, getting yet paler where it was always covered by her clothes and palest of all where it was usually hidden by her pubic bush. She spread the dress neatly over the chair and there was nothing more to do. As she turned away from the chair, the receptionist also turned and the horror returned as she took in the sight of Julie standing there, naked, shaved and ready. Julie tried a nervous smile, but at that moment they heard the dining room door opening again and the guests, in a clamour of anticipation, spilling back into the lounge. There was a hubbub of seating

184

arrangements before Chrissie appeared at the arch again, and smiled smugly to see her instruction had been obeyed.

'Good. Come on through.' And she disappeared again.

Twelve

Julie walked up to the doorway and stopped, hidden just behind it as she prepared herself for the reality of an entrance which her imagination had never understood. The laughter and chattering were showing no sign of dropping, so finally she took a deep breath, stepped forwards and pushed open the door.

The end of the room to Julie's left lurked in half darkness while, down at the other end, the chatter died away into silence and every face turned towards her. Some were grinning, some tense, some salacious, but all animated. The chairs and sofas had been arranged in a semicircle round the open fire which crackled and spat as rain dripped down the chimney and, although most of the spaces were filled, there were not forty-two people at all; there were scarcely a dozen, roughly equally balanced between men and women. Peter was back again, sitting quietly to one side, and Julie could not work out how he could have got in without passing her – unless he had arrived while she was in David and Chrissie's room. Or unless he had never been away. On the opposite side, David was holding a small video camera pointed directly at her and behind him Chrissie was grinning in triumph. As well as them, there were eight or ten others, all dressed as formally and elegantly as David and Chrissie were – the men in dinner jackets, the women in magnificent evening dresses – but the

186

gathering was so much smaller than Julie had been preparing herself to face that she was disappointed. Yet the contrasts were so great, this must surely be part of a larger plan. The formality of their dress showed up even better the contrast with her own complete nakedness so that she shivered, and felt herself special. At the same time they could not have devised a greater contrast between the magnificence here and the squalor in the cinema and the video shop. Elegant coffee cups and brandy glasses were scattered round the little tables, dainty mint-chocolate sticks were arranged in gleaming silver dishes, graceful candles flickered in their antique candlesticks along the mantel. The image was practically identical to the cover of the stupid publicity brochure Julie had been reading earlier, except that in that photograph no young woman was standing naked in the candlelight, waiting for whatever ordeal the others might choose to inflict upon her.

She hesitated until Chrissie came up and took her hand to lead her down to the centre of the semicircle.

'Rather than playing games, or having a volunteer as we normally do after our dinners, tonight we've got Julie,' Chrissie announced to everyone, turning her to face the guests on all sides. 'She's Peter's, really, but he's offered her to us all to share.'

Several of the guests clapped, some grinned or cheered, but more than one of the women, particularly the younger ones, simply stared in horrified delight, clinging tighter to the protection of a partner. The young couple who Julie had met in the sauna, Linda and Barry, were there and the blonde girl from the changing room with her boyfriend. They had their arms round each other as they clung together and the girl hid her face in his shoulder but still peered out with a sparkle in her eye that gave no reassurance. The rather unlikely couple, Graham and silent Judith whom she had met in this very room, shared a great overstuffed chair, Judith

187

perching stiffly on the arm while Graham lounged back in it, his hand resting on the expanse of leg which had emerged through the slit in her skirt. The woman who had made her expose herself, Margaret, sat on a little two-seater with a girl who could not have been much over twenty, but sitting so neatly together that Julie even wondered whether they were a couple. As Julie stared round she found Peter always watching her carefully, his eyes almost expressionless, but sitting just sufficiently out of the circle to show that nothing which happened would be his fault. David had moved down opposite her again, the silver camera still in front of his face, its round black eye staring down unblinking at her. As well as them were people Julie had never seen. A man, middle-aged, hair silvering at the temples, leaned nonchalantly beside the curtains which hid the doors to the little conservatory, but his attention seemed half taken by another couple, respectable and much older, practically as old as Julie's own parents, who sat stiffly side by side on another settee.

Chrissie didn't introduce any of them but, as Julie was turned to face each one, so that each person there could see clearly her full heavy breasts, her proud erect nipples and her clean hairless pubis, she was also turned away from the person sitting opposite, to expose her bottom, round, clear and inviting. And when, at the end, she was turned away from all of them, she was also brought round to face the mantelpiece and the huge gilt-framed mirror hanging above it, in which her shame and the anticipation of her audience were reflected back. The woman on the chair arm ducked down to whisper into the ear of her companion, at which he smiled and patted her thigh. A waitress entered from the dining room with a cafétière and stopped dead. As young as the receptionist, and dark – perhaps Greek or Egyptian, probably a language student – but equally aghast at the image that confronted her, she stopped in her tracks.

188

For a moment her reflected eyes met Julie's before she crept back through the door, the coffee pot still clutched in her hand.

Chrissie was still there, turning her back to face them all again and holding her hand almost as if they were friends. 'Julie has never been here before, but I'm sure that need not stop us having fun.'

Then Chrissie was gone again, following the terrified waitress into the dining room, and Julie was standing alone, surrounded by a blur of unknown faces who were calling out to her to turn this way or that, to show her front again or her back, and she meekly obeyed, because nobody was left to appeal to. There were so many of them but it all seemed so aimless, so confused and unstructured. Soon Chrissie was back with the waitress in tow. They crossed over to David and, after a short whispered conference, the girl took up the coffee pot again and went round the room refilling cups, trying not to look at the lonely, naked figure who was so obviously the focus of everyone else's attention.

Chrissie took charge again, moving Julie out of the way so that two of the men could bring through a table from the dining room and place it in front of the fireplace. Then Chrissie summoned Julie back to the centre, steered her towards the table and round to the end, so she was facing the centre of the semicircle, and everyone was facing her. The arrangement made the sequence inevitable. Julie was made to stand at the end, made to sit down, made to lie back and eventually made to bring her legs up and spread them wide apart until her knees were dangling off the edges and she was opened up and exposed to everybody. She felt her face flushing red, the embarrassment spilling down in hot waves over her neck and her chest, felt her sex drawn tight by the stretching apart of her thighs and felt the lips themselves slowly peeling open in the warm sticky blatancy of her exposure and her arousal.

189

'Now, then,' said Chrissie, as brightly as if she were about to demonstrate a television recipe, 'let's start by seeing how responsive she is. Who wants to be first?'

There was no immediate response; then came a movement from the young couple who Julie had seen coming out of the sauna. Huddled together on the end of the sofa, they slowly started to unwind under a barrage of good-natured teasing and encouragement, pulling themselves upright and coming forwards until the girl, the perfect blonde girl who had so casually displayed herself practically naked in front of Julie in the changing room, was towering over her, the piercing blue eyes scanning the whole expanse of offered skin. The boy loomed up on Julie's other side and Chrissie slipped back out into the circle.

Julie tried to be calm and settled back on the table but, as she stared up at the solid beams across the ceiling above her head, the row of iron rings seemed much less innocent.

Everything and everybody else, the circle of watchers, the soft murmurs and gentle clinks of coffee cups, the occasional crackle of the burning logs, all this became muffled, floating off somewhere into the background of her consciousness while the two people on either side moved in until they filled her vision. The boy, too young to be called a man, barely twenty-one or -two, was watching her intently as he took off his jacket and hung it over a chair. He smiled over to his girlfriend or fiancée or whatever she was, as she took a final sip from the glass of some garish liqueur she was clutching and balanced it on the mantelpiece somewhere behind Julie's head. Then they both turned back to her, ignoring the many people sitting all round them, ignoring the one person lying between them, but grinning across her to each other. They moved together, their graceful slim bodies almost identical in their golden androgynous perfection and, for one divinely wicked moment, Julie wondered if they might even be twins. Their movements were perfectly synchronised so that they seemed too perfect, hardly human, barely able to know the glorious squalor of real lust, but they had stepped up close, within easy touching distance and then, still moving together with a practised ease that betrayed prior experience of these joint operations, they simultaneously flexed their fingers and lay them down on Julie's breasts.

Julie shut her eyes and felt her entire body melting into memories of her visits to that mythological building in London. She had done everything that had been asked of her and, from here on, she was a passive victim. Her part, standing alone in that public reception area and slowly taking off her clothes, waiting trembling to be called in before the gathered watchers, passively offering herself up on the table for their enjoyment – all of that was past. Now, as she lay on the table, her naked body surrendered without reservation, she was melting. Their fingers were still stroking her breasts, a hand on each, slowly circling the sensitive round mounds and floating up over to her nipples, where they paused and circled there, drawing the final little tender point out to a sharp urgency before slithering back down to encircle the rest of her breast again. Yet, all the time this was going on, two other hands were circling lower down across the soft skin of her chest and her stomach, circling like dancers in symmetrical spirals across her warm skin. They never drifted too low, never quite reached her hungry crease, but always circled tantalisingly close before spinning back up again. Every circle down brought a promise that her sex opened to receive; Julie could feel her lips opening like a flower to receive the caress that never quite arrived. Every retreat up her body left her trembling in frustration as she seeped in sad disappointment and choked back the frustration.

Without warning, the girl ducked down and Julie felt the warm lips encircling her nipple for a second, a firmer pinch as the teeth nipped lightly, a light flick of her tongue, and then it was gone and she had straightened up, her smile across the table now triumphant, challenging. The boy followed her example, but he took much longer. Once his lips had enclosed her nipple, and his tongue was running rapid circles round its point, he stayed, both hands now holding her breast, completely enfolding it and squeezing it to push up more of the soft flesh to his lips. When he finally released her again, and his hands had returned to the dance, leaving Julie cold and abandoned, she turned in expectation to the girl on her right, even half lifted her body to offer that breast for the same treatment, but she was ignored and when she fell back to the table again and sobbed in frustration, they merely laughed.

Still the boy had not finished with her, not for her arousal or his own pleasure, for his hands now moved away from her breasts and the next circle confidently slid straight across her stomach, over the hairless velvet of her belly and tucked straight between her thighs, the fingers curling back to enfold her lips. The fingertips danced menacingly across the super-sensitive space between her bottom and her vagina and then slithered up the sides of her swollen lips, met again at the top and pulled backwards. She felt the air being sucked into her lungs – she couldn't help it – as her skin was stretched unbearably tight and then he was fiddling about again and she knew that even the shining wet tip of her clitoris itself was now exposed to the avid eyes. He pinched her between the very tips of his fingers, smirking down at her as his finger stroked along her wet crease, the tip, the sharp little nail, grazing along the skin and then flicking up to her clitoris again. Julie sighed, sucked in her breath and it came out in a low moan that caused a little ripple and giggle from the row of heads craning closer.

Yet Julie couldn't help it. There were people down there watching her being aroused, doubtless sneering at the easy way she responded to a stranger's caresses; at the speed and intensity of her reaction; at the way her legs fell open so readily to expose herself to them; at her sex laid bare and inviting and wet and pulsing and seeping and wanting more of the fingertips so that her own hands were fidgeting to stay still as they gripped the edges of the table, although she longed to reach down there and penetrate herself; she was fighting the craving and only just holding herself in check when she heard the noise.

A low humming was coming from just beside Julie's ear and, when she turned to see, there stood the girl – the smarmy perfect little blonde in her elegant sheath evening dress, not a hair out of place, not a smudge on her lipstick – and she was playing with that disgusting plastic toy that Julie had been required to use on herself earlier in the day. Having found the switch and the speed control, Julie watched the girl moving away, trailing the thing over her breasts briefly, and on down towards her hips. Julie shut her eyes. She felt the fingers – cool, graceful fingers – gently slipping between her legs to press open the narrow mouth of her vagina, felt the sticky sides peeled apart and then the crudely throbbing plastic was pressed there too and, without hesitation, pushed slowly deep inside. The sound changed, almost muffled once most of the thing was inside her, but the quivering shaking was unbearable.

Other fingers – presumably the boy's, although Julie did not dare open her eyes to look – were still flicking over the top of her clitoris, weaving little circles round and round and then, when the weakness of the sensation grew frustrating, returning to a direct blunt attack which lifted her up another level as her hips writhed to twist closer. More fingers were down there now. She could feel them touching and pressing and pushing and probing and the long point of a graceful nail had skimmed down beyond her vulva, reached to the delicate star of her bottom and was scratching for an

193

entrance even in that untouched place. Julie shivered, disgusted at the prospect of so obscene a threat, but it was all becoming too much. The image dropped into her brain of being breached even there, while everyone watched her, seeing not only the plastic vibrator humming in her pussy, but also the fingers strumming at her clitoris, one hand – whether his or hers, Julie no longer knew or cared – grasping her breasts and pawing them now with little sensitivity, only a determination to push her further. With all that – and Julie was unable now even to pretend any resistance – she could hold on no longer and cried out in a single wail as they continued to push her further and harder and higher and better, and it went on and on and over and over and would never, ever end.

At last they stopped. The vibrator slowed and died away completely as it was withdrawn and Julie brought her thighs up to hug them together, squeezing herself in a comforting enclosing embrace as the couple stepped back to meet a small ripple of applause from all around the room. Julie wondered whether the applause was for her or for them, but did not dare to open her eyes to see. She just relaxed, grateful that at last it was over and, if she was ashamed at having been brought so easily to orgasm, ashamed of having succumbed so publicly to the caresses of another girl, it could all have been much worse. In the end it had been the boy's fingers which had brought her to the peak and, although she had not been as repulsed as she ought to have been by the girl's assistance, nor by the presence of so many faceless women among the circle enthusiastically watching, she could always pretend that her arousal had been in spite of their presence. She would believe that, even if she was alone.

As Julie felt herself coming down from the peak, Chrissie was back again, her superior smile aimed down as she callously turned her attention to Julie's open sex, mauling at the tender lips and stretching them wide open as she peered inside. She snorted, released them and delivered a sharp slap across the whole exposed surface which rang out in a shamefully wet splat as she turned back to the little audience.

'Right now; stage two. Barry? Linda? Would you like to take over?'

Julie's heart sank and she sagged back on to the table. She already felt wrung out, her whole body limp and drained as if she had run a thousand miles. The prospect of undergoing that all over again was too much to bear and yet . . .

Wasn't that the appeal? Not that she would have enough, but that she would have too much? That she would reach her limit and be pushed on beyond that? That she would beg them to stop and be ignored? It had been good, certainly – being so exposed in front of everyone, being masturbated, being made to climax with so many people watching her. And yet to have to do it again, to be so abused again: that would be something special. But did Chrissie mean once more, or more than that? Could every couple there be waiting their turn, quietly taking their places in a dignified queue, ready to come up and . . .? What? Could they all be as sparing as the first two? Would there not, almost inevitably, come the moment when she would hear the rasp of a zip being unfastened beside her and see a man's face leering down?

Julie closed her mind to that prospect. She noticed that Chrissie was sidling back to her seat and that somewhere down in the corner people were now moving, standing up, coming closer to where she lay. She shut her eyes.

The two figures were moving up closer. Julie could hear the footsteps and rustle of clothes, smell the perfume and the wine, feel the shadow fall across her face. She felt them close and dared not open her eyes

195

until a new sound came: a rattling of metal, and when, unable to stay calm any longer, Julie opened her eyes, a pair of dangling leather cuffs came dancing into her view, their shiny steel clasps jingling. Beyond them, Barry was grinning down at her, grinning just as he had in the sauna when Julie had first been made to expose herself to him, grinning with anticipation as he gave the cuffs another shake.

'I think we'll have you standing up, Julie.' He offered a hand so that she could sit up, swinging her legs across and off the table – but when he stopped and frowned, she followed his gaze to see a glistening smear right across the table where she had been lying. Without any comment, Barry ran his finger straight through the incriminating mark and then brought her out into the room.

Barry offered one of the cuffs over to Linda and she, with a quick nervous glance to see if Julie was going to object, followed Barry's example in buckling it round her wrist. Then Barry pulled her arm up in the air and swiftly clicked the catch through one of those rings in the ceiling beams which Julie had so scorned. He took her other wrist, clipped this into the same ring and then stood back.

By some inexplicable logic, Julie felt more exposed now than when she had been stretched flat in front of everybody with her legs apart. Now she was held, stretched up, utterly unable to defend herself. She could turn if she wanted to; she could pull at the leather, rattle at the cuffs as hard as she liked, but she could not do a single thing to protect herself. The posture lifted her breasts enticingly, offering them out to the people in front of her. When Barry reached up and pinched her nipple between finger and thumb, pinched so hard that she winced, tried to pull away and finally, as he deliberately twisted the nipple round, cried out – when he did all that, she could do nothing to stop him. When, with that same utterly pitiless expression, he scraped his fingernail down from her breasts, slowly tracking across her stomach towards her sex, Julie could pull back – she could pull back as far as she liked, but she could not get out of his reach so that the vicious smack when his open palm whipped down across the puffy cleft mound of her belly left her crying out again.

'Quiet, now,' he muttered in a voice of wheedling calm, as if to a tetchy child, and took her hips in his hands to twist her right round so that she found herself facing her own reflection, staring into her own eyes and, beyond that, circled the staring eyes of too many people.

Barry stepped up beside her and rested his hand on her shoulder before it started slipping down her back, reached her bottom and there it stopped, lurked, waited and the fingers spread open like a fan. He took a great handful and squeezed, steadily squeezing tighter so she could feel her bottom being contorted in his fist and could see him watching her reflection in the mirror as she screwed up her eyes against the pain and sucked in her breath and finally gave in and cried again. He released her, took his hand away and then brought it straight back in a stinging slap that rocked her and again she cried out. In the background, the audience stayed motionless and she saw Barry smile as he turned away and ambled across to a grubby brown holdall lurking beside the door. Julie didn't turn round, just watched him in the mirror rummaging in the bag. She didn't turn round until she saw him turn back towards her and saw a long black riding crop was dangling from one hand. Then Julie turned to confront him, stared at the crop and stared at him.

'Oh, no, you don't! You are not going –'

'Have you ever been beaten before, Julie?' His tone was soft but he simply ignored her protest, as if she hadn't spoken a word.

'No, but look, I –'

197

'Then you'll need this.' He held up his other fist in front of her face, closed at first, but then opened it to allow a bizarre leather strap to drop down and dangle in front of her. It swayed hypnotically, too short to be a belt – too narrow, for that matter – and besides halfway down its length a large red ball was fastened. After letting the thing sway directly in front of her for a few seconds, he silently passed it across to where Linda was still patiently standing, watching with an expression of increasing nervousness as if she half expected to find herself the victim at any moment. Linda took the strap and, before Julie had fully realised what was happening, it had been passed round her head, the ball pushed into her mouth and the strap buckled up at the back. Julie protested, but found immediately that the gag was supremely effective; she could not form words and she could not call out with any volume whatever. Her helplessness was now complete.

Barry still held the riding crop in his hand as he strolled round her, tapping it against his leg as he walked. Having completed one full circuit – and those long moments while he had been out of sight had lasted for hours – he came back in front of her and took a step back, his head cocked to one side as he appraised the sight, frowning. He was considering Julie in a way that would not have frightened her – would not have frightened her at all – if she had not seen, just drifting across the corner of her eye, Linda's childish little face wrinkling into a twist of dismay, and seen her take a step backwards away from culpability.

The tip of the crop was now lifted up, circling and hovering like some malevolent insect right in front of her, moving through the air as it sought out a place to land until, without warning, a single flick lashed out, caught Julie a searing crack straight across her right nipple and then was hovering again. The pain was excruciating, stinging and biting into her in flesh that was used only to being nurtured and embraced. Never had she known or imagined such an attack on so sensitive a part and, forgetting her incapacity, she screamed out in a pathetic impotent grunt of gagged outrage. The sound, little more than a muffled squeal, did no justice to the burning misery of her treatment but, as she glared out, determined that somehow the power of her rebellion must be – would be – communicated, she could see quite clearly that he was lining up for an assault on the other breast. She squealed and turned away before the stroke came down but, although she turned away, he was quicker and the crop flicked out and back, fast as a snake, the tongue licking across her to leave an immediate scarlet weal where it had landed beside the other nipple. Julie wanted to cry, but she couldn't. She could only snort and mew and feel herself dribbling from the corners of her mouth. Meanwhile the tip of the crop was circling again, lightly running down her body, just as his nail had done towards her sex. Barry stepped to one side, giving everyone in front of her a clearer view and bringing himself within arm's reach of Linda. He slid his arm round her shoulders, but his hand reached down a little further so that he was holding her breast and squeezing that as hard as he had squeezed Julie's own bottom as he lifted the crop away, smiled into Julie's eyes and flicked it back down on her again, perfectly aimed, perfectly timed to bite at the very top of her crease.

Julie recoiled as far as the unforgiving cuffs would let her, mewed out another impotent squeal and felt the tears starting to run from her eyes as Barry lifted the crop again. It wasn't the pain, because that was bearable – Julie had known worse – it was the humiliation of being held so exposed, so powerless while he toyed with her, trailing the vicious little crop across her body wherever he liked, tiny stinging flicks landing at will – on her hip, on her thigh, on her stomach, on her arm.

And all she could return was a pathetic mewing sob at everyone and a glare of fierce defiance that he totally ignored.

Finally he stopped and turned with a flourish to hand the crop to Linda, the picture of a variety magician with his glamorous assistant, before coming back to Julie, running his hands down her body from her shoulders to her hips and then turning her back to face the mirror once more. This time, he even pushed his foot between hers and kicked her legs apart – wide apart – so that she would have toppled over if she had not been supported by the cuffs.

'Stay there,' he muttered into her ear.

His hand ran back over her again until it was resting on her bottom once more, squeezed it once more, released it once more and then whistled back. Julie cried out again at the shock of the stroke but almost immediately there was another one, and another, and on and on, blow after blow from his hand raining down. He had stepped back and settled into a steady rhythm that could have continued for as long as he wanted. Her skin was growing warm; she knew it must be turning red and felt the heat spreading as Barry continued distributing the blows across the full width of both cheeks, and up and down them as well. Some blows were directed down on to the upper surface and some were aimed up at the undercurve; a few were aimed even lower than that, right across the top of her thighs. Julie had long since lost count of the number of smacks; she could feel no more than a continuous merciless rain that beat down with no indication it would ever stop.

And it hurt. She was sore and must surely be glowing out like a beacon but, as if that indignity was not enough, Julie found she could no longer stay still. With each slap, she was twisting away, turning and spinning, trying to get away from the last one, trying not to present herself for the next. Through the steady beat of his hand on her skin, beyond the grunts that escaped from her mouth, she heard the muttered comments from the rest of the room, the little gasps of delight when a stroke made an unusually sound and ringing contact, when a specially low one tore another squealed protest from behind her gag, or when a particularly hard stroke sent her spinning with greater vigour.

Yet suddenly, with no warning, no signal at all, he stopped. Julie cautiously lifted her head and saw, through the blurred tears, the faces of her admirers reflected back at her in the mirror. They were all watching eagerly to assess the effect that the treatment had had on her. She could see that some were focusing on her bottom; others were watching her face and she tried to hold up her head, to blink back her tears, but their casual, spiteful gaze was impossible to endure. The young golden couple who had already abused her were snuggled back together, their arms around each other as they watched; the boy was grinning as he whispered to the girl and, although she smiled obediently, Julie saw her hands clutching tighter at the boy's arm as she peered closer. Even the waitress was watching, her initial disgust now forgotten as she lurked in the corner beside Peter, her arms wrapped tightly over her chest as if in self-preservation but in a position which, Julie knew from her own experience, easily allowed surreptitious caresses of one's own breasts. A movement right next to her caught Julie's attention and she realised that she had been distracted from what was happening close to. Now Barry had taken the crop back from Linda and was stepping back up. He rested his hand on Julie's shoulder, kicked her legs apart again, and the cool leather tip of the crop was back sliding down her spine. Julie shut her eyes and waited.

He knew exactly how to keep her in suspense. Two, three, four times the crop trailed up and down her back until finally it stopped and drew little circles across the burning skin of her bottom. When it lifted away, she braced herself for the blow, gritting her teeth, clenching her buttocks against the pain and the crop landed in a single searing stripe right across her shoulder blades. She would have screamed if the gag had let her, but scarcely had time to acknowledge the shock before another stroke had landed, a good six inches lower, midway across her back. She tried to scream again but another came, lower still and another and the one after that was straight across the middle of her bottom again, across the same tortured skin that he had so thoroughly tenderised – and this, she realised, was the first one that really hurt. With all the others she had protested at the outrage, at the treatment, but in truth there had been little pain and, compared with that last one, which still burned like fire, Julie understood that they had been applied very lightly.

Barry's hand was back, massaging her slowly but squeezing harder than was necessary. 'You'll have five more,' he said, 'for now.'

Julie absorbed the words without collapsing, snorted a huge breath – although her nose was running from the tears she had already shed – and might even have lasted but for Linda. Doubtless Linda was sincere, intended her gesture to be kindness, but when Julie saw the girl come round in front of her, such sympathy and terror on her face, Julie knew that Linda had suffered the same at some time, knew that she understood what was to come and that it was unbearable.

She tried to offer some comfort, lifted her dainty little hand, and wiped the tears from Julie's face. 'There, I'll be with you.'

For some reason, this kindness broke her where the cruelty had failed and she did cry at that. Then she cried at each of the strokes as Barry applied them, as he stopped between each one to run his fingertips along the line he had just made, as he planted his open palm across each cheek and grasped a full round handful. She cried when he tapped the crop back to let her know the next one was coming; she cried when he lifted it away; she cried when he waited as she puckered up her bottom in fear and despair and agony when the next stroke landed. Yet she counted the five off in her head, and at the end knew she had survived the ordeal. She hung from the wrist-cuffs and heaved and sobbed and felt the dainty little fingers stroking away the tears with a sympathy that can only have come from sharing a similar treatment. 'There, it's over now. It's over now. He's done.'

But it wasn't over, and Barry wasn't done. His hands snaked out to Julie's hips again and twisted her back to face the room, a silent room now as everyone considered the single naked figure hanging in their midst. After a brief pause while his fingers ran across her body, over her breasts and down to her stomach, he finally pushed her feet apart again and, although Julie shook and twisted and growled what objection she could, he reached in between her legs, fluttered along the top of her lips and then dug deep between them.

He didn't say anything, not a single word, but his eyes came up to hers, his eyebrows arched up and he smiled. Julie could only look away in abject humiliation. It was not her fault if she reacted that way; it was an entirely physical response, utterly beyond her control, and she would have argued with him if she could. Still, he said nothing, merely turned to face everybody else and, having their full attention, lifted his hand, sliding the slippery fingers together, and then wiped the incriminating evidence down her cheek. She had been found out and shamed and the triumph on the smug faces ranged across the room showed her defeat was general knowledge.

Barry turned away again, his eyes scanning round the room and finally coming to rest on the waitress. She shrank a little further into her corner, squeezed her arms a little tighter and watched in terror as Barry advanced towards her. Julie could not hear what he whispered, but saw the girl glance over towards her, frown and then turn to scamper from the room.

For the few minutes that she was away, Barry left Julie in peace while Linda wiped her eyes and stroked her cheeks and even ran soothing cool palms over the blazing agony of her bottom. When the waitress returned, she held, of all things, a duster, a ridiculous feather duster. In other circumstances, Julie might have been amused, but these weren't other circumstances – these were very bizarre circumstances in which Julie felt utterly defeated so that even something as innocuous as that held a threat. Barry indicated that the waitress was to hand the thing to Linda and the girl immediately scurried back to her corner, where Julie just caught sight of Peter beckoning her closer to him before her view was blocked by Linda standing straight in front of her.

When the feathers first brushed against her thighs, Julie was almost moved to giggle, but the sensation was different from that; lighter than a caress, more intense than a tickle and yet it was both, and such a contrast to the vicious punishment which she had just endured that she was ready to sink down into the softness and accept everything they gave her. Even if they continued until she climaxed again, she felt ready now to let them do it, although even as that thought came to her she realised the stupidity and impotence of her decision. Standing naked, bound and gagged, she would have no choice.

Julie looked down to where Linda had shoved the thing between her legs, was pushing it back and forth like a piston and twisting it round as she went. Already the tips of the feathers glistened with a silvery sheen that shimmered in the flickering candlelight like raindrops on a fern. Julie shut her eyes to keep out the shame and hold in the stimulation and as she offered her hips forwards just a fraction, ready for a firmer touch, the crack of the crop flicked down on her inner thigh. Julie flew back, crippled by so sudden, so barbaric and excruciating a strike when she had offered herself for a sweet and gentle caress. Her legs crumpled beneath her. As she recovered her balance and her vision, there stood Barry, calmly peering down as he examined the place where the leather had struck, examining it as if it were a matter of no more than academic interest, the crop twirling idly between his fingers, preparing to strike out again at any moment. Linda had not let up for a second; the feathers were still twisting between Julie's legs, already soothing away the sting with the soft seduction of their touch, stroking along that most exquisitely sensitive strip at the very top of her inner thighs, ruffling over her swollen lips, wafting over her clitoris so delicately that it was almost heaven but always just frustratingly short of that. Julie moaned in despair at the inadequacy of the touch, heard herself whimpering, begging incoherently for more and harder and faster and the crop struck again, this time across the smooth mound of her belly. She twisted away, agonised beyond bearing as the fire of the sting spread out from the contact, awakening every nerve, enlivening all her skin so that through the pain she was stimulated and ready. The feathers still pursued her, refusing to be shaken off and continuing to roll and press with the same seductive lightness that Julie embraced and welcomed and yet knew would never do more than excite her and, if that was all there was, would never be enough.

But that wasn't all there was; there was more.

There was the presence of everybody else – everyone watching as she showed off her shamelessness, opened her legs wide and allowed another woman to masturbate her with this obscene implement, as they saw the juice of her arousal running down her thighs, as they witnessed her abandoning herself to whatever was asked of her. She closed her eyes again, to concentrate better on the feelings within, to allow the gentle pleasure growing between her legs to take over. She was almost ready to give in to them, seduced by the delicacy of so inadequately light a caress, already disregarding the recurrent treachery of the crop, and she had even offered herself forwards again when the vicious little loop of leather flicked out once more, overwhelmingly strong, directly across her nipple, and immediately across the other one.

Julie sobbed out in agony and climaxed. With the tears washing down her face and her legs unable to support her a single moment longer, she sagged down, quivering and lost and squirming her thighs together to clamp the stupid feathers in place, to squeeze herself against the harder core within, to grab whatever extra feeling could be grabbed from whatever implement was available at that desperate instant of total agony and unsustainable pleasure.

They let her down after that, unclipping the cuffs from the beam although, ominously, they remained buckled round her wrists. They removed the gag and let her perch on the edge of the table as Linda rubbed some cream into the livid red weals where her wrists had pulled at the leather bands and even fetched her a glass of wine. The room was quiet, with no more than a low murmur of scattered voices, and Julie hardly dared look up, fearful of the derision she expected on the faces of everyone there. But when Linda was finally done, and she found the courage to confront them, that was not what she found at all. The young golden couple were entirely immersed in each other, eyes for no one else. The old man and the young wife were deep in conversation but, when he pointed in Julie's direction with a gesture, she looked up and there was admiration on her face. The waitress was now sitting on Peter's lap but, even as Julie watched, their heads came together in a kiss and Peter's hand snaked up under her skirt; the girl showed no surprise and did not recoil or attempt to remove it, so the hand had probably been there before.

Yet it was the other side of the room that caused Julie the greatest fear. David, Chrissie and Barry huddled together, laughing as they poured themselves more wine. Once they all glanced round at her, Chrissie staring down with as much poison as ever before so that Julie could not stand it and quickly looked down. Yet even when those three had turned back to their private world, she could feel other eyes appraising her. She dared not look up, but it was with sickening dread but little surprise that she heard the cultured Scottish tones ringing across the room.

'Julie, dear, will you lay yourself back on the table for me.'

Thirteen

The very calmness of Margaret's request was what was so chilling. A voice that could, with so little emotion, demand something so depraved, was a voice that could demand anything at all. It was the voice of a woman who knew exactly what she wanted, was used to being accommodated and would stand for no refusals. For a few moments Julie stared at her as she considered the options. Her bottom and her sex were still throbbing with the aftermath of the treatment they had received; her breasts ached from an excess of arousal. Whatever came next, whatever the woman demanded of her, would be further suffering heaped on skin already pushed beyond bearing.

There was nowhere she could run to. The hotel was closed, the doors bolted, the curtains drawn against the night, while outside the rain was pouring out of a bleak grey sky on to the cold ground. Nor would she find any refuge inside: the guests were all sitting patiently in the warmth of their log fire, in the yellow glow of the soft lights and flickering candles while they waited for the next scene. Julie was utterly alone.

She climbed back up onto the table, turned and obediently settled herself down, trying not to wince at the pressure on her bottom and trying to convince herself that the woman would probably only want to look, as she had done in that same room only a few hours earlier. Margaret got to her feet and the room dropped into silence again, the focus closing in from the scattered huddles to Margaret's slow progress up to the one centre of attention. At the first light touch on her ankle, Julie shivered and clamped her legs together, an involuntary reaction that brought a smile to the other woman as she lightly trailed her fingertips the whole length of Julie's body up to her face. All the while, as the fingers brushed over her skin, dawdling just a little longer at areas of particular sensitivity and particular interest, Julie felt the strength of the woman's scrutiny.

Margaret continued idly caressing Julie's cheek, examining the figure laid out for her. Then at last she glanced round and reached over to the mantelpiece and carefully lifted a single slender candle out of its holder. For a moment, while it was still burning, she held it up, brilliant red and erect, proudly phallic and uncompromising, the intention so obvious that Julie turned her head away and relaxed her muscles in preparation for the insertion.

'Amy! Come here by me, if you please.' In silence, the girl followed the path to where Julie lay and appeared on her other side. 'Here you are. You know what to do.'

She passed the candle across and then Margaret stepped back, her fingers lingering for as long as possible in contact with Julie's skin, sliding across her cheek and neck and shoulder until finally contact was lost. Margaret had withdrawn out of Julie's sight and the young girl, Amy, was standing clutching the candle, its flame waving as it trembled in her hand, a worried frown creasing up her face.

She held up the candle again, held it as a votive offering directly over Julie's chest and then tipped it slightly so that a single drop of molten wax reached the lip of the candle, gathered there, paused and then dropped. Julie saw it in slow motion tumble through the air until it landed right in the middle of her chest. Before

209

Julie could react, Amy had moved the candle across a short distance so that the next drop, equally slow, equally reluctant to leave the heat of the guttering flame, finally broke free and splashed on the swelling of her breast. Julie cried out, clutching at the edges of the table, trying to hold herself still and arching her back in an involuntary reaction, almost as if she were offering herself up for another. Amy glanced up to gauge the reaction and another drip fell, just alongside the last.

The pain was exquisite; not unbearable, but so precise that it switched on the nerves in that one area where the drop landed, focusing Julie's attention on that single spot; the round red circle served also to point the place up to the watchers. Where each drop landed was unmistakable; where the next would land was readily discernible. As Amy tipped the candle further, the wax melted faster, the drips turning almost into a trickle that trailed right round her breast as the flame flared, circling her in a sequence of tiny stings, each one followed by a tiny clawing grasp as the wax congealed and puckered at her skin.

Then Amy paused, holding the candle upright and motionless for a moment, before lowering it to no more than six inches above the centre of Julie's breast. The next drop landed directly on her nipple. Julie shrieked out in protest, twisted away and would have leaped up but for Margaret's hand firmly pressing her back down on to the table as she seethed and gasped. Every nerve rebelled and screamed; the entire nipple throbbed and burned and already another drop was landing. With the candle so close, the wax was so much hotter and again she twisted, scrambled to escape, the tears now flowing from her eyes. Though she wailed and implored Amy to stop, another fat drip was already hovering at the lip of the candle and finally tumbling over to land on her pulsing flesh. Yet her nipple was already erecting beneath the hardening coating of wax as it responded to

210

the intensity of so absolute a caress. Another drop, another scream at the shock of such calculated cruelty inflicted so deliberately on so sensitive and intimate a place. Everybody knows how delicate a woman's nipples are, so how could anybody behave in that way? Worse than that, how could one woman inflict such treatment on another? How could any woman order another to do it? Yet Margaret ordered and Amy willingly obeyed and Julie suffered and, as the candle was waved across in front of her, she knew that the other breast was about to be treated similarly.

Julie held her breath, closed her eyes, unable to watch and opened her eyes, unable to resist. Again the whole tender surface of her breast was first subjected to a steady trickle of dripping wax, every drop an individual attack, every one dragging out a cry as she sucked at her breath and tried to withstand the pain of this in the knowledge of how much worse was yet to come.

Amy glanced at her a moment, and then the candle was turned back upright and held while a better pool of wax gathered. Tearing her eyes from the flame, Julie peered down between her breasts, beyond the wavering candle, beyond her legs. Down there – in that respectable area of the hotel lounge where nobody was naked, where nobody was stretched across a table while being alternately tormented and stimulated, where nobody was freely available to receive whatever beatings, whatever pain, whatever humiliation anyone desired – down there, Julie was the focus of every attention. They were all craning round for a better view: David, Chrissie, Graham and his wife, all watched with amused interest the replaying of a scene which for them was evidently nothing new. Yet for the younger ones, the girls, who doubtless could all imagine for themselves the agony that Julie suffered, the nightmare was utterly different and immediate. Linda was clutching at Barry as if he were the Titanic's last life raft; the golden blonde had stuffed her knuckles into her mouth as she stared in wide-eyed horror at the spectacle unfolding; even the waitress had torn her attention away from Peter and now gaped, eyes sparkling in animated dread, her own hands clutched protectively over her own breasts in sympathy, her own fingers slowly stroking at the little points where her petrified nipples showed through her uniform dress.

Julie turned back to see the candle being dipped down to hover six inches above her breast again, the height it had been for the left breast, and here it paused. For a second Julie waited in hypnotised terror, staring at the smooth curve of pure white skin, topped by the eager pink nipple, erect as if reaching up to embrace the agonising assault it was about to receive. She caught a brief glance exchanged between Amy and Margaret and then the candle dipped lower; four inches, three inches, until Julie could feel the heat of the flame on her skin before at last it tipped. The splash landed full on her nipple and Julie twisted away, a tortured cry wrung from her even as the next drip landed. She writhed again to escape the next but was held there while the candle weaved inches above her, seeking out any remaining white skin, while drip after drip of molten wax, so hot it felt it was boiling, seared into her nipple, ran into every crack and coated the delicate flesh with burning, stimulating fire.

Margaret lay her hand back on Julie's shoulder, pressing her down until, once Julie was still and the tears had been blinked back, she could be released and Margaret could reach over instead to pick with dainty nails at the little red scabs which were spattered all across her skin. As each was torn away, it sent another tiny shudder through her body, another tiny stimulation that lifted her another tiny step. But the candle was still there, still burning, and the next drop landed not on Julie's nipple but right between her breasts, the next on

212

her breastbone, the next on her stomach and then, after a pause while the candle hovered over her, an excruciating trickle poured into her belly button. The drop after that was lower still, and lower again, until one drop landed right on the very top of her hairless crease where the valley began, where there was no protection at all.

Julie turned to Margaret in agonised despair at what the woman intended to make Amy do but, instead of sympathy or safety, Margaret pushed her out on her own. She smiled with that same understanding as when she had ordered Julie to undress, then took hold of her hand, raised it once to her lips and kissed her, like a Victorian gentleman. Then she looked into her face and gave her a choice.

'It's up to you, dear.'

Julie stared at her. How could the woman offer such a choice in such a situation? What choice was there? Cowardice or humiliation. What Margaret asked would be nothing like the sting upon the delicate skin of her breasts or the sharp burn on her tender nipples. The pain of this would be unmistakable and unbearable on flesh of such supersensitivity. The whole idea was simply unthinkable.

She looked up, to see Amy still holding the candle, patiently waiting for Julie to decide; for a moment, Julie had a picture of young Amy lying in this same position, as Margaret applied the wax, and wondered whether Amy too had been offered this choice and, if so, what choice she had made. Beyond her, in a broken mist at the other end of the room, swam the faces of so many strangers, still motionless as if none had moved or breathed since last Julie had looked: Chrissie, arrogant and confident she would fail; Graham, calmly pretending no more than academic interest in the outcome; the three girls drawn speechlessly to the sight, yet with an eager, jealous horror in their faces that gave Julie

213

courage and pride. How could she come so far and then walk away without experiencing the epitome? Yet how could she volunteer to a torture of such agony that she would be unable to bear it without screaming and weeping and making such an exhibition of herself that any credit for her agreement to try would be drowned in ridicule at her failure to conclude? How could she agree, here in front of everybody, agree purposely to be so maltreated, so abused and in a way which would inevitably cause such clear and obvious signs of her own arousal at the humiliation and even at the agony itself?

It was simply impossible and Julie lay back, while tears welled in her eyes at the shame of it all, at the pain she had endured, the beating, the burning, the humiliation and she gripped Margaret's hand tighter and slowly edged apart her thighs to open her vulva to the view of everyone.

'Good girl!' whispered Margaret. 'Good girl!'

As Julie's feet reached the edges of the table, dropped over and still she pressed her legs wider, she felt the lips of her sex peeling open, felt the inevitable trickles of a wetness that she could not control running down her skin, felt the cool, cool air washing at her lips and her vagina and the hard fullness of a clitoris that had not yet been scorched and was as full and hard as if she had been attending to nothing else.

Amy shuffled and adjusted her position as she prepared for the next act. Julie heard scurrying from the far corner and suddenly the golden blonde was standing at her side, her dress half unfastened, her hair straggling loose, her eyes blazing in horrified glee as she pushed up closer to see more, to see better, to see everything.

Amy licked her lips. Margaret nodded. Julie dropped her head back and shut her eyes.

The inside of her thighs was agony; the thick outer lips were agony; the thin inner lips, despite being protected by the wetness of so much arousal, were agony and, at every drop, as they fell faster and faster, Julie cried and sobbed and twisted. Margaret held one leg in place and first Amy and then both Amy and the golden blonde held the other one, but the drops were too much and too hot and the flame was now so close to her skin that Julie felt herself in danger of being burned even by that, and all the time the wax was building up, coating her completely so that she could feel pools of it forming and solidifying like vile growths on her flesh, pulling and dragging at her lips.

Eventually, inevitably, Amy moved on to the one little area that was still untouched; the delicate little fingers reached down and Julie felt the hood of her clitoris being peeled back, felt the cold of the evening air on the tip of that little place and knew what was in store next. For a while they stayed like that, perhaps just looking, perhaps more, Julie dared not open her eyes to see, then a finger touched her. It could have been Amy, or Margaret or even the blonde girl, and for a second she caressed and stroked and petted and stimulated to an even greater fullness – and then the finger was gone. A second later she was on fire, stung beyond bearing by the first splash of molten wax, and Julie screamed out loud, sat up, tearing her hands free and reached down to cover herself, to protect herself, to hold on to whatever shreds of dignity were left as she shoved the girls away, tugged her leg out of Margaret's grasp and sat there nursing herself as a paroxysm of pain built in that most tender place. She tore away at the vile crusts of solid wax, tearing at what tiny downy hairs were left, tearing at her skin, rubbing at the injuries, rubbing most at the one little nut which was most injured, most maltreated, most sensitive and the agony grew until it was all through her and was no longer pain at all, it was just totality, all sensations merged in one overwhelming rush that washed over her in an unstoppable uncontrollable wave.

She heard the gasps from everyone, sensed the two girls scatter and sat there alone, sobbing, cradling her brimming, burning vulva in her hand. Yet Margaret had not deserted her. As the woman's hand slipped down to cover Julie's own between her thighs, she felt a strong arm coming to circle round her shoulders and the soft Scottish lilt in her ear.

'Well done, dear! Well done!'

Julie turned her face into the great warm soft bosom and wept.

When she had recovered, had finished shamefully picking away the last scabs of wax from all over her skin, she finally made herself face the gathered guests again.

Amy was skulking against the wall, no trace any-where of the candle, as she looked in terror from Margaret to Julie and back, seeking reassurance for what she had done. The golden blonde had returned to her place with her boyfriend, where their heads were locked together in fevered description of her part in the shameful proceedings. Chrissie was watching from the back, her eyes flashing anger at Julie's success and stamina so far.

Yet that was her eyes; Chrissie's mouth smiled sweetly at the rest of the company. 'All right, everybody? Who wants to be next? Maurice? Mary?'

The older couple declined; this was their first visit, they explained, and they would sit this one out and perhaps take part next time, if that would not cause offence. Clearly Chrissie was not used to her invitations being declined, but she brushed over it.

'Fine. Fine. Suit yourselves. Graham? Judith?'

These two were less bashful. Judith pulled herself up awkwardly, and Graham too got to his feet. As they approached where Julie was sitting, Margaret dropped a last little pat on her shoulder and the places were swapped over: Graham and Judith were looming over her, just as so many others had done, and with the same look of selfish anticipation.

'Turn over. Hands and knees.' Graham's mild tone did not hide the determination of his demand. 'Head here.' He rapped his knuckles on the end nearest the fireplace, and Julie worked round and came face to face with her own reflection again. Her knees were immediately pulled apart, again peeling open her sex and Julie hung her head as she tried to imagine what could be coming next. The man's great rough hands ran all across her skin, over her back, her bottom, and down her thighs, wrapped round inside to run up into her crease and then along her stomach to grasp each of her hanging breasts. Eventually satisfied with what he had found, he returned to her thighs again, pulled them even further apart so that Julie was certain everyone would be able to see right into her vagina, and then, the final indignity, moved up to her bottom again. Only this time both hands were there, one resting on each round cheek and then they spread these apart, opening her even there, revealing even that most private spot. She felt his finger reach down and touch it, deliberately touch that secret, dirty place, actually pressing against the tightly closed gates. Never in all her life, never even in her fantasises had she ever permitted access there. The wickedness of such an invasion was unspeakably alluring, finally exposing to a crowd of onlookers that most intimate and private part. In the mirror Julie watched him turn his head this way and that as he examined her further. Without looking up, he spoke to Judith.

'Take off the harness.' His eyes didn't flicker, didn't check that his instruction was understood or being obeyed – and Julie knew why not. His manner, his bearing, his tone all made such a check unnecessary. No one would think not to obey him.

Even so, Julie did not understand what he had asked, only deduced from Judith's nervous glance back down the room that it was a matter of some shame. It became clearer as Judith reached down to the hem of her long evening dress, started to bundle it up and her legs appeared, her knees, her thighs and then there should have been knickers. To Julie's horror there were none. Instead, there was a contraption of thick leather straps like the ridiculous athletic support that Mike sometimes wore for sports.

The dress was now round Judith's waist bringing the whole harness into view and Judith was reaching round to the side where a brass buckle held the thing in place. As Julie watched Judith fumbling with the buckle, Graham relaxed his grasp on her bottom. For a moment he was not touching Julie at all and then his hand whipped back in a smart stinging slap. Julie screeched, at the surprise of the blow and the strength of it; considering it was delivered only from his hand, the power of his stroke was as punishing as any she had received before. She sobbed.

'Would you like to be gagged again?' Graham's voice came from close to her ear, his words not a threat, but a genuine concerned enquiry as to what would make the experience best for her. Would she? Did she want that foul object forced into her mouth again, stopping her talking or protesting, making her dribble like a toothless old woman with every gasp that was torn from her throat? Yet there was also a freedom in being gagged; she could scream then, for little sound would come. She could protest, she could remonstrate, she could make whatever demands were necessary to ease her conscience, and all would be entirely impotent and completely ignored. In meek acquiescence, she nodded.

Judith had now unfastened the buckle, and was pulling away the thick black belt from around her waist. In the middle of her back, this ran through the loop of another wide strap which passed down between her legs, studded for those critical few inches where it curved under her crotch, and came up to fasten on to the belt in the front. It certainly would be a most uncomfortable belt to wear for any length of time, but Julie's attention was distracted again.

Graham was back with the ball gag, pulling her upright, yanking her head back and pushing the ball into her mouth before fastening it tight behind her. The leather was still damp from before. He left her there and Julie turned round to watch Judith again. The belt was now completely unthreaded but it hung down by her side, although the central strap was still in place. She seemed to be waiting for permission to carry on and, perhaps at a signal from Graham, perhaps at no signal to stop, Judith bent her legs into a squat, reached down and eased the strap down. As it came away, Julie saw a huge black phallus gradually emerging from Judith's vagina. It was at least nine inches long and thicker than any real penis could surely ever be yet, in horror, Julie realised that it must have been planted in there all evening. As she tried to meet Judith's eye to try to pass some silent sympathy, she saw that the process was not over; worse was yet to come. Judith reached round behind her, winced as she delicately pulled the strap there, and a stubby bulbous plug was slowly squeezed out from deep within her bottom, a conical plug whose rounded point swelled to a thick shoulder and then narrowed into a neck at the base. It glistened obscenely as Judith stood up, flexing her legs, squeezing her thighs together at the relief, and offered the obscene object across.

Graham didn't take it from her, but his hand clamped down on Julie's neck, pressing her down on to all fours and then to her elbows. Her bottom was blatantly thrust up into the air and, as hands hauled her thighs open again, she knew what he planned to do. One foot was lifted and the harness passed up her leg, thick and heavy as it scraped over her skin.

They did her vagina first, stretching it wide open and then presenting the phallus, still wet, still warm from Judith's body, to the opening. Despite her arousal, Julie could not prevent her muscles contracting in protest at the invasion of something so monstrous and for a moment they let her wait, let her relax, let a little more of her stickiness gather to ease the path when, inevitably, she felt the thing pressing on, forcing its way through and steadily further and further in, until it was banging against the very top of her womb. She was utterly filled and its base was pressing against her lips.

It felt huge inside her, brutal and alien – and yet before she had any chance of becoming accustomed to that, they were moving on. A fingertip trailed round her lips, slurping through the honey, and then it was back on her bottom. She could feel that little mouth pulled tight, the skin all round distended and stretched to the limit and then the finger was there, right in the very centre, worming its way inside through the terrified little entrance.

'Relax,' he said, but she couldn't.

'Relax!' he insisted and slapped down on the nearer cheek so that, momentarily distracted, she flinched from that and he had suddenly pressed harder and the fingertip had pushed through. She felt it inside her, stirring in that inadmissible cavity, pressing on unstoppably against her writhing evasions, against her muffled protests, against her screaming muscles, until it was so far inside that his hand was pressed tight against her bottom.

'Relax,' he coaxed and she finally found she could. At first every movement made her automatically clench up and it was a struggle to relax again, but after he had several times pulled back and then pressed back in again, she was eventually able to tolerate movement, foul and foreign though it was. Then his finger withdrew completely and the bulbous end of the stubby plug was pressing against her, colder and slimy with a grease she could not contemplate. The rounded point pressed for entry with a relentless persistence that ultimately nothing could resist. It pressed through, stretching her wide, agonisingly wide, as if an entire fist were thrusting in, and still the further it penetrated, the wider she felt herself stretched until she was crying again, the tears rolling out of her – she would have screamed if the gag had let her – as the stretching became so tight that one more touch would tear her open and then the widest part of the plug was through, her anus closed round the narrower neck, hugging the thing and holding it tight where it could not go forwards, and neither could it go back. It was excruciatingly uncomfortable, as if she badly needed to relieve herself and could not do so, but it was in.

The straps were now being fastened, the belt wrapped round her waist, slotted through the loops and buckled tight.

'Good. You can get up now.' The man's kind mellow voice mocked the obscenity he had just forced on her, but Julie turned over to her side and slid carefully off the table, earnestly ensuring that no pressure was put on the disgusting objects inside her. Graham helped her off the table and steadied her on her feet, where she stood half stooped and bandy-legged. Graham pulled her hands behind her back and clipped the leather cuffs together, so they were held there and she was further humiliated, further unable to protect herself, further displayed in her total powerlessness. That done, he slapped her smartly on the bottom, right in the middle, sending waves of pressure up the plug in her bottom which defused right through her in a way that was simultaneously punishing and intensely stimulating.

He turned to the other guests. 'Short refreshment break, do you think –' he smiled and turned to slap Julie again, sending her up on to her toes, almost over on to the floor, '– before we continue?'

Fourteen

For Julie, the break provided little comfort. The wait-ress leaped up from Peter's lap, hurriedly refastened her dress and returned incongruously to being a waitress again, but otherwise it gave the guests an opportunity to stretch their legs and move around. Julie could barely stand, let alone stretch her legs, while impaled on the two rubber plugs. Several guests took the opportunity to go out to the toilet and, despite the embarrassment of walking naked through the hotel corridors, Julie would have liked to go too, but was not allowed to remove the harness. For a short while they removed the gag and she was given more wine to drink, and some water when she asked for that, but soon the gag was back again although she knew she would need to be allowed out of the harness soon.

While the guests circled and chatted, and one or two ventured out to the sun porch to watch the storm clouds still swirling over the Fells, others drifted up to see how Julie was coping. They came in ones and twos; some-times in couples, sometimes two of the girls or two men, and they pressed at the broad round shield over her vagina, pulling at the straps of her harness to turn the objects inside her; slapping her buttocks just to see them quiver and send shock waves up the plug in her bottom, or drumming on the shield in front to vibrate the phallus which so stretched her vagina. She passed from hand to hand as each guest had another idea. After whispering together for some minutes just inside the door, Linda and the golden blonde came up together, egging each other on as they got closer and then reaching up simultaneously each to take hold of one nipple and pinch as hard as they could until the tears rolled down her cheeks again. After this, they each took one of the candles from the mantel behind her and each dripped wax on to her nipples until they were encrusted like the wine bottles in an Italian bistro.

Even the quiet couple, unknown, unnamed, despite having declined the invitation to participate, strolled casually up to see her, smiling happily. Ignoring the gag, they gaily chatted to her as if this were a village fête, asking if she was enjoying herself, but they also both reached up to caress her breasts, pulling at the nipples, tweaking them back to full erection and then flicking them from side to side. And they both eased the straps away from her sex to push an inquisitive finger into the groove and feel the slippery wetness of her clitoris where the strap rubbed continuously with enough bite to arouse her and not nearly enough to satisfy her. And they made her turn round and bend over and pulled away the belt behind as well to see how distended was her anus where the thick plug still penetrated so far inside. When they were done, they let her stand up again, thanked her kindly and the wife petted her cheek softly and told her what a brave girl she was and then slapped her straight across the breast as she turned back to her seat. The blow was so unexpected, so uncompromising and so sharp that Julie almost collapsed, staggered sideways and would have fallen had not the woman's husband been there to catch her.

Chrissie stayed well away, but Julie saw her talking earnestly with David and knew something more was in store. So when, after twenty minutes or so – once the stragglers had drifted back in from the sun porch and the wanderers were back from their rooms or the toilets or wherever else they had drifted away to, when everyone was starting to settle back into their seats, when even the waitress had returned with a proprietorial smirk to her place on Peter's lap – when Julie glanced up and saw David, arms folded, perched on the side of a chair, unsmiling, unfrowning, watching her intently, the knowledge that he would be next came as no great surprise.

David started picking his way up the room, but halfway through the rows of seats he stopped and turned round, considered the array of available faces and available bodies and then homed in.

'Peter! May I borrow Shalina, please?'

Peter smiled with perfect generosity although the waitress looked up, startled and uncertain as David stretched out a hand and Peter pushed her up off his lap in an unequivocal donation. Julie was pleased to see her being dragged away from Peter's increasingly possessive attention, but had no idea what plans David might have for them both. Nor could she hear what he was whispering as he led the girl closer. She had no idea what was expected or planned, only that Shalina glanced back, just once, nervously towards Peter and the safe refuge of his lap, and then stood entirely still before quietly reaching back to unzip her black dress and starting to pull down the sleeves off her shoulders.

David left her to that, and came up beside Julie. He had never touched her before, but now he ran his hands in slow circles over her skin and then started unbuckling the gag while he spoke softly into her ear.

'You know something, Julie? I think this has all been too easy for you.'

Behind him, Shalina was pulling the top of her dress down her arms, revealing an expanse of smooth skin; then over her breasts, revealing a black lace bra, but David was still talking and pulling the disgusting gag out of her mouth so that, although Julie could now breathe more comfortably, could lick her lips and flex her jaw, she couldn't concentrate on anything else.

'Up to now,' David continued, 'you haven't had to do anything. Everything that has happened has been done to you, but done by somebody else.'

Shalina had pushed the dress down to her waist and the top of her knickers appeared – black, matching the bra, a very thin waistband which suggested there would be little more than a thong – but still David wouldn't be quiet.

'Many people – and I think this applies to you – find it's quite easy to tolerate practically anything, provided they do not take an active part, provided it is all done to them while they remain passive.'

Shalina was pushing off her shoes, stepping out of the dress and looking round for somewhere to put it before finally dropping it on the floor. For a moment Julie caught her eye, but no communication was possible and even this much was embarrassing so they both quickly looked away again.

'So, for the last bit, I want to make things a little more challenging for you, give you something more to aim at and more of a sense of achievement when it's done.' His tone was still low and wheedling and he had started fiddling with the cuffs behind her back, but his hands still occasionally ran up her side, or straight across her breasts, before slithering back down her arms to draw wide circles on her bottom.

Meanwhile Shalina had unclipped her bra. When Julie looked over she was already turning back, her breasts now exposed, her thumbs hooked into the waistband of her knickers. She turned first away from Julie, but that was towards the guests; then away from the guests, but that was towards David. Finally she turned to face the wall and Julie couldn't see.

'I think you'll enjoy this,' David was droning on, the first wrist now unbuckled, the second on its way, 'and

225

Shalina will be able to help you, because she's at about the same stage as you.'

Shalina had now pushed her knickers down, dropped them on to the pile and turned back entirely naked to face everyone. At first, she squatted down to sort out her clothes, folding them neatly, and her movements were so unhurried, so effortless that Julie was, for a moment, jealous. Shalina was not as shy now as her earlier behaviour had suggested she should be; in fact, she appeared entirely at ease. Once she had finished, she stood, happily facing her audience and waiting for the next instruction. She was not ashamed, not embarrassed or shy – merely patient. She stood with her arms down, her hands happily clasped in front of her so that, although this partially hid her pubic fleece, the pose seemed more for comfort than modesty and she made no attempt to hide her nakedness. Her fleece was, like the hair of her head, quite black, but neatly trimmed and sparse, the hairs laid neatly so that they all pointed downwards, inwards and focused attention on the little pink nut at the apex of the triangle. She was very slim and her breasts, although small, were round and proudly high-set, with tight little nipples set in a smooth but swollen pale brown halo.

However, David was now pulling at the belt of Julie's dreadful harness. 'Shalina, help Julie out of all this.'

So then Shalina's slender little fingers were fiddling with the buckles and Julie was shoved this way and that as the thick belt was unfastened and pulled clear of the loops, every movement sending further tremors through the plugs in her bottom and her vagina. When at last it was all unfastened, it hung like some baby's fouled nappy, the weight dragging at her. Shalina was now kneeling down in front of her, and tugging at the phallus as Julie, humiliated at the way her own body seemed reluctant to release the thing, dropped down into a grotesque half squat that opened her up obscenely right in front of this other girl. When it finally emerged, wet and shining, the scent wafted unmistakably through the room while David leaned down to run an amused and inquisitive finger along its length.

Shalina stayed where she was and, placing her hands on Julie's hips, made her turn round to present her back. She made Julie part her legs, made her lean forwards and drop down again to another half squat while the thick plug was pulled from her bottom. The swollen middle caught and again Julie's muscles seized up in automatic revulsion at the strain of its being drawn out, so that there was a struggle as Shalina pulled at it and pushed at it and eased it back and forth before eventually it emerged back into the light. Julie felt that her body was hers again and she could at last move more freely.

Then David had them stand side by side and, for a moment, while the two of them suffered the scrutiny of the rest of the room, nobody spoke. Julie tried to take comfort in being no longer the sole centre of attention, no longer the only one naked; but, although David had said this was the last stage, his comments had made it all too obvious that it would not be easy on her. She understood too that the possibilities were hugely expanded by there being two of them standing naked and available, and she was only too aware of the appeal of so total a contrast. Julie's skin was so very pale, and her hair, not quite the fiery red of some of her family, still shone a rich auburn. Shalina was dark, her skin rich olive and her hair pure black. Then there were the two other differences. Julie's breasts were full, round and heavy with a clear crease beneath each one, where Shalina's were slight and pert, with neat dark nipples in a circle of swelling brown. Yet, most obvious of all, Shalina had a neat triangle of black hair at the top of her sex and Julie had no covering at all – just an invitation, half open, half revealed. For a minute Julie wondered whether the contrasts between the two of them were really too great to be coincidental. Had there really been time to arrange so much?

David in the meantime had rearranged the table, turning it sideways on and now, in a calm, entirely businesslike tone, he directed their next event.

'Come and get up on the table, please, Shalina, and sit facing down towards Julie. You too, Julie; you sit facing up towards her. That's it. Move in closer together. Now there's no need to be shy – legs apart so we can all see what is going on. That's good.' His manner was like a school teacher; his meaning was not. 'Now then, let's see who can be first to make herself come. Off you go.'

Yet Shalina again seemed much more at ease than Julie could believe possible. With only the briefest hesitation, she drew one knee up and bent the other leg out so that she was turned to display herself entirely to the room. As she leaned back on one hand, her other hand reached down and, after rubbing all her fingers flat across the mouth of her sex a couple of times, she started to work her middle finger deeper into the crease. Julie could see now that the careful trimming was even more evident right between her legs and that the lips themselves were entirely free of any covering. Glancing up, Julie found the girl watching her intently and, as she did so, Shalina allowed her eyes to drop, very obviously, down to Julie's vulva. The gesture was entirely unambiguous and Julie edged her legs apart, just a fraction at first, and moved her hand down to her thigh. Yet when she glanced up again and caught Shalina's slight frown, she realised that Shalina was right: the best way was just to dive straight in.

So Julie reached down and gently ran the tips of her fingers down the length of her crease in a slow wide circle a few times before reaching further round under her lips to the most sensitive point where her lips joined again and where a small drop of her honey was already gathered. But then she stopped again.

David had been right. Julie could withstand almost anything if it were done to her; the real ordeal came in having to act herself, and here, doing something so private and so shameful, was unbearable. It had been difficult enough when only Peter had watched, but in front of all these people, several of them women, and in a vile staged competition, this was too much. Julie's movements hesitated and faltered and slowed and stopped. She could accept being watched, being handled, but there were limits she could not pass.

Suddenly David told Shalina to stop. 'We don't want you getting too far ahead in the race, do we?' He retrieved the black riding crop from the mantelpiece and laid it carefully on the table directly between the two girls. 'There. That's for the loser. Now carry on, both of you.'

He had put a fraction of extra emphasis on the word 'both' and clearly meant what he said. Julie also realised from his expression that David would be perfectly happy if she lost the race and would have no hesitation in applying the crop without mercy if the need, or the opportunity, arose. At the end of its long smooth stem lay the narrowing tassel of woven leather which curled sinuously across the polished table; she did not want to be on the receiving end of that when it was applied for punishment, not stimulation.

So she copied Shalina's position again and copied too her actions. Julie knew she was already wet but, glancing down between Shalina's thighs, she could see that her competitor was even more glisteningly aroused than she was herself. Had this too been planned? Had it been pure coincidence when Shalina had been pulled down on to Peter's lap and his hand had disappeared so easily up her skirt? Was that all planned too, to start Shalina from a position where Julie was at a disadvantage?

Directly in front of her, Shalina's hips were beginning to quiver and her bottom was starting to lift in small circles over the table top. Julie could hear her breath beginning to come in rasping sighs and saw the girl bite her lips as her moment came nearer. Feverishly, Julie tried to concentrate better on her own action, on the years of longing for such public misuse – displayed across a table in front of a gathering of strangers, manipulated, probed and tested without thought for her own wants or desires. Now at last she was living that – had been put through everything she had dreamed of, plenty she had never dreamed of – and her life was suddenly new.

As she was sinking deeper, approaching the possibility of obeying the command, David interrupted them again. 'Put your fingers up inside, both of you.'

Julie did not need a second asking. Her sex was crying out to be entered and filled and she immediately pushed two fingers deep inside herself, twisting them round the sleek, pulsing walls of her vagina. She could feel how sticky and liquid she had become, how deeply the tremblings were beginning to grow within her and how easy it would be, if she were allowed to continue, to take this on for ever. Two fingers inside her was good, but it was not good enough. Her clitoris was now deprived of attention and so she sat up straight, brought her feet up in front of her, soles pressed together, and brought her left hand round to join in. With the fingertips there working her hooded clit, and her other hand still churning deep within herself, she was oblivious to the rest of the room. Suddenly a hand clasped her wrist and pulled her fingers out and Julie opened her eyes to see Chrissie reaching out similarly to Shalina, also pulling her hand away. For a moment Julie thought the game was over and she let out a little cry of frustration at being so cruelly prevented from finishing what she had initially been so unwilling to start. Then she found that

Chrissie was tugging at the two girls' wrists and pulling them closer together and crossing their arms over. At first, Julie could not work out what strange arrangement she was trying to achieve until Chrissie's next instruction to them both.

'Open wide!'

Chrissie was holding Shalina's hand up to Julie's mouth and had similarly pulled Julie's wrist up directly in front of Shalina. It was clear now that it was their mouths that Chrissie wanted them both to open, and Julie found that already she could smell the sweet perfume of Shalina's arousal on the fingers being offered to her. It was unmistakably similar to her own scent – and she had no other woman's scent with which to compare it – and yet equally unmistakably different, sweeter and less viscous. As she hesitated, she felt a warm probing tongue circling inquisitively round her own fingers and looked over to see Shalina smiling at her as she licked carefully at the treat she was being offered. Julie followed suit, lapping around and between the slender fingers that were held out to her, relishing the taste she was given and the glorious decadence of sampling it, relishing this even more than those few times when she sneaked her own guilty fingers to her lips after they had been moistened from her own caresses.

As soon as they were released, both girls returned immediately to a more direct and deliberate performance. Julie no longer cared – if she was even entirely aware of them – about the people watching. The need was far too strong and the arousal on Shalina's face, the sounds and scents that she was producing, goaded her and lifted her. Shalina was groaning now and three of her fingers had disappeared up inside her although Julie watched hypnotised as, with every thrust, the shining knuckles reappeared briefly before shooting back home. The girl's thumb was thrumming over a clitoris that pushed forwards so eagerly and willingly that for a

231

second Julie wanted to touch it, pictured herself actually reaching out with her fingers, even her tongue, to touch that most intimate part of the girl right there, and that image, laid on top of the completion of her life's fantasy and the sight of Shalina now rocking in her own orgasm, was enough. Julie gasped out herself, shoved fingers of her own hand inside in a substitute for that great black phallus which had filled her before and she too cried out as the climax engulfed her.

Once they had calmed down and turned, both of them, to acknowledge shamefacedly the applause of their audience, they climbed down off the table. Julie was now seriously in need of a toilet but first they had to deal with everybody else as they were surrounded by welcoming, if sometimes intrusive, hands and kisses. Yet Julie could stand all of that, and sipped her wine and watched Peter's approach with confidence. She had done everything she had been asked, passed every test and acquitted herself well – a feeling which was underlined by seeing the venom sparkling in Chrissie's eyes. Peter had agreed to help her only if she accepted 'anything' and she had done that. Now she would reap the rewards for her loyalty and her strength. Now he would take her upstairs and these games would be over; she had earned her place. She proudly returned his warm embracing smile.

'Well done, Julie. I'm very impressed. Excellent. Now, just one little thing more.'

She almost wept.

Fifteen

He might have been Moses. At his words, everyone parted like the waters of the Red Sea, leaving just Julie and Peter standing there while all the others pulled back to watch. Even Shalina, happily naked, lounged against the table to see what would develop.

'But David said we'd finished!' Julie knew her protest was pathetic, ineffective and pointless but she made it anyway; too much disillusionment and despair were gnawing at her for any self control.

'Oh, this will just take a moment.' His easy smile and considerate tone should have sounded like reassurance but already, in just two days, she had learned they meant the opposite. He tipped back the last of his wine and handed her the glass. 'Here you are. Fill this.' In the background, Chrissie giggled and that giggle, coupled with his brief nod down towards her nakedness, were all that showed what he meant. Even so, she could not bring herself to believe it.

Since this grotesque weekend had begun, Julie's eyes had been opened to many different discoveries, and from several incidents and comments she now knew that these people did not regard even something as private as that as beyond their reach. Were there really no limits?

'Why?' She had meant to say she couldn't; that she wouldn't; that she refused – but the demand so surprised and shocked her that it was all coming out wrong.

Peter didn't even bother to answer. He just left her standing there, holding the glass while he went back and sat down. Shalina was still perched on the table, but otherwise the whole room seemed to have settled back into their seats where they could watch as she submitted to this final indignity. They were perfectly calm, nibbling at chocolate mints, sipping wines and cognac as they waited; but the comfort of their position, the elegance of their dress, was what marked them as being on one side of the divide – in control. Julie's nakedness marked her as being on the other side – the servant. Indeed, the only other person in that room who was naked was a servant – the waitress. Yet even she seemed more at ease with her situation than Julie.

But now this, the ultimate humiliation, was the most potent proof possible that Julie's body and all its functions, however intimate, existed only for their entertainment. She had a vague recollection of reading that, when making one of the popular fly-on-the-wall type of documentaries on television, most volunteers would agree to anything being filmed except this. They would allow themselves to be seen naked, bathing, even making love. The only prohibition was being seen on the toilet. So far beyond the bounds, that one thing alone would be withheld. So far beyond the bounds, now Julie was commanded to perform even that. Although she would have liked to say it was not possible, she knew really that she did want to go, and that everyone else would know that too. It had seemed so innocent, the glasses of water and wine she had been given so freely during the evening, the easy excuse which had prevented her from going to the toilet when everyone else had taken a break. How naïve she had been, surrounded by such devious planning.

She placed the glass between her legs, pressing the hard rim against her skin and nothing happened. She tried to relax, tried to forget everybody was there, tried to remember how much she wanted to go. Nothing would happen. Nothing would come. She looked up and felt the humiliation of standing there naked in front of them all, when they had seen her do so much – seen her whipped until she cried; seen her penetrated with an artificial phallus; seen her masturbate; seen her lick the juice of another girl's arousal off her fingers. When they had seen so much, now she shamed herself yet again by being unable to control her own body enough to pee when she needed to, when she wanted to, when she was ordered to – just because other people were watching. The knowledge was – just – enough and she felt a little trickle spurt from her into the glass; then another before the sense of shame became too much and she seized up again.

Still she lifted the glass to show Peter. Barely half full, admittedly, but it was something. She had accomplished the task.

'Good! Well done.' He didn't move from his seat, nor did anyone else. It was as if they expected something more to come. 'Now drink it.'

Julie stared. The glass was warm in her hand, warm from the heat of her own body, and that made it even worse than if it had been cold. For a moment all she could do was stare – at Peter; at the half-full glass; at the circle of faces, silent now and intent. None of them was shocked or disgusted or outraged. They were interested, one or two even looked intrigued, but Julie detected no real understanding of the enormity of Peter's request. It was so far beyond anything Julie could have envisaged before this weekend began that there was no benchmark to compare it with. What would the other Julie, the real Julie, say about this? The one who worked for Quinlon & Withers; the one who pushed a shopping trolley round the supermarket with Mike, her loyal and boring fiancé; the one who drove to Cheltenham to visit her mother; the one who Julie had been for the last twenty-five years, all her life until yesterday morning, when she had walked into Peter's office and said, quite clearly, quite deliberately and quite knowingly, that she would do anything. She had known the stakes were high, but to do this?

Yet this was just another step in a long line and she had expected none of them. She had anticipated that he would strip her, take her to bed; she had known enough of his tastes to know he would tie her up, that he would spank her. Yet from the very start, when she left the security of her own house, she had been in another world. From those vile creatures at the cinema to this was a succession of impossible steps and she had managed every one. This was the last one; this was the highest level. They could do nothing after this. She let her imagination run and knew there was nothing beyond this. She had reached the peak that all her fantasies and years of desperate, lonely frustration had led to. When she raised the glass, calmly put it to her lips and drank, she would know utter obedience, utter humiliation, utter satisfaction. She could feel herself trembling at the prospect, feel her vagina starting to fill again, to swell and seep and open in anticipation of the glorious rush that would come from performing so obscene an action. She parted her legs a little and then she was ready.

And at that moment, as she knew she was going to do it, as she turned to meet the patient faces in front of her, the glass was snatched away. She had barely noticed the movement, just been vaguely aware of someone else there, but now Shalina was standing beside her, still naked, her little breasts pushed forward proudly, and she was now holding up the glass and drinking. Calmly and happily, while Julie looked on in horror and everyone else looked on in surprise, Shalina swallowed down the pale contents without the slightest hesitation or concern until finally the glass was empty.

For a moment she held it up for everyone to see, but even after that she didn't give it back. Instead, she put it down between her own legs and, after no more than a moment's pause, Julie saw, and heard, a thin trickle splash back in as it was refilled, refilled this time right to the top.

Shalina held it up again, but still nobody spoke and for Julie everyone else faded into mist. There were just the two of them standing naked in the firelight, and Julie felt that the challenge had been thrown. They had been rivals before when David had made them masturbate; were rivals, it now seemed, for Peter; now they were to be rivals again in sinking to the lowest possible point of humiliation. Shalina had succeeded; now Julie must prove whether she was worth as much. She reached out for the glass and held it for a moment, warm and sticky where it had overflowed. Shalina was staring at her, daring her, taunting her hesitation. So Julie raised it to her lips and without a pause drank it all down, feeling the warm liquid, sour but surprisingly not bitter, tipping into her mouth and down her throat. She didn't stop until the glass was empty. Only when it was finished could she look round at all the other faces and learn what she had done. Several were impressed, but from Linda there was something more. From her, there was simply disgust.

This time, that really was the end of her ordeal. Although the evening continued for some while before everybody drifted off to bed, Julie was not allowed to dress, but then neither was Shalina, and Julie was not sorry that she received so much attention. The two of them stayed close together; indeed Shalina stayed closer than Julie found comfortable, and the frequency with which Shalina slipped an arm round her waist or lay it on her hip began to be disquieting. However, Julie was saved by a cry from the far end of the room, a protest and a soft command of insistence, before Barry reappeared, leading Linda out to the space before the fire.

Julie was allowed to sit and watch now as Linda was first stripped and then the cruel double-horned harness was strapped on her. She struggled against this, her tightly cropped golden hair framing her tortured face, her breasts looking far too heavy for so weak a figure, but finally she accepted the phallus in her vagina. The plug for her anus proved much more difficult, and eventually Barry had to put the gag on her, before he bent her right over double so that the little brown ring of her anus was opened to them all and he could apply a liberal coating of oil all round her bottom and up inside it. After that the cone was finally squeezed in and the harness strapped up tight, but Linda was still squirming and mewing inaudible protests so that Julie was concerned until the golden blonde, who had come up to the front to get a better view, told her not to worry.

'She always fusses when he does that, but Barry would stop at once if she gave the real signal. Anyway, she doesn't really mind this part; it's what she's got to do next that she really does dislike.'

She had calmed down now, so Barry took the gag off again before he turned back, scanning the room carefully. Whether it was because she was already naked, or whether he had some other reason in mind, he finally settled on Shalina, led her forwards and had her lie back on the table, just as Julie had done, so that Linda could be led round and pushed down between Shalina's wide-spread thighs and, despite her tears and protests, Linda's mouth could be pressed up to Shalina's shining open sex.

Shalina did come, eventually, but it took a long time, or maybe she was fighting it, because there were more moans of protest from Linda than of pleasure from Shalina. If Linda slackened in her attentions, Barry flicked her with the riding crop across her bottom and once, when she stopped completely, flicked it up between her thighs.

After that, everyone began to drift away. First the quiet couple, who explained they had an early start back to Plymouth in the morning; then Graham and Judith, who were not staying at the hotel at all and returned to their cottage further up the valley; then the young golden couple whose names Julie still hadn't learned. Soon there were just David and Chrissie, Barry and Linda, Peter, Julie and Shalina. After all that had happened, Julie was eager to go too. She wanted a shower and a warm, soft bed. She wanted to lie by Peter's side and feel the security of his arms around her. She wanted a reward for obeying him so completely.

Then Shalina had come and smiled as she slipped her arm round Peter's waist; Chrissie had come and smiled as she produced a tartan rug and the two of them led Julie out to the bleak cold sun porch where she shivered in the dark and the silence as she heard the door locked behind her and saw the lights going off behind the thick curtains until she was left on her own. She held back the tears until they were gone but, once the hotel had settled to sleep and the stillness had settled round her, she gave in. She curled up on one of the cane settees, and with one hand clutching the blanket under her chin for warmth and the other between her legs for comfort, she eventually fell asleep.

It couldn't have been more than an hour later – for the night was black and a few tiny lights were still burning far down in the valley – when Julie was woken by the door being unlocked and two shadowy figures crept out from the lounge. Both, she realised, were in dressing gowns as they slipped out quietly, furtively. They were whispering, so it was impossible to recognise the voices, but the girl seemed to be in charge. She threw away her own dressing gown, then tugged the rug off Julie and tossed that away too.

'Here,' she whispered, 'lie down on the floor.'

Half asleep, too startled and unprepared to resist, Julie slid off the settee on to the cold stone floor where she lay on her back, her arms up protecting her breasts, as she tried to see what they intended.

The girl came up and stood over her, stood right over her with her feet either side of Julie's head and then, in one single swoop, she squatted down until her sex was hovering, peeled open and inches in front of Julie's nose and mouth. Julie could smell her arousal; it was unmistakable and so close that they were almost touching, and they were practically one single tableau, each feeding off the other's proximity and arousal. She was so close that Julie could, had she wanted to, actually have poked out her tongue and licked her. Naturally she didn't, and when she licked her lips it was only from nervousness. Only then the girl pushed down a little lower, and her lips dangled cold and damp against Julie's tight-shut mouth.

'Open your mouth,' the girl whispered, 'and lick me.'

So Julie obeyed the command and opened her mouth, and pressed her lips and her tongue to the place, and it was all hot and moist and sticky with a debauched abundance that was like cream on top of everything that had happened so far, so that Julie was not at all surprised when her mouth was immediately filled by the girl's pee, gushing hot and sour. Yet it seemed not so much an act of humiliation – although it was that, and Julie knew it would be even more like that in the cold light of day – as an excess of desire which the girl needed to share with someone and Julie was perversely honoured that she had chosen to share it with her.

And when, at the same time as she was pissing into Julie's mouth, the girl, whoever she was, reached down and started clawing at Julie's sex, there was no reason not to open her legs, not to offer her body completely to someone who was making such a selfless gift of herself. All Julie's revulsion at such intimate contact with another girl had evaporated, and she realised that the only reason that she had been spared this during that long evening was that, for everyone else, it was too mundane to be interesting and they had judged her by their own standards. Only Julie – and, apparently, Linda – still found such an action so outrageous and objectionable that it held sufficient value to be worth repeating.

The pee streamed on, stopping every now and then whenever the girl leaned forward and applied extra pressure, or slipped another finger deep inside her, but Julie took it all and swallowed practically all of it. When it seemed to be finishing, even though there was only a hand and not a mouth between her own legs, Julie too let herself go and the girl dabbled her fingers in the stream and licked them and dribbled them into Julie's own mouth and rinsed them again until there was no more to play with.

However, at the end, neither of them had climaxed and, as the girl stood up, reluctantly, Julie couldn't help believing, her companion immediately started to pull her away. He had previously taken no part, but now he emerged out of the shadow, anxious and fearful.

'Come on, Lucy.' He too was whispering. 'Someone will hear us.'

The girl let herself be dragged away and Julie heard the lock click over as they left her alone, lying in the mess they had made. She climbed back up on to the seat and hauled the rug up round her shoulders but her skin felt clammy and tacky; her hair clung together in sodden rat's tails and, when she pulled the rug right up over her head, the smell from all over her body surged up to remind her.

But in her mouth the taste was still there, the sour bitterness of the girl, and though a surreptitious finger-tip soon scooped up some of Julie's own flavours, the

241

stronger tang still lingered, full and unmistakable. In spite of everything, it was not altogether unbearable. In fact, it was a taste that Julie thought she might eventually grow to like. With that in her mind, it took much longer this time before she fell asleep.

Sixteen

Julie awoke to the sound of a vacuum cleaner being started up. She blinked at the dazzling light and peered round. This was not her bed. In fact, this was not any bed. She was naked. It was broad daylight.

In a wave, the memories came flooding back – scattered images of what she had done, what she had suffered, of everything they had put to her – and, gradually, swirling like particles in a toy snowstorm, it all settled back into an even manageable layer. Eventually it was something she could look out on with equanimity, even pride. After all, she had endured it all.

She turned over and peered out on the world. She lay covered by a thin blanket, curled up on one of the cane seats in the long sun porch and above her the sun was burning down from a brilliant cloudless sky. The day sparkled bright and new and the rain was a memory as distant as her own humiliation. In a far-off village church bells were ringing to greet Sunday morning while, closer to, all across the garden, the grass, the leaves, the trees all twinkled like Christmas, refreshed and revitalised.

Peering round the back of the settee, Julie could see through the windows back into the lounge. All the curtains were now open and two women were moving about inside, one vacuuming the floor, the other dusting the tables, fluffing up the cushions and returning the

chairs and sofas to their rightful positions. There was no
knowing whether they had already noticed her or not,
but Julie did not want to parade through the hotel
wrapped only in the blanket, so she settled down to
wait. With luck, they would not be long, because she
badly needed to get back inside, to retrieve her clothes
and find where Peter had got to. Most pressing of all,
she needed to go to the toilet.

She pulled the blanket closer round her and noticed
in front of her two sticky damp patches on the
flagstones: a wide one that she had made herself, a much
smaller one where she had been unable to swallow it all.
Now she needed to go again, and there was an extra
richness in knowing that most of what she needed to
expel had already been expelled by someone else. Surely
on a Sunday the cleaning women would be quick.

Ten minutes later, the vacuum cleaner stopped, so
Julie waited a couple of minutes more and then peered
round again. There was no sign of either of the cleaners
so she stood up, drawing the blanket round tighter, and
hurried to the door.

It was locked.

In despair, Julie ducked down out of sight again. The
doors out to the garden were locked – not that she
thought she could face stepping out there wrapped only
in a blanket – and it seemed she could not get back into
the hotel. Even if she did get back inside, what then? She
could go up to Peter's room, but would Shalina be
there, in bed with him? Would she run into David and
Chrissie and, if so, would they allow her to go to the
toilet, or would they want to use her need for their own
entertainment and her greater humiliation? Would it not
be better to stay out of their way until she was less
vulnerable? She squatted down and dropped her head in
her hands. This whole business had already gone utterly
wrong. Peter had taken advantage of their agreement to
pass her from hand to hand as a plaything for his

friends. She was supposed to be a responsible, professional woman and yet here she was, crouching naked on a stone floor and suffering whatever anybody, man or woman, demanded, unable even to pee when she wanted to.

Finally, with no hope of finding any better prospect, she crept down to the furthest end of the room, positioned herself carefully astride a straggly bamboo, hoisted the blanket out of the way and released a pent-up jet of pee. The relief was magical and, if she couldn't call it comfort, this was the first time since the changing rooms at the sauna yesterday that she had been able to pee in private. It was not until she had finished and was scrabbling to wrap herself back in the blanket, that she turned to see two horrified faces peering out at her from the lounge. The disgust in the two women's eyes showed there would be no point in attempting any explanation, and Julie slunk back to her seat.

She had heard the distant church strike nine before finally she was released. Shalina appeared, back in her waitress dress again but with an unashamedly satisfied smirk across her face. She told Julie that everyone was in the dining room having breakfast.

'No need to get dressed,' she added. 'Everyone's seen it all already.'

However, that was too much for her to face, and Julie hurried back upstairs where she was able to find her clothes and her overnight case, have a shower and get dressed before she risked the dining room. With nobody to tell her otherwise, she put on a T-shirt and jeans, but didn't risk a bra.

About half of last night's guests were there, assembled at a single long table. A couple of used places showed where some had already come and gone; clean places showed where others had yet to appear. One of these was next to Peter and, although Julie felt she no longer owed him anything, it would have been very pointed not to have taken it.

'You really didn't need to put all that on, you know. We're going out later and you'll only have to take it all off again. Would you like some orange juice?'

Margaret and Amy reappeared, having been down to Ambleside to buy newspapers; Graham and Judith returned from a short walk to say it was fine but breezy and, after some discussion, it was agreed that they would all walk over Wansfell to Troutbeck. By the time this had been settled and a route had been accepted by all parties, and the golden couple had finally emerged, tousled and grinning, from their bedroom and the papers had been read and more coffee had been ordered, and everybody had at last been gathered together in the one room, and the proposal had been explained again to the late arrivals, the bright morning sun had gone. Clouds were gathering dark and laden over Coniston and, just after eleven o'clock, the first spots of rain were again trickling down the glass.

Peter went to investigate. 'It looks as if this has settled in for the day,' he reported. 'I'm rather afraid we'll have to make our own entertainment.'

Nobody said anything else, but Julie immediately felt all the eyes turn towards her.

In fact, by midday the cloud had lifted enough for the party to risk a trip down to Ambleside where they settled into a pub, had lunch and a couple of drinks. However, on finishing, they found that the clouds had closed in again and this time there looked to be no real prospect of improvement. Several of the older members seemed happy to stay on in the warmth and comfort while they prepared for the rest of the weekend, discussing plans and ideas; but the younger ones, whose wishes anyway counted for nothing, had drunk as much as their heads or their bodies could take. Eventually only Linda, Amy, the blonde girl and Julie herself set out ahead of the rest to trudge back up through the rain to Scourfield Lodge.

The hotel appeared to be completely deserted. None of the staff was on duty at the reception desk, nor in the kitchen; so, having the place to themselves, the four girls headed out to the sun porch, throwing their outdoor clothes over every available surface. There was some suggestion of playing cards or seeing what other games might be lying about the hotel but, with no real enthusiasm for that, the afternoon settled down quietly while Julie and Amy read the newspapers, the blonde girl stretched out on a settee and fell asleep and Linda tackled a jigsaw puzzle spread out on one of the tables, started but uncompleted by some long departed guest.

At last Julie could feel secure and content. The instigators of all her ordeals over the last couple of days had been left behind in Ambleside and now, in the present company, all girls and all at least a year or two younger than her, she finally felt she could relax to a quiet comfortable lazy Sunday afternoon.

Then Amy started fidgeting. She was crossing and uncrossing her legs, but this had been going on for a good fifteen minutes before she finally broke the gentle silence of the afternoon. 'Shall I show you what Margaret does sometimes?'

Since the question was not addressed to anyone in particular, nobody felt a duty to respond. Finally Julie answered.

'OK. What does she do?'

'Well, come and sit here in front of me. You can be me and I'll be Margaret.'

Julie took up the position, kneeling on the flagstone floor where she was shown.

'No, not so close, move back a bit. Now you have to stay there, all right?' Puzzled and intrigued, Julie grinned round to the other two and agreed. Linda, one piece of puzzle clutched in her hand, had turned round and even the blonde girl opened her eyes and lifted herself up on one elbow to watch.

Amy tossed back her mousey hair and pulled up the hem of her long skirt. However, it was not until the skirt was bunched round her waist and a dainty little pair of pink knickers had been uncovered that Julie realised the intimate nature of whatever it was Margaret did. Amy pushed her hips forwards to the edge of the chair, spread her thighs wide apart and reached down to pull her knickers aside. Her vulva, a neat, pink tightly closed little sideways smile, was now displayed, the lips themselves entirely hairless and all the rest of her hair neatly trimmed and cropped short. Without the slightest hesitation, her fingers pulled the thick lips apart before pulling up even on the smaller ones so that they too peeled open to reveal a warm damp inside. Just once Amy's long middle finger smeared down and back up the centre of her sex, then a look of rapt concentration came over her face, and a jet of pee shot straight out, catching Julie straight in the chest.

Julie immediately started to scramble up, but Amy stopped her. 'No! I told you! You agreed!' she shouted. 'You must stay still!'

The pee was still shooting out, but already it had soaked the whole front of Julie's T-shirt, turning it practically transparent and showing off the darker rings of her nipples, nipples which were quickly responding to the revelation and to the pounding warm jet, by erecting into sharp points. But Amy wasn't finished. By twisting her hips she was able to direct the jet wherever she liked and was soon aiming her stream directly on to first one of Julie's nipples, then the other and then down into her lap so that a great dark stain appeared in the front of her jeans. Suddenly the spray stopped.

'Hold on,' Amy said, readjusting her position and hauling her skirt up again. 'I'm not quite finished.' Her face contorted into a concentrated frown and then the spray shot out once more, hitting Julie's chest again

248

before Amy lifted her hips right up, the spray followed and finally caught Julie in the face. She could even direct it there, over Julie's cheeks, her eyes and even up into her hair before it died away, the force no longer strong enough to reach so far and it subsided into a trickle before stopping completely.

Amy was still holding her knickers open with one hand, but she smeared the other across her sex, wiping away the last drops of pee before putting that hand to her mouth and licking it clean. 'There! Mind you, Margaret can hit me from much further away than that and she can keep going for hours. I'm absolutely dripping head to foot by the time she's finished.' She smoothed her skirt back down over her knees.

Amy may have felt she was not as proficient as Margaret, but the other two girls were impressed. They gathered round to inspect Julie where she was still kneeling in a growing puddle, her T-shirt drenched and pee still dripping down out of her hair, off her face and down her shirt to collect in a little yellow pool between her thighs which gradually soaked into her jeans. Julie too used her hands to wipe the pee off her face but she certainly did not go on to lick them clean.

'Can I have a go?' Linda was most enthusiastic.

'You can try,' answered Amy, 'but you need to wait until you are quite desperate before you can get it to go much of a distance. You could bring the chair closer.'

They entirely ignored Julie, or what she might want or not want. The pee was drying quickly, already she was cold and shivering, but they took no notice. Amy dragged the chair a little closer and then sat back where Linda had been to watch as Linda started unzipping her jeans and pulled them down her legs.

'I wish I could wear jeans,' Amy said softly, 'but Margaret won't let me.'

Linda was no more modest than Amy had been. She perched on the edge of the chair with her legs wide apart, pulled the gusset of her knickers aside and Julie couldn't help but stare as the girl opened up her vulva, one finger pressing her clitoris up so as to open the little dark eye. At first nothing happened. She was concentrating, straining to start but with no effect. When it did come, it came in a rush. A single narrow jet shot across, hitting Julie's shoulder with such force that drops spattered in all directions, some even splashing her face. Julie flinched away, but immediately both Linda and Amy called out to her to turn back again and she did. For no possible reason at all, she obeyed them, turned back and let Linda direct a spray of urine all over her breasts and then up all over her face. She closed her eyes and felt the stream washing over as if she were in a shower, but knew that the two girls were watching closely, witnessing her humiliation and enjoying her suffering as she kneeled there, dripping.

When the spray finished, and Julie had again used her hands to wipe her face as best she could, she looked down to see the mess she now presented. Her jeans were an almost even colour, as wet as if they had been dunked in a bucket; the puddle was spreading all round her, running into the gullies between the flagstones and flowing towards the door; her T-shirt was plastered to her chest, clearly outlining her breasts and the dark rings of her nipples. Yet her nipples were unmistakably erect now, and the whole curve of her breast – bigger, rounder breasts than those of the girls sitting round her – was also visible. Julie put her hands up to cover them, but she was also cradling them, and would, if she could, have stroked herself.

There was a movement from behind her, the third girl, who Julie had forgotten all about, came over, stepping carefully over the puddle. She said nothing, but bent down to Julie's waist, took hold of the sodden T-shirt and pulled it up, right up and over Julie's head. For a second, the material was completely covering her,

wet and stifling, starting to smell of the other two girls'
pee, and then it dragged all across her face and, when
Julie gasped, it scraped over her lips as well. Now she
could even taste them. The girl held it for a moment, so
saturated that it was still dripping, then, keeping it right
over Julie's head, she squeezed it tight, twisted it and
wrung it out. Another torrent of pee, cold now, poured
over Julie's shoulders, running down her breasts, trickling off her nipples and landing in her lap. Julie
shuddered.

The T-shirt landed with a wet splat on the floor next
to her and then the girl leaned over and gripped Julie's
cold wet breasts, one in each hand, squeezing her tightly
and then openly caressing her nipples with her thumbs.

'Aren't you going to pee as well?' asked Amy.

'No.' The girl answered. 'I've already done that.
Haven't I?'

When Julie didn't answer, Amy pressed on. 'When?'

'Last night. After everyone else had gone to bed.'

'You sneaky thing!' Amy was obviously impressed,
but the girl just laughed at the compliment.

Linda hadn't bothered putting her jeans back on, but
she sat open-legged on the settee, both her hands stuffed
down inside her knickers. 'I wish Barry would come
back.'

The girl finally released Julie's breasts and stood up.
'There's Julie, if you like.'

'Oh, no, thanks.' Linda answered quickly. 'I'll wait.'

'Suit yourself. Amy?'

'No, I'd better not. Margaret can get very jealous if I
mess about with other girls.'

'Quite right! I can!' The unmistakable voice boomed
out from the doorway and Julie whipped round to see
most of the rest of the party gathered just inside the
lounge, peering out at the four guilty faces. Julie hated
to think how long they might have been there watching
it all unfold – a thought which had presumably chilled

251

everyone, for a mortified stillness had dropped over the little gaggle. 'And I think,' Margaret continued as she came marching in, 'that you need to be reminded what happens when you disobey me.' She grabbed Amy's wrist and hauled her to her feet. The squeals and protests of innocence could be heard long after the two of them had disappeared back inside and up the stairs.

Barry now pushed his way to the front. 'You too, Linda!' Startled, she hastily dragged her hands out of her knickers, but too late. Linda too was hauled away, grabbing unsuccessfully for her jeans as she was chased back through the lounge in a torrent of slaps and cries.

Julie did not move. Sitting in a puddle of two other girls' pee, her breasts shining wetly in the dim light, her jeans saturated, her hair straggled and still dripping, what possible explanation could she give? She turned to the doorway. Thankfully there was no sign of either David or Chrissie, but Graham and Judith were standing there, and so was Peter. None of them looked the least displeased at the sight she presented.

Graham turned away, but clapped Peter on the back as he did so. 'Well done, Peter. I trust we will have the pleasure of Julie's company for another weekend soon. I'm sorry you have to start back so soon, but I will leave you to get her cleaned up and to deal with any other matters that might occur to you. Safe journey.'

Seventeen

They barely spoke on the Monday morning. What could Peter find to say after they had experienced so much in so short a time? He needed to get away and decide how to continue. This was the end of the agreement, but was it the end of everything? If he asked her out that evening, would she accept? Should he risk a rejection? Even if she agreed, the relationship would have returned to normal. She would expect to be wooed and flattered, entertained and indulged. He could not face so conventional a relationship. Hard though it would be, he preferred to end amicably now rather than risk a degeneration into acrimony later.

Besides, physically she was not his type at all. That waitress, Shalina, with her dark complexion, thick black hair and tiny breasts, was his ideal. Julie was just the opposite in almost every respect: fair, tall and auburn. Admittedly, Beth had also been fair-skinned, and her hair was even redder than Julie's, but Beth was different. Beth could be permitted anything.

He watched Julie emerge from the shower for the last time, catching glimpses through the swirling towel of her breasts, her slim back, her smooth buttocks, her sweet smooth vulva, and he almost wept. Just once he interrupted her, kneeled on the floor and clasped his hands round behind her as he buried his face in the damp fragrant warmth between her thighs. He kissed her crease, pushed his tongue for a final time against the divine ridges of her lips, stood up to kiss each nipple and then bent to lay one last caress on the fullest, roundest smoothest part of her exquisite bottom. For a few seconds his fingers traced the twelve long stripes which he had laid across her after they returned home last night as a final mark, a final memory to carry back for when next they met in the office, one final picture of her writhing naked across his bed. He kissed each swollen weal.

Then he hid away in the bathroom and, after washing his face again, emerged with a new determination to face the day and Collis and the week.

Their contract did not end until nine o'clock, so when she was getting dressed and asked to be allowed to wear underclothes again, he was able to refuse. She held up the two scraps of pale blue cotton that were all he had permitted her to bring and asked if she could take them with her in her handbag to put on once the deadline was reached but he refused that as well. He wanted to spend one more day with the knowledge that she was naked under her dress, and it would be better still for being an extra day, a stolen day. She did not argue but silently placed them in the overnight case that they had brought from her own home and zipped it closed.

The traffic was heavy, so it was well past quarter to nine before they reached the office. They climbed the first flight of stairs together and at the top she looked at her watch. There were still eight minutes to run.

'Do you want me to come up?'

'No, it's all right. You go on.'

'Right.' She hesitated, as if she too now felt something needed to be said, but no words would ever be enough. Finally she turned towards her office while he climbed the remaining stairs to his but as she reached her door, Julie stopped and whispered, 'Thank you, Peter.'

For a moment he wondered if he could have heard her correctly. She had paid a very high price for the work he had done for her, much higher than she could have been expecting, and had little need to add thanks.

Up in his room he threw down his briefcase and strode across to look out across the little carpark. Robert Collis's Volvo was just coming down the road and Peter watched it pull up opposite the carpark entrance, so heavy and self-possessed, the orange lights blinking patiently while it waited for a stream of oncoming cars to pass. It turned slowly across and pulled up in its allotted space. In the room immediately below him Julie would be sitting and waiting or perhaps looking out at the same scene.

Why had he forbidden her to wear underclothes? It was an unnecessary humiliation for her that now seemed petty and futile and gained him nothing. He could not even run down and tell her to put them on; they were left in the overnight case in his car. So now Collis would notice; he would see she was not wearing a bra, and he would say nothing, but he would gain pleasure from it all the same. He had probably been indulging secret fantasies about Julie for months; might even think she had chosen this for his benefit, a welcome back. What should have been their private bond now seemed sullied and cheapened.

Peter watched the top of the bald head as the man climbed out of his car, locked it carefully and strode across the gravel to the office. Peter turned back to his desk and miserably turned his diary to see what the week would offer.

The pages were blank. There had been no need to write in the deadline for the Parkinsons project, but now that the prospect of facing Collis with his incomplete notes loomed closer, he had none of the confidence which had sustained him over the weekend when other distractions had clouded his judgement. He decided to postpone the encounter for as long as he could and it was gone ten o'clock before his phone rang and Collis's voice asked if he could 'pop down for a minute to discuss Parkinsons'.

'Certainly, Robert. Two minutes.'

Two minutes. The carefully prepared excuses were decomposing before his eyes: the pressure of other work; the need to consult Collis on certain key points; the difficulty of getting replies. Collis was going to be very angry that so little had been achieved in the time. For a moment, Peter regretted letting himself become enmeshed; and yet, as he pictured Julie stretched naked over the hotel table, dangling by the wrists while the crop whispered up and down her body, writhing in ecstasy as wax dripped on to her proud nipples, he knew that any reprimand would be worth it.

Collis's office led off Julie's and so it happened that, when Peter finally went down, Collis was explaining something to Julie in her room. She looked up when Peter appeared, but he could read no concern in her eyes; if anything she was amused, smug, even excited. Peter had been looking for sympathy and support during this trial, and resented her evident complete confidence that he would take on to his shoulders the whole blame for her failure. The Parkinsons file lay prominently on her desk, thin and incomplete, but she picked it up.

'Here's the Parkinsons file you wanted, Mr Collis.' She offered it up to him, then turned to Peter and she beamed. That file held his career prospects and his whole life and she had handed it across without a care. In that single moment, he felt the blinds had been lifted. His resentment turned to suspicion and suspicion turned to clarity.

Like the end of a play, the girl he had fallen for had stepped forwards and smiled, had admitted she was only an actress and that everything which had gone before was pretence. As the lights came up, reality was revealed. All the events since she had knocked so timidly on his office door three days ago emerged out of the darkness: the entirely out-of-character tears; the half-smile right back at the start which he had seen but been persuaded to ignore. In the bright light, none of these stood up to scrutiny.

His stomach cramped up as if hit by a fist. How could he have been so deceived? He should have seen that it had all been too easy. She had been too acquiescent, but it was only now, when his reason was not overwhelmed y his lust, that he began to understand.

Julie was far too experienced and too well organised to have made such a silly omission in the first place. And she was certainly smart enough to cover her tracks completely if something did happen.

And she was devious, and quite vindictive enough, to lay a trap of that nature.

The whole scenario had been set up deliberately for one purpose: to get him into trouble. But why? Jealousy? Spite, because he had rebuffed her first advance?

In the few seconds remaining to him while Collis leaned over her shoulder and showed what he wanted done with a thick pile of letters he was holding, Peter tried to grasp what she had done, why she had done it, and how great was the damage she had caused. Could she really be so deceitful? Was she that good a liar?

As she sat there, cheerfully smiling up and nodding, 'Yes, Mr Collis. No, Mr Collis,' there was nothing to suggest any guilt, any remorse – not even a slight concern. Surely she could not be so proficient? More than that, could she really have endured so much over the last few days? Surely no one would be prepared to pay so high a price for so little gain. This alone was almost enough to convince him as he frantically searched for clues, his eyes searching over her serene untroubled face, her relaxed body, her fingers idly toying with a pen, her blouse pulled tight over her shoulder, and over the clear outline of a strap. She was wearing a bra.

Although it had been barely an hour since she had meekly obeyed his command to leave the item behind, she must have known even as she did so that she was not going to obey. Perhaps she kept one in her office, or perhaps she had stuffed it into her handbag when he was not looking; it did not really matter. Either way, she had lied, and her duplicity over this pointed an accusation at all the rest of her behaviour; at every word, every gesture, every smile, every tear. As he studied her face, feeling the hollow bottom dropping away from his life, he caught her eye. She smiled over Collis's shoulder. Like a cat who has stolen the cream, she smiled and puckered up her mouth into a kiss.

He would have struck out at her but that simply would not have been adequate. A kiss. After they had shared so much, while he waited for his sentence to be handed down, a sentence for a crime which she had committed, she now offered an exaggerated kiss. There were precedents for such a betrayal, but who could stoop so low as to bait the trap with their own body? She must have been watching the growing panic on his face, but still she smiled, just smiled. In fact, she was trying to keep from laughing and Peter could only stare. At last Collis turned, spoke words to him and Peter jerked his attention back to the present.

'Ah, Peter, just the man. No problems while I've been away, I trust? Good, good. Now then, Parkinsons. A project that's right up your street, I should imagine. I meant to let you have this before I went so you could mull it over while I was away but I forgot. No matter, there's no rush for it. Have a look at what they want and come and have a chat in a week or so to sort out how we'll tackle it.'

Peter stared. What was going on? Nothing made sense. Had he made another blunder? 'Did you say Parkinsons, Robert? No rush?'

'Yes, that's what I said: Parkinsons. What on earth is the matter with you? You've turned white as a sheet. You should have yourself a holiday.' He grinned and poked Peter in the ribs with the file. 'Now then. Second thing and much more interesting. How do you fancy six months in Barcelona?'

'Barcelona?' It rang a bell, but he couldn't remember why.

'Yes, Barcelona. Douglas and I have decided it's time the firm embraced the opportunities of the European Union, so we're merging some of our operations with a Spanish outfit. You're practically fluent in the language so you're the obvious choice to represent us. Here.' He waved a second file, much fatter. 'It's all in there. Read it through and then we'll get our heads together. You'll need some help, of course, so I suggest you take Julie; she did Spanish at university, she tells me, so if you can stand spending six months in the sunshine with her, she'll be the best choice. I'll make do with dear old Janice.'

Peter could only stare at the two faces grinning up at him.

'Really, Peter! You should see your face! I'm sorry to spring it on you but I couldn't say anything until it was tied up at the Spanish end, so Julie was sworn to secrecy. Anyway, come and talk when you've got over the shock and read the papers.' He collected a handful of letters and turned back towards his office before stopping again. 'Of course, we'll have to take you formally into the partnership before you go, but I don't imagine you'll object to that too much, will you? Come through, would you, Julie?'

Peter turned to her for an explanation, but she ducked away and started to push past.

'Julie?'

Her reply was too low for Collis to hear. 'I'm sorry, Peter. I must have made a mistake about Parkinsons. I

259

realise it's my fault, and I'll accept the punishment, but we couldn't think of any other way to see if you'd be suitable. Please don't be too hard on us.' She shoved something into his empty hand and was pushing past him towards Collis's office as he unravelled the bundle. It was one ridiculously tiny bra and two identical pairs of pale blue knickers.

'Us? Who's "us"?' He shook his head: anything to clear the fog. 'And whose are these?' He flapped the little blue scraps in the air.

'Mine!' she answered. 'Well, mine and Liz's.'

'Liz? Who's Liz, for heaven's sake?'

'My sister! She's come over to stay with me for a couple of weeks. She arrived yesterday while we were away.'

'Your sister?' Just as the mist had been starting to clear, something else had swirled up to obscure everything even further. 'What does your sister have to do with Parkinsons?'

'Parkinsons?' Julie was practically laughing as she collected the files and edged round to the door. 'Nothing! Only the whole weekend thing was her idea. Honestly it was. She said I'd enjoy it, and she was certain you would.'

'I would? But I've never met your sister!'

'Yes, you have! Liz! You know, Elizabeth!' She squeezed through into Collis's office and started to shut the door behind her. 'Beth!'

NEXUS NEW BOOKS

To be published in March

WHIPPING BOY
G. C. Scott
£5.99

Richard and his German girlfriend Helena have cocooned themselves in the English countryside, to live out their private – and elaborate – fantasies of submission and domination. But their rural idyll is threatened by the arrival of Helena's aunt Margaret – an imperious woman with very strict house rules and some very shady friends, who always gets what she wants. And what she wants is Richard . . .

ISBN 0 352 33595 5

ACCIDENTS WILL HAPPEN
Lucy Golden
£5.99

Julie Markham embarks on a game whose rules she does not know, and in just three short days her life is turned upside-down. On Friday she was happily engaged to be married. By Monday, she is crouching naked on a cold floor and suffering whatever any man or woman demands. The two days in between have been a very wet weekend – and the best of her life.

ISBN 0 352 33596 3

EROTICON 3
Ed. J-P Spencer
£5.99

Like its predecessors in the series, this volume contains a dozen extracts from once-forbidden erotic texts – from the harems of the Pashas (*A Night in a Moorish Harem*) to the not-so-chaste devotions of a French nunnery (*The Pleasures of Lolotte*). A Nexus Classic.

ISBN 0 352 33597 1

To be published in April

DEEP BLUE
Aishling Morgan
£5.99

Old-fashioned seaside smut blends with the strange and bizarre in Aishling Morgan's most fantastical and pervy book yet: peeping Toms, dirty old men, girls with inadequate bikinis, all in the mix with erotic pagan ritual and strange marine encounters. The perfect beach read.

ISBN 0 352 33600 5

NURSES ENSLAVED
Yolanda Celbridge
£5.99

When European nurses are interned by the Japanese on a Pacific island during World War Two, they are forced into cruel familiarity with their captors' almost feudal codes of punishment. But their submission becomes a matter of pride, forcing their captors to question who's really in control, until only one thing's for sure – no one's in a hurry for the war to end.

ISBN 0 352 33601 3

THE NEXUS LETTERS
£5.99

From the intimate correspondence of our readers come the *true* tales of cruel punishments, ritual humiliations, and initiations into the world of domination and submission. Nexus readers share their most intimate secrets – from slaves who'll do *anything* they're told, to ice-cool supervixens; from husbands who like to watch, to the men – and women – who pleasure their neighbours' wives – it's all here, in our kinkiest and most perverse collection yet.

ISBN 0 352 33621 8

EROTICON 4
Ed. J-P Spencer
£5.99

Like its companion volumes, a sample of excerpts from rare and once-forbidden works of erotic literature, featuring maids, whores and rakes, ranging from Bella in *The Autobiography of a Flea* to the adventures of Spartacus and Clodia in *Roman Orgy*. A Nexus Classic.

ISBN 0 352 33602 1

Nexus

NEXUS BACKLIST

This information is correct at time of printing. For up-to-date information, please visit our website at www.nexus-books.co.uk

All books are priced at £5.99 unless another price is given.

Nexus books with a contemporary setting

THE BLACK MASQUE	Lisette Ashton ISBN 0 352 33372 3	☐
THE BLACK WIDOW	Lisette Ashton ISBN 0 352 33338 3	☐
THE BOND	Lindsay Gordon ISBN 0 352 33480 0	☐
BROUGHT TO HEEL	Arabella Knight ISBN 0 352 33508 4	☐
DANCE OF SUBMISSION	Lisette Ashton ISBN 0 352 33450 9	☐
DARK DELIGHTS	Maria del Rey ISBN 0 352 33276 X	☐
DARK DESIRES	Maria del Rey ISBN 0 352 33072 4	☐
DISCIPLES OF SHAME	Stephanie Calvin ISBN 0 352 33343 X	☐
DISCIPLINE OF THE PRIVATE HOUSE	Esme Ombreux ISBN 0 352 33459 2	☐
DISCIPLINED SKIN	Wendy Swanscombe ISBN 0 352 33541 6	☐
DISPLAYS OF EXPERIENCE	Lucy Golden ISBN 0 352 33505 X	☐
AN EDUCATION IN THE PRIVATE HOUSE	Esme Ombreux ISBN 0 352 33525 4	☐
EMMA'S SECRET DOMINATION	Hilary James ISBN 0 352 33226 3	☐
GISELLE	Jean Aveline ISBN 0 352 33440 1	☐

Nexus books with Ancient and Fantasy settings

Edwardian, Victorian and older erotica

Samplers and collections

NEW EROTICA 4	Various	☐
	ISBN 0 352 33290 5	
NEW EROTICA 5	Various	☐
	ISBN 0 352 33540 8	

Nexus Classics
A new imprint dedicated to putting the finest works of erotic fiction back in print.

AGONY AUNT	G.C. Scott	☐
	ISBN 0 352 33353 7	
BOUND TO SERVE	Amanda Ware	☐
	ISBN 0 352 33457 6	
BOUND TO SUBMIT	Amanda Ware	☐
	ISBN 0 352 33451 7	
CANDY IN CAPTIVITY	Arabella Knight	☐
	ISBN 0 352 33495 9	
CHOOSING LOVERS FOR JUSTINE	Aran Ashe	☐
	ISBN 0 352 33351 0	
CITADEL OF SERVITUDE	Aran Ashe	☐
	ISBN 0 352 33435 5	
DIFFERENT STROKES	Sarah Veitch	☐
	ISBN 0 352 33531 9	
EDEN UNVEILED	Maria del Rey	☐
	ISBN 0 352 33542 4	
THE HANDMAIDENS	Aran Ashe	☐
	ISBN 0 352 33282 4	
HIS MISTRESS'S VOICE	G. C. Scott	☐
	ISBN 0 352 33425 8	
THE IMAGE	Jean de Berg	☐
	ISBN 0 352 33350 2	
THE INSTITUTE	Maria del Rey	☐
	ISBN 0 352 33352 9	
LINGERING LESSONS	Sarah Veitch	☐
	ISBN 0 352 33539 4	
A MATTER OF POSSESSION	G. C. Scott	☐
	ISBN 0 352 33468 1	
OBSESSION	Maria del Rey	☐
	ISBN 0 352 33375 8	

------- ✂ ------------------------

Please send me the books I have ticked above.

Name   ....

Address   ....

                ....

                ....

         .... Post code ....

Send to: Cash Sales, Nexus Books, Thames Wharf Studios, Rainville Road, London W6 9HA

US customers: for prices and details of how to order books for delivery by mail, call 1-800-805-1083.

Please enclose a cheque or postal order, made payable to **Nexus Books Ltd**, to the value of the books you have ordered plus postage and packing costs as follows:
   UK and BFPO – £1.00 for the first book, 50p for each subsequent book.
   Overseas (including Republic of Ireland) – £2.00 for the first book, £1.00 for each subsequent book.

If you would prefer to pay by VISA, ACCESS/MASTER-CARD, AMEX, DINERS CLUB, AMEX or SWITCH, please write your card number and expiry date here:

....

Please allow up to 28 days for delivery.

Signature ....

------- ✂ ------------------------